Teddy. Where are you?

Daniel stood in front of the old-fashioned picture window. A reviled man in a self-imposed solitude.

Fear was a cold knot in his stomach. Resolutely he blanked from his mind an avalanche of obscene possibilities if Teddy had really run away. But she couldn't have. Wouldn't have. Nowadays, any thirteen-year-old knew about the danger that lurked everywhere. Beth was permissive to the point of neglect, but she would have—

He rubbed a hand over his face. How did he know what Beth had or hadn't told his children? He'd spent so little time with them in the past five years.

I'll do whatever it takes, I swear. Sell my soul to the devil, anything to have my children in my care again.

He picked up the phone and dialed. "Joey? It's Dad. Tell your mom I need to talk to her. Tell her it's urgent."

ABOUT THE AUTHOR

Karen Young is the talented author of a dozen Superromance novels and is hard at work on her second mainstream book for MIRA. Always a popular romance writer, Karen often challenges her readers with moving and controversial topics. *A Father's Heart* is a case in point. The hero, Daniel Kendrick, has been wrongly accused of a crime that turns his whole life upside down. He can no longer pursue his career as a high school principal and he can no longer be a real father to his children. The woman whose testimony so drastically affected his life has to come to terms with her mistake and learn to trust her instincts...and her heart.

Karen recently moved to Mississippi with her husband, Paul, so they can be close to their daughter and three grandchildren.

Books by Karen Young

HARLEQUIN SUPERROMANCE
500—THE SILENCE OF MIDNIGHT
532—TOUCH THE DAWN
602—ROSES AND RAIN
606—SHADOWS IN THE MIST
610—THE PROMISE
681—HAVING HIS BABY
712—SUGAR BABY

MIRA
GOOD GIRLS

A FATHER'S HEART
HEART
Karen Young

Harlequin Books

TORONTO · NEW YORK · LONDON
AMSTERDAM · PARIS · SYDNEY · HAMBURG
STOCKHOLM · ATHENS · TOKYO · MILAN
MADRID · WARSAW · BUDAPEST · AUCKLAND

ISBN 0-373-70786-X

A FATHER'S HEART

A FATHER'S HEART

CHAPTER ONE

DANIEL KENDRICK'S EYES snapped open. He lay for a second in that oddly paralytic state between sleep and reality, his heart knocking in his chest. He rubbed a hand over his face. What—

The peal of the doorbell brought him up on his elbow. Groggily he peered at the green numerals on the bedside clock. It was 2:05. He threw off the covers and grabbed his pants. In the hall, he hit a light switch and nearly stepped on the gray-striped cat that darted between his legs. By the time he reached the foyer, his visitor was banging on the door. He knew none of his neighbors. He was on nodding terms with the folks at the lumberyard, the hardware store, the library and the grocery store, but that was about it. He couldn't remember the last time anybody other than FedEx had rung his doorbell.

"I'm coming, I'm coming," he muttered, still groggy with sleep. He could see the outline of his visitor through the glass oval in the door. A cop in uniform. He flipped the lock and pulled the door open.

He was young—black hair, jutting chin, spit-and-polish neat and about forty pounds overweight. "Sheriff's department." He flashed his ID. "Are you Daniel Kendrick?"

"Yeah..." Daniel glanced at the name on the ID. Dwayne Duplantis. He barely had time to read it before it was slapped shut and buried in the deputy's pocket. "What's wrong?"

"Had a helluva time finding this place." Duplantis peered around Daniel to see inside. "It's the old Pertuit horse farm, right?"

"Yeah. Why were you looking for me?"

"Maybe we should talk inside."

"Why?" Daniel repeated. He glanced at the acreage surrounding the house. "Nobody's listening."

"It's about your daughter."

Daniel's heart stopped, then slammed into overtime. "Teddy? What about her?"

Duplantis looked beyond Daniel to the dark foyer. "I'll need to take a look around. Are you alone?"

"It's me and the cat." Daniel pulled the door open and flipped the light on. The cop stepped inside, looking quickly around as he pulled a small black notebook from his shirt pocket. He pushed the bill of his cap back with his thumb and frowned at his notes. "Teddy Kendrick, age thirteen, light brown hair, brown eyes, four feet, ten inches tall, seventy pounds." He looked up. "Does that sound like your daughter, Mr. Kendrick?"

Vital statistics. Daniel felt disoriented, fearing what would come next. "My God, what's happened? Is she hurt? Has there been an accident?"

"Well, she's missing, best we can tell."

Daniel stared, uncomprehending. "Missing? What do you mean, missing? She lives in New York with her mother, not here."

"It was...um..." he consulted his notes again "...Beth Carson who called."

"Yes. Beth. My ex-wife," he acknowledged impatiently. "What did she say?"

"You'd have to ask Sheriff Wade. He's the one who talked to her." With a creak of leather, he shifted his weight from one leg to the other, but his gaze never left Daniel. "She seemed to think your girl might be here."

Daniel gazed blankly around the foyer as if Teddy might somehow materialize from a shadowy corner. On the table beside the door where he stacked his mail, a birthday card stood propped open. The face of a whimsical yellow cat suspended on a tiny wire spring bobbed in perpetual motion. It had arrived Monday. This was...what? Wednesday. Teddy. My God. How could she be missing?

"When did this happen?"

"Coupla days ago, according to Ms. Carson." Movement from the living room caught his eye, and Duplantis took a step toward the arched entrance. The cat perched on the back of the sofa calmly grooming itself. "You say nobody else is here?"

"No." Shaking his head. "No. I haven't seen Teddy."

"Well, has she called?"

Daniel rubbed the back of his neck. "No."

"Because your wife seemed to think you would know something about this."

Daniel looked directly into Dwayne Duplantis's porcine eyes. "I don't."

"I should remind you that if your daughter was to

be here, it would be in violation of a court order, Mr. Kendrick.''

"Beth has…her mother has custody if that's what you mean.''

"And you have only supervised visitation rights.''

"Yeah.'' Impotent anger swelled in Daniel's chest. "And I'm not about to do anything to jeopardize what little time I do have with my kids, Deputy. I haven't left Louisiana in months. How could Teddy be with me? She'd need to fly to get here. If Beth didn't provide an airline ticket, how could a young girl travel fifteen hundred miles?''

"Your wife…ex-wife thinks she could have hitch-hiked.''

"Hitchhiked? She's thirteen, for God's sake. A child. There's no way she would have done something so dangerous. She and Joey both understand the risks of trusting strangers. No, this is crazy. She's probably just trying to scare her mother. Has Beth tried her friends?''

"The sheriff didn't say, but it's the first thing most folks would do. She had NYPD on it before she called us.'' Duplantis closed his notebook. "Kids do crazy things. Maybe she thought she'd try hanging out with her daddy if things weren't going the way she liked with her mama. Your wife—''

"My ex-wife.''

"Yeah. Ms. Carson seems convinced the kid is headed this way.'' He slipped his notebook into his shirt pocket. "If she shows up, you'll need to notify Sheriff Wade.''

"Right.''

Duplantis squinted at the pale light coming from

the kitchen and dining area on the opposite side of the hall. "Where you from, Kendrick?"

"The court order says Florida." *As you know, you bastard.*

"Yeah, but that's five years ago. City directory says you've been here about three years. You rent anywhere else local before you found this place?"

"A few months in an apartment."

He grunted. "You come directly here from Florida?"

"I did some construction work in Texas." *And Arkansas and Oklahoma and New Mexico.*

"I'm gonna make a round inside," Duplantis said. He gave Daniel a look that said clearly that both knew he had no search warrant, but any refusal to cooperate would cast even more suspicion on him.

Better not push it, Daniel told himself. The last thing he needed was to get some young hotshot deputy riled at him. He moved to the foot of the stairs, crossing his arms over his chest. "Go ahead."

It took Duplantis about twenty minutes before he was satisfied there was no thirteen-year-old girl concealed in the house. Or being concealed. "I'll check back in a day or two," he said, settling his hat back on a level with his eyebrows. He opened the door, and just before stepping out, turned back to Daniel. "You'll want to stick around, Kendrick. Wouldn't look good if you were to take off somewhere with the kid missing, if you get my drift."

"I'm not going anywhere."

"Just in case you might be thinkin' that."

"Yeah."

FRUSTRATION AND RAGE warred in Daniel as he watched Duplantis back the police car out and drive down the lane. In moments, the taillights had disappeared and he was alone again. But temper was no asset when he needed to think clearly. He went back inside, closed the door and locked up, righted a few things Duplantis had disturbed in his walk-through, then turned out all the lights and went to stand in front of the old-fashioned picture window. A reviled man in a dark, self-imposed solitude.

Teddy. Where are you?

Fear was a cold knot in his stomach. Resolutely he blanked from his mind an avalanche of obscene possibilities if Teddy had really run away. But she couldn't have. Wouldn't have. Nowadays, any thirteen-year-old knew about the danger that lurked everywhere. Beth was permissive to the point of neglect, but she would have—

He rubbed a hand over his face and hurried down the hall to get to the phone in his bedroom. How did he know what Beth had or hadn't told his children? He'd spent so little time with them in the past five years. Guilt was added to his fear as he reached for the phone, but even as he touched it, it rang.

He snatched it up. "Yeah, hello!"

"Dad, Dad, it's me, Joey."

"Joey?" He sank to the side of the bed, glancing again at the green numerals on the clock. "It's two o'clock in the morning, Joey. Where's your mother?"

"She's asleep, Dad. That's why I had to wait so late. 'Cause she doesn't want me to call you."

No, she wanted the cops to come to my house to

tell me my daughter was missing and hopefully hassle me a little, to boot.

"It's okay, Joey. Go to her bedroom and wake her up. Tell her I want to talk to her."

"*No!* She'll know I called. She'll be mad."

"She won't, son. I'll explain."

"No, Dad, you don't know what's going on." Joey's tone dropped. "Teddy's run away, Dad."

Gripping the phone cord, Daniel stared hard at his bare feet. He hated the fear in Joey's voice, hated the way his eleven-year-old son had to master that fear for his sister, hated that a phone call to his father was forbidden. And he, Daniel, who should have been there for both his children, was fifteen hundred miles away. He raised his eyes to the ceiling. "Has she really run away, Joey, or is she just hanging out with a friend somewhere?"

"No, honest. She's run away, Dad."

"How do you know, son?"

"'Cause she told me a couple of days ago that she was gonna do it. She and Mom had this big row 'cause she didn't want to go to Mom's art thing. There was this party at her friend's house and she wanted to go to that instead."

Daniel drove a hand through his hair. "That's not reason enough to run away, Joey."

"Teddy's got a thousand reasons, Dad. Me, too."

Daniel stared at his bare feet, cursing fate and a system that had devastated his kids' childhood. "Joey, what can you tell me about where Teddy might have run to?"

"Nothing for certain, but I think she's coming to see you."

He stood up with alarm. "How do you know that, son?"

"She said it all the time, especially when she and Mom were fighting."

"Explain, Joey. How were they fighting?"

"You know...Mom yelling and Teddy yelling, back and forth and back and forth. It's a pain, Dad."

"I know, but people can disagree, Joey. Especially kids and their parents. It's not cause to run away."

He heard the boy sigh. "You say that 'cause you don't hear them going at it, Dad."

More guilt. More rage. Daniel began pacing with the phone. "I wish I could be there, Joey. You know that, don't you?"

"Yeah, I guess."

"How long has this been going on, son?"

"A long time. Forever."

"Why didn't Teddy call me, Joey? I've told you before that if you have a problem, tell me. That's what dads are for, son."

"Maybe in a reg'lar, normal family, Dad. But it's different with us and Mom and you. You know that. Teddy just decided the only answer was to split."

"And come all the way to Louisiana? How, Joey? Did she tell you that?"

"Hitchhike. We heard those guys that drive eighteen-wheelers are pretty nice."

Except for the ones who weren't. Daniel felt the chill of true terror. This couldn't be happening. It had to be a nightmare. He moved to the window and looked out. A full moon illuminated the farm's rolling fields with cold winter light. Fallow now, the fields looked barren and empty. He was no farmer, but he'd needed the barn, and the acreage had come with it. Over three years now and he felt as if he'd been in this tucked-away spot all his life. The years that had gone before were like someone else's past.

"Joey, I need some honest answers to a couple of questions. Will you help me out?"

"Okay, I guess."

"Has your sister called you since she left?"

"No, Dad. And that's the honest truth."

"Do you have any idea how we could reach her?"

"Uh-uh."

"Is there any place or any person she might have mentioned that we could call? It's important, Joey. It's not a good thing for Teddy to just walk away from her family, no matter how upset she was."

"I don't know *anything,* Dad. Swear to God. She left and she told me she'd call when she got to your place. She said not to worry, she'd be fine."

"You're sure about this, Joey?"

"Do you think she's hurt?" The boy's voice went sharp with concern. "Maybe, you know, kidnapped or something?"

To lie or not? Daniel drew in a breath. "Not kidnapped, son, but the truth is that nobody seems to know anything right now. That's why I need you to help us figure out how to help her if you can. If Teddy said anything, now's the time to tell it."

"She didn't say a word to me, Dad." He paused a second. "You believe me, don't you? I wouldn't lie about something like this, Dad."

"Okay, son. I believe you. But if she does call, you tell your mom first thing and then pick up the phone and call me, too. You got that?"

"Yes, sir." The boy paused for a beat or two. "Dad, when can I come down there?"

"Joey, Joey, you know you can't come unless your mother brings you."

"She won't ever!" Joey cried, suddenly losing it. "She likes it *here!* She likes this stupid city and her stupid artsy friends and that stupid private school where we have to wear dumb stuff and act like the rest of the world's strange when we're the strange ones. It's awful, Dad."

"But you know the rules, son."

"I hate the rules. The rules are unfair! Why can't I visit my dad like other kids? Me and Teddy aren't the only divorced kids. There's lots of 'em in our school, and they all get to visit their other dad or mom, even if they live far away, like you, Dad."

Daniel drew a deep breath. How to soothe his son's pain? What words to magically transform the bitter reality of his children's lives so that they would grow up reasonably healthy? His worst fear was that one day he'd try to explain the circumstances that had robbed them of a chance to be a family and his children would be so warped by the years of deprivation that they'd never understand. Or forgive. Would they cut him out of their lives then?

He raked a hand through his hair. He saw them as often as possible, but always with Beth in the room or, worse yet, one of her lawyer's handpicked stooges. He longed for a weekend, just a single weekend, where he and Teddy and Joey could go to the zoo or to an amusement park, a museum—anywhere—just as long as they were alone. But the chances of that happening were as slim today as they'd been five years ago.

"Dad?"

"I promise I'll talk to your mother, Joey. I'll try my best to get her to bring you here."

Whatever it takes, Joey, I swear. Sell my soul to the devil, anything to have my children overnight, in my care, for the first time in five years.

"Now, go in and wake your mom and tell her it's me on the phone, that I need to talk to her. Tell her it's urgent."

TESSA HAMILTON and her daughter, Keely, plowed through the tangle of tourists on the Bourbon Street sidewalk. Veterans of the French Quarter scene, they were oblivious to the tacky souvenir shops offering everything from T-shirts printed with tasteless slogans to racy undies. Keely waved a friendly refusal to a pitchman who tried to lure them into a smoky bar. They were half a block farther along when Tessa tossed a dollar bill into the open guitar case of a street musician, hoping he'd spend it on a po' boy to eat, but from the look of him—emaciated and dirty—he'd probably blow it on heroine or cocaine. Tessa had promised Stephanie, her sister, that she'd meet her at Mr. B's, one of New Orleans's best bistros, but unless you were lucky enough to get a parking space nearby, the walk was not pleasant. Especially at this hour.

Reminded of the time, she glanced at her watch. "No way we're going to make it, Keely. We should've called and canceled when we got tied up by that accident on the Causeway."

Keely, a good three inches taller than her mother,

draped an arm around Tessa and squeezed. "Relax, Mom. You worry too much. A lot of neat people hang out at Mr. B's. Aunt Steph and Uncle Tal are killing time in the bar. So what if we're a tad late. They aren't watching the clock worrying about us."

"An hour and fifteen minutes isn't a tad late, Keely."

"So they'll be all mellowed out." Keely dodged two obviously inebriated senior citizens, stepping quickly to the side to avoid a head-on collision. "Whoops, watch out, ladies."

Her remark produced a goofy smile from one white-haired matron. "Sorry, dearie. My friend had one too many of those pink things they serve at Pat O'Brian's."

"Hurricanes," Keely said with a smile. "Better be careful drinkin' those things. They're deadly."

"Too late," said her companion, giggling. Slightly off balance, she stumbled on the edge of the sidewalk and was saved from a nasty spill when both Tessa and Keely caught her.

"Whoa. I hope your hotel is close," Keely said.

Tessa frowned with concern. "Can we help you get a taxi?"

"No, no, we're fine." One of them waved nonchalantly, and after they'd steadied themselves, they linked arms and started off in the same direction they'd come.

"They're going the wrong way," Keely said, still smiling.

"I hope they don't get mugged," Tessa muttered.

Keely gave an exasperated sigh. "Chill out, Mom!"

"Okay, okay." With another look at her watch, Tessa picked up her pace. "It's just that two women like that, elderly, unsuspecting, unused to drinking...it's just asking for trouble. Why in the world respectable people who would never dream of getting tipsy in...in..."

"Poughkeepsie?" Keely quipped.

"Yes, in Poughkeepsie, smarty. Why they come to New Orleans and totally lose their good sense is beyond me."

"Tsk, tsk. Those naughty old ladies." Shaking her head, Keely caught her mother's hand and swung it like she used to do as a little girl. "It's called letting your hair down, taking a break from reality, relaxing Big Easy style. You ought to try it sometime."

"No, thanks."

This time, Keely's look at her mother was one of understanding. "Too much relaxing when you were my age, huh, Mom? So now, you have to live your life all prim and proper to make up for those years in your wasted youth."

"My daughter the philosopher," Tessa grumbled, but she was smiling. Keely could always make her smile. Studying her profile, she saw a beautiful honey-blond eighteen-year-old with a stunning figure and a sparkling personality. She still found it hard to believe she'd given birth to this lovely creature. God, she was so lucky to have a second chance with Keely.

Keely's smile suddenly vanished as she spotted the group of grungy teens approaching. "Uh-oh. *Now* I say a little caution is the thing. Let's cross over." She tugged her mother toward the curb to allow the teens all the room they wanted.

Because of New Orleans's moderate climate year-round, the city had more than its share of runaway teens. The group headed toward them was typical. Most were bizarrely dressed with strange hairdos and an abundance of body piercing. One boy's ears were decorated with a dozen or more loops and studs. And one girl wore a see-through shirt which displayed the tiny rings in her pierced nipples.

"Just a minute, Keely." Tessa pulled away from Keely and singled out one of the teens, a girl who looked about sixteen years old and who was obviously pregnant. Tessa smiled at the girl. "Hello. I'm Tessa Hamilton and this is my daughter, Keely."

"Yeah? And Madonna's my mom. So?" With a sulky look, the girl crossed her arms over her stomach. Knowing better than to touch her, Tessa reached into a pocket inside her shoulder bag and plucked out a card. She held it out to the girl. "I can see you're pregnant. And in case you aren't seeing a doctor regularly, I thought you might want to know about the prenatal services at the clinic on Esplanade."

The girl's eyes flicked to a tall boy who'd stopped when Tessa spoke. A smaller, very young girl was plastered close to his side. The boy nodded and the pregnant girl studied a passing taxi. "Why would I want to know that?"

The boy spoke up. "So you could see the doctor, Shelly! Haven't I been telling you that?"

"Shut up, Brian!" Still sulking, the girl tossed her long hair over one shoulder.

"How far along are you?" Tessa asked, still offering the card.

"How should I know?" the girl replied, adding,

"Who cares?" Turning, she started to go, but the boy stopped her.

"Wait up, Shel." He glanced at the card but didn't take it. "If she went, how much would it cost?"

"It's free. It's part of a program at Women's Hospital." She looked at Shelly again. "They have classes about parenting, too. And a diet for you while you're pregnant."

"I don't need any classes to tell me how to eat." Shelly exchanged a quick look with the boy. "Brian can tell you that."

"She's not talking about how much you eat," Brian said with patience. "She's talking about *what* you eat. Healthwise and all that. You need to think about the baby, Shel."

"Why should I?" Shelly asked, holding her long hair up away from her neck. "You worry enough for the both of us."

"Here." Tessa had her pen out and was scribbling on the back of the card. "I'm the director of Sojourn, a hostel located on the north shore. You might want to check us out." She passed the card to Brian. "Give me a call, either one of you, or come over the Causeway bridge and take a firsthand look."

Suspicion replaced the sulkiness in Shelly's expression. "I don't want nothing to do with the cops."

"If you've done nothing illegal, we don't involve the police unless you ask us to call them," Tessa said. That was always the complication. These kids were listed on the missing-persons roster in every police department in the U.S. To get help, they had to go through the juvenile department. The system automatically posted names and photos, which in turn exposed them. Many were running away and didn't want to be found. It was a catch-22 and something Tessa dealt with daily. If they were runaways, she tried in counseling to get them to reconnect with their parents.

"Come on," Shelly said suddenly to Brian. "I told you it's hopeless, didn't I?" She snatched the card from Brian, ripped it in half and threw it on the sidewalk. The small girl scrambled into the gutter and retrieved the torn card, tucking it into her pocket, then hurried to catch up with Brian and Shelly. At the corner, she turned and gave Tessa a quick, furtive look, then she was gone.

"You never give up, do you, Mom?"

"Hmm?" The small girl's eyes had been large and blue. Something about her reminded Tessa of Keely in her preteens. There had been a dark smudge high on her cheekbone. Tessa hoped it was dirt and not a bruise.

"You're going to try and save all the poor runaways in the world, aren't you?"

With a smile, Tessa fell into step beside her daughter. "Not every one, honey. No one can."

"That pregnant girl—Shelly—she's about six months along, I bet."

"Good guess. And I bet she's never seen a doctor."

"I wish she hadn't thrown the card away."

"The younger one picked it up. There's hope."

Suddenly Keely threw up her arm and waved. "There's Uncle Tal. See? There, in the entrance at Mr. B's. Come on, Mom. I'm starving!"

CHAPTER TWO

THE NEXT MORNING, Daniel crossed Lake Pontchartrain via the Causeway bridge along with the rush-hour crowd. He usually didn't have any reason to drive into New Orleans unless one of his clients wanted special material for a custom piece, and as he jostled for position alongside regular commuters, he was glad his business was one that allowed him the convenience of working at home.

That hadn't been the reason he'd settled on the farm in Abita Springs—a village on the north shore of Lake Pontchartrain, about forty-five minutes from the city. When he'd finally sobered up and decided he needed to get a real life, he was already renting the farmhouse. The reason he'd stayed was because of the barn, which had a concrete floor, a necessary foundation for the equipment and tools he needed for woodworking. He'd always had an interest in carpentry, but it had been only a hobby until his world had collapsed around his ears. When his career had gone down the drain with his marriage and he'd been denied access to his children, he had spent a couple of years wandering through the southern states, picking up work on construction sites to eat, pay rent and child support and keep himself sane.

Reaching the end of the Causeway, he merged into

the traffic in Metairie at Interstate 10 and headed east to the heart of the city. Ten minutes later, he exited at Tulane Avenue and soon turned in to the parking area at the police department. He was still steaming from his conversation with Beth last night. He shouldn't have been surprised that she took no responsibility for Teddy's disappearance. She complained that Teddy was so difficult, moody and stubborn nowadays that not even a trained counselor would have guessed she was thinking of running away. "I refused to cater to her silly moods," Beth had stated with belligerence.

"It's normal for thirteen-year-old girls to be moody, Beth," he'd argued wearily. "They're entering adolescence, they're dealing with a whole new world of ideas and sensations. They're bombarded on all sides with negative messages. Peer pressure is another major influence. Did the two of you ever talk?"

He recognized her sigh as the sound of exhaled cigarette smoke. He wondered if she still smoked two packs a day. "Have you ever tried to talk to a thirteen-year-old, Daniel?" she snapped. "No, of course, you haven't. You don't have to cope with any of this. You're cocooned in that primitive place, puttering in your stupid wood shop, sanding and sawing away while I have to deal with the kids every day. You can't imagine how stressful it is, Daniel."

"Then bring them here to me, Beth!"

"And live in Louisiana? Be serious. You're not even in New Orleans proper. No, I would never be able to paint again, Daniel. You know how it was when we were in Florida. My creative juices just dried up! No, no, I couldn't do it."

Bending his head, he'd struggled to hang on to his patience. "I'd be happy to take the kids off your hands forever, Beth. Just say the word and we're back in court."

"Don't be ridiculous! After what you did, that's impossible."

"I didn't do anything, Beth. You know that."

"What about the witness? What about that girl?"

"She lied! How many times do I have to say it?" He breathed deeply. "We're off the subject, Beth. I want to know about Teddy. Where she might have gone. Why she left. You must have some idea."

"If I had an idea, don't you think I would have told the police? I don't know anything. I came home from an engagement and she was gone. No note, no nothing. Kids are so insensitive, Daniel. They think only of themselves. Things have changed since you were around. I know Teddy thinks of herself as Daddy's girl, but if you spent as much time with her as I do, you'd soon see how selfish a teenage kid can be."

As selfish as her mother?

"Have you tried her friends?"

"Of course. And nobody knows a thing." She blew out smoke, then added, "As crazy as it sounds, I'm beginning to wonder if she's headed down there to try to see you, Daniel. She's just silly enough to do it."

"How? Did she have any money? Could she have charged an airline ticket?"

There was a small silence. "I don't think so."

"Don't you know? My God, Beth, she's thirteen. She wouldn't even know how to purchase a ticket."

"She's tried it before, but I—"

"Tried to fly here to New Orleans? When?"

"Oh, a couple of months ago, but the airlines have safeguards about kids flying without parental approval. I told her if she tried anything like that again, I'd have to consider sending her to a good boarding school. If she's so set on defying me, let's see how she likes the strict discipline she'd find there."

Before the conversation had deteriorated any further, he'd hung up. It was useless raging at Beth. Sometimes she was like a teenager herself, but he'd been left seething. Instead of worrying about Teddy's safety, instead of trying to deal with the problems that would drive their daughter to run away, Beth focused only on how her own life was impacted by her missing child. Art, not her troubled teenage daughter, was the ruling force in her life. Why she'd even agreed to have children still mystified Daniel. It had been him who had wanted them, and he'd lived to regret ever persuading her to change her mind. As in any divorce where there were kids, Teddy and Joey were the true victims.

His stomach was in a knot as he climbed the broad steps that led to the front door of the building. He didn't know what else to do except check with the police department in New Orleans. Bright and early this morning he'd been in Sheriff Wade's office with a picture of Teddy. The man had been clearly skeptical when Daniel denied having seen or heard from his daughter. He'd left convinced that even if they found Teddy, he would be the last person the authorities would notify. Battling frustration and rage, he pushed at the doors and went into precinct headquarters at NOPD.

He stood for a moment to get his bearings. The front desk was straight ahead, manned by two female cops and a big, burly sergeant with a heavy paunch. Both women were busy with an irate citizen who was arguing over something in an accident report he was waving in front of them. The desk sergeant was tied up on the phone. On a long bench against the wall, two handcuffed thugs sat, ankles chained to the bolted legs of the bench. When the sergeant slammed the receiver down, he bellowed a name, and instantly a uniformed cop came out of the door from the men's room across the hall.

"Take 'em to central booking, Mike. Sweeney's waitin'."

"Thanks, Sarge." He bent and freed the chains from the bench, then pointed both prisoners toward a turn in the hall. Without expression, they shuffled ahead of the cop, the chains on their ankles clanking with each step on the hard tile floor.

Daniel approached the desk sergeant, glancing at the name tag on his shirtfront before speaking. "Sergeant Naquin, I'm Dan Kendrick. My thirteen-year-old daughter's missing. She lives in New York, but it's possible she might have headed down to New Orleans. Who in the NOPD can help me?"

"That'd be Juvy," he said, running a finger down a duty roster. "Marly Toups." He glanced at a big bulletin board on the wall. "She's signed out right now, yeah."

"What do you suggest, Sergeant?"

"We're pretty swamped at the moment. Marly got

a call, I think. She's probably down in the Quarter trying to flush out a couple of runaways. Them kids keep her jumpin'. It's a cryin' shame, the trouble we got tryin' to keep tabs on all the little jerks who take it in their heads to run off to the Big Easy. Like the weather here, yeah. And the Mardi Gras, the Quarter. Hey, let the good times roll. What they don't like is stayin' in Boise or Mayberry and doin' homework and havin' to listen to Mom and Dad tell 'em what they can and can't do." He turned to one of the women. "Sandy, didn't Marly head out a few minutes ago to check on some juvies hangin' out on Jackson Square?"

"Yeah, ten minutes ago, I think," Sandy replied, giving Daniel an interested look. "You want me to try to raise her?"

"No, she'll check in once she's back in her unit." He turned back to Daniel. "Just take a seat over on the bench, and when she shows up, you can give her the vitals. Never can tell, the kid might be here."

Trying to control his frustration, Daniel asked, "Does Officer Toups work alone? Or is there a clerk or a secretary, somebody who answers her phone when she's away from her desk?"

The folds of Naquin's fat cheeks almost obscured his eyes as he gazed at Daniel. "You in a big hurry?"

"Every minute my daughter's missing increases the chance of her being harmed, Sergeant. She's thirteen. I need to find her before something tragic happens. I've got a picture here and I can give you her 'vitals,' as you call it. I could get the formality of filing the missing-persons report behind me and save Officer Toups some time."

"Hell, that's her job. But if you wanna try to get Jerry away from that freakin' computer—he's her clerk—have at it. Room 216 on the second floor. The elevator's over there. Don't worry, it's off-limits to prisoners and safe as the cemetery at midnight."

"Thanks." Not trusting himself to speak, Daniel strode to the elevator and punched the Up arrow viciously. Five years hadn't improved the quality of the Neanderthals manning the front desks of America's protectors. He hadn't been in a police department since the night of his arrest in Florida, but the good news was that at least he wasn't in handcuffs this time.

With a *ping*, the elevator opened and he waited for a couple to exit before stepping inside. A woman followed behind Daniel, facing away from him when the doors slid closed. As he punched the button for the second floor, he was aware of her perfume—something light and flowery. It came to him suddenly that he hadn't been with a woman in a long time.

"Two, please," she said in a husky voice.

"Done," he said, nodding at the button he'd already punched. He glanced at her, but she was busy rummaging in her handbag, her honey-blond hair screening her face so that he glimpsed only the curve of her cheek and a firm chin. When the elevator stopped, she hurried out.

He followed, beginning a search for Room 216, and found himself taking the same direction as the woman, who was long gone. It took him a few more minutes to find the door marked Juvenile Services. He turned the knob and went inside.

The office was windowless and barely big enough

to accommodate a desk and two battered filing cabinets. In baskets stacked three high on the desk overflowed with papers. Daniel felt instant dismay. If this was the best NOPD could do for missing kids, he probably wouldn't get much help here. He tried not to look at the walls. Plastered on every available inch of it were pictures of kids of all ages, most captioned with the chilling phrase *"Have you seen this child?"*

The young clerk manning the desk was studying the computer monitor in front of him. Behind him was an open door, Toups's office, Daniel guessed. He could hear sounds of shuffling papers and the squeak of a chair. Maybe he was in luck for once today. Maybe she was in. The clerk looked up. "Yes, sir, what can I do for you?"

"I'm Dan Kendrick. I'm trying to locate my daughter, Teddy. It's possible she's run away, and her mother thinks she could be in this area. I was told by the desk sergeant to see Officer Toups."

"Marly's out right now, but I'd be happy to try to help. I'll need her name, age, general description, when she was last seen, what she was wearing. That kind of stuff."

Daniel reached into the breast pocket of his jacket and withdrew Teddy's picture. "This is a photo taken a couple of months ago. I'd like to get it out onto the street right away, show it to the cops patrolling the city, especially the Quarter." After handing over the photo, he glanced at the computer. "What do I have to do to get her picture into the system?"

"Very little," Jerry said, propping Teddy's picture against his coffee cup. "And second to one of the patrolling units eyeballing her, this'll be your best bet to try to find her. There's some paperwork, forms and stuff. They're in Marly's office.'' Without getting up from his chair, he zipped backward to the office directly behind him, leaned into the open door and yelled, "Tessa, bring some of those forms out here, will you?''

There was an instant of silence, then the sound of a file drawer sliding open. Apparently it wasn't Marly Toups in Marly Toups's office. Daniel looked curiously at the open door as a woman emerged.

It was the woman from the elevator, he realized. Tessa Hamilton.

IT HAD BEEN sheer impulse that brought Tessa to the police department. One of the kids at Sojourn had finally caved and given Tessa permission to call her parents in Indiana. Once the reconnection between parent and child was made, Marly's office would handle official paperwork, airline tickets and the like. Tessa often assisted Marly and Jerry with the details. She frequently encountered homeless kids and juvenile officials from other jurisdictions in Marly's office, but she was totally unprepared to meet Daniel Kendrick. She blamed the man and the tangle she'd been plunged into because of him for many a sleepless night. What perverse quirk of fate had brought the two of them together after five years?

She braced herself for the moment their eyes met. "Hello, Mr. Kendrick.''

For a beat or two in time, she saw confusion. Disbelief. And then icy fury. His gray eyes went as cold as sleeting rain. His hard, square jaw clenched, thinning his well-shaped mouth. And then he mastered whatever emotion raged inside him and gave her a nod, a quick, barely civil movement of his head. "Ms. Hamilton. It's been a long time."

Not long enough. That's probably what he was thinking. And how could she blame him? "Yes."

"You live in New Orleans?"

"Covington."

Something flickered in his steely eyes. He turned to Jerry. "About that paperwork."

"Here." She dropped the forms on Jerry's desk and was turning to leave when her gaze fell on the picture propped against the coffee cup. "Who's this?" She reached for the picture.

"My daughter," Daniel said. "Teddy."

"This is the child who's missing?"

"That's why I'm here."

"She lives with her mother?"

"I think you know the answer to that."

"In Florida?"

"Beth left Florida when we were divorced. The children, Teddy and Joey, are with her in New York."

"Why do you think your daughter might be in New Orleans?"

"Why are you asking so many questions, Ms. Hamilton? Are you suggesting, because of what you think you know about me, that I don't have a right to search for my daughter when she's run away from home?"

"I don't know anything about your relationship with your children, Mr. Kendrick."

Jerry stood up, frowning at them. "Hey, wait a minute. You two know each other?"

"Not really," Tessa said. "We've met, but it was a long time ago."

"About that paperwork, Officer." Daniel reached for the forms. "I'll fill it out now, and if there's some way the picture could be circulated, I would appreciate it. I know Officer Toups is in charge, but surely there's no reason to hold the picture."

Tessa studied the features of the young girl. In this photo, her hair was neatly pulled away from a gamine face, clipped above each ear with barrettes. Her white blouse had a lace-trimmed Peter Pan collar. Around her neck she wore a heart-shaped locket on a thin gold chain. There was very little resemblance to the wary-eyed, dirty young girl Tessa had seen yesterday afternoon in the Quarter.

"I've seen this child."

Daniel straightened abruptly and gave her a sharp look. "Where? When?"

"I was in the French Quarter yesterday with my daughter, and we talked to a group of teenagers, one of whom was pregnant."

Daniel drew a harsh breath. "Not Teddy!"

"No, another girl, older than your daughter. I didn't speak to Teddy. She stood off to the side while I talked to the boy and the pregnant girl, trying to persuade them to see a doctor at the clinic or to come and stay at Sojourn with me."

"Sojourn?"

"Tessa runs a halfway house for kids in trouble," Jerry explained. He looked at her. "You think you could find these kids again, Tessa?"

"Who knows? They can be here one day and in

Houston tomorrow, Jerry, but it's certainly worth a try.''

Daniel studied her from silver-sharp eyes, the forms in front of him forgotten. "Are you sure it was Teddy?"

The plight of his daughter was taking more of a toll on him than Tessa would have believed. She tried to recall him as he'd been five years earlier. Had there been so much silver in his dark hair? Had those lines bracketing his mouth always been so marked? Or had the consequences of the crime he'd committed been worse than he expected?

"She was dirty and tired and scared, Mr. Kendrick, but the face is the same. She probably realizes she's in over her head. She picked up my card after the other girl ripped it apart and tossed it. I saw Teddy slip the pieces into her pocket. I'll retrace my steps and see what I can find out." She reached for a sticky note on Jerry's desk. "Give me a number where you can be reached and I'll keep you informed." She glanced at him. "Are you staying in a hotel here in the city?"

"I live in Abita Springs."

She was startled. "Really? For how long?"

"What difference does it make, Ms. Hamilton? Here's my phone number and my address, but you won't need to contact me, because I'm going with you."

CHAPTER THREE

IT WAS HIGH NOON by the time Tessa left the police department with Daniel, tense and silent in the car beside her. She let him ride along with her to look for Teddy rather than tolerate him tailgating her in his beat-up truck all the way to the French Quarter. That would have been almost impossible in the congestion in the business district at lunchtime. She didn't relish making conversation with a man she wished only to forget, and was glad to concentrate on driving.

Daniel waited while she stopped for the St. Charles streetcar, then asked abruptly, "About Teddy, Ms. Hamilton—how did she look when you saw her? Was she...did she seem...okay? Her mother wasn't sure she had any money with her."

"She looked scared, Mr. Kendrick. Like most runaways, she was probably clueless about what life is really like on the streets, but once there, too many kids prefer to take their chances rather than call home. That says something about the dismal circumstances some of them are running away from, doesn't it? The only encouraging thing I can tell you is that she was with kids who seemed streetwise."

"Streetwise! How is that encouraging? There's no telling what they do to survive. They could be into drugs or crime or...or prostitution. I don't want Teddy exposed to that.''

"She's already exposed to it, Mr. Kendrick. She entered that world when she left home. And *survive* is a good word. These kids can astound you by their ingenuity when it comes to surviving. By encouraging, I meant that the teenage boy seemed to have the welfare of his pregnant girlfriend at heart. And if he cares about her, it's reasonable to think he might take a scared thirteen-year-old under his wing, as well.'' She glanced into her rearview mirror and signaled a left turn. "He wanted to keep my card.''

He rubbed his eyes. "I can't believe Teddy has done this!''

"How do you think she got all the way from New York to New Orleans?''

"Probably her mother's credit card,'' Daniel said in a hard tone. "According to Beth, she tried this once before at the airport, but Beth discovered what she planned and stopped her in time. She could take a bus, she could hitchhike. Who knows?''

"She sounds like a desperate kid,'' Tessa said, watching him with interest. "Why do you think she wants to get away so badly?''

He was shaking his head. "Joey said she and her mother haven't been getting along, but Teddy's not foolish enough to take off without having some kind of plan. She's young, but she's not stupid.''

"I take it her plan is to find her father.''

Daniel's bitter gaze was focused on a street artist. "Even if she made it safely to my door, you know better than anyone that it would be impossible for her to stay with me.''

"It was the judge, not me, who decided that, Mr. Kendrick."

He turned and looked at her coldly. "I was innocent, Ms. Hamilton. I didn't lay a hand on that student."

"That's not what she claimed."

"She lied, and you drove the final nail into my coffin when you convinced the judge to believe her."

"I testified to what she told me, Mr. Kendrick, no more and no less."

Daniel looked at her with a fierce expression. "She was a troubled kid, you knew that. Why would she be at that shelter otherwise? I don't know why she said what she said, but it wasn't true. As for your complicity in her little scheme, you should have known better. It's because of your testimony that I lost custody of my children. That girl's accusation would have been dismissed for the fairy tale it was if you hadn't supported it."

"You delude yourself if you think my word has that much power, Mr. Kendrick. Have you forgotten your wife? She believed the girl, too."

"We were in the process of a divorce, for God's sake! A custody battle. If I'd gotten custody of our kids, she wouldn't have been morally free to run off to New York. Beth's a great one for keeping up appearances, but she's a very selfish, self-centered individual. Art is the motivating force in her life, not Teddy and Joey."

Even knowing she had done the right thing, the look on his face—and his argument—made her uncomfortable. Tessa kept her eyes on the street, reminding herself they were looking for a little girl.

"If Teddy's run away, it's not me who's to blame," Daniel said in a quietly bitter tone. "It's you and the judge and Beth and the whole screwed-up system that destroyed any chance of my kids' happiness when my marriage went down the tubes."

He'd hit a nerve. Tessa had lived with enough guilt and uncertainty over Daniel Kendrick to last a lifetime. She didn't like having new fire stirred up from old ashes. "You're saying you would have been a better parent?"

"You're goddamn right I would!"

She stopped the car with a jerk. "We're here," she snapped. She got out of the car before he could say another word.

FOUR HOURS LATER, Tessa admitted defeat. After an exhaustive search of the Quarter, including the alleys, every hole in the wall, the many byways and hidden corners she'd come to know after two years in New Orleans, there was no sign of the grungy group she had seen yesterday.

"There's still hope," she told Daniel, driving back to the police station to pick up his car. He had been tireless in seeking out every kid under the age of sixteen whether they looked as if they were homeless or not. "Teddy has my card. From what you've told me about her life back in New York with her mother, I think it's clear she'll be looking you up, Mr. Kendrick."

"No, she knows she can't stay with me, though she doesn't know why I'm prohibited from taking care of my children like a normal parent."

"What you did *wasn't* normal," Tessa snapped.

He'd been taking verbal potshots at her all day and she was fed up with it. It wasn't her fault that he was in this mess.

He gazed thoughtfully out the passenger window. "Maybe she'll use that card you gave her," he said, ignoring her retort.

"I sincerely hope so."

"What exactly do you do at Sojourn?" Daniel asked when she stopped for a red light.

"We offer an alternative to incarceration for troubled teens who have broken the law but haven't committed violent acts. To stay with us, they have to contribute in a meaningful way. Sojourn tries to teach them basic skills in getting along in the outside world, about meeting obligations, obeying rules, respecting authority, contributing to the good of the group. For some of these kids, these are alien concepts."

"How do they come to you? How do they find you?"

"We work through law enforcement mostly—Marly Toups's office, for example. And, naturally, Social Services. You would be amazed what some kids can survive and still function with near normalcy."

"On the other hand, some who may look normal are way out in left field," Daniel said, studying the pedestrians crossing in front of them. She recalled suddenly that he was once a high school principal. "So, how do runaways fit in?" he asked.

"Originally they didn't—not at Sojourn, but word gets around. Sometimes they just show up looking for a free meal or shelter for a couple of days, but there are no freebies here. If they want to stay, they have to abide by all the rules, same as the hard juvies. Which is to share in housework, cooking, maintenance and upkeep, as well as encounter groups and talk sessions.'' She gave him a small smile. "We're very big on communication at Sojourn."

"Sounds like an ambitious project."

"I feel overwhelmed at times, but the small victories make it all worthwhile."

"Such as?"

"When a runaway is reunited with his family. Or when a teen decides to go back to school after dropping out. When a teenage girl rejects promiscuity. When a teenage boy acknowledges that sexual prowess is no indicator of real masculinity." She pulled into the parking lot at the police department. "Some of these kids have had no parenting. They've been forgotten. They're innocent victims of a society gone haywire."

"And some aren't so innocent." Without giving her a chance to argue, Daniel reached for the door handle to get out. "One of your unfortunate victims turned my life upside down, Ms. Hamilton. With your help." He got out of the car but leaned in to look at her before closing the door. "The question is how to tell the innocents from the miscreants? For the sake of the public at large, I hope you're better at telling the difference now than you were five years ago."

He slammed the door and walked away.

"Hi. Got a minute, Steph?"

Dr. Stephanie Robichaux looked up, removed her reading glasses and smiled. "Tessa! Come inside. You almost missed me." She glanced at her watch.

"I've got twenty minutes before I have to meet a group of Alison's friends at Basin and Canal for a cemetery tour."

Tessa frowned. "Not alone? That cemetery's notorious for its muggings. What kind of security have you arranged?"

"Hah! I pity the mugger who would dare approach twenty fifteen-year-old girls."

"I'm serious, Steph."

"Relax, Tee. The school has engaged two security guards."

Tessa wrapped her arms around herself and shuddered. "I hate those old cemeteries. They're weird. And so are the people buried there. Marie Laveau and Lestat don't hold any fascination for me."

"Marie Laveau's crypt is there, Tee, but Lestat isn't buried in New Orleans."

"Fine. That's one less weirdo."

"What's wrong?" Stephanie could always sense Tessa's mood. They were twins, identical twins, and even though they'd lost contact for many years, there was still a bond between them that a hundred years couldn't sever. "I'm headed for a cemetery, but you look like you've seen a ghost."

"I suppose I have, in a way." Tessa sank into a chair. "I've just spent the afternoon with a man who hates me, Steph."

Stephanie frowned. "Who? Nobody hates you, Tessa."

"This man does, and when I explain, you'll agree he has good reason."

Stephanie glanced at her watch again. "So tell me. I've still got eighteen minutes."

"I testified against him in court, and my statement helped cause him to lose custody of his children when he got a divorce."

"Wow. What did he do that was so bad?"

"It was when I was the administrator of Cypress House in Florida. He was the principal of the high school at the time. There was a girl—Judy—I've never forgotten her. She said he had come on to her, that he'd tried to seduce her." Tessa was rubbing her arms through her shirtsleeves. "She was sixteen."

"Not much older than you were when you were raped."

Tessa closed her eyes for a moment. "Uh-huh. I wasn't sure whether she was telling the truth or not, but she insisted and begged me not to tell anybody. Then I was called to testify in the custody hearing during this man's divorce. I suppose someone told his wife's lawyer. I repeated exactly what Judy had told me."

"Which is what you should have done."

Tessa rubbed her forehead, sighing. "It was a difficult call, Steph. His wife seemed almost casual about it all. Not like an outraged mother at all. He told me today that immediately after the divorce, she moved them to New York."

"And so the wife got her divorce and the kids, and he got what was coming to him. Why do you look so upset, Tee? You did the right thing."

"He still claims he was falsely accused. After five years." She gazed through the window into the glossy dark leaves of a magnolia tree. "He's so...strong in denying it."

"They all say that, Tee."

"He looks ten years older," Tessa murmured, her gaze still on the tree.

"He was found out. The world tends to frown on that kind of behavior."

"I suppose so." After a moment, Tessa turned back.

"How on earth did you happen to meet up again?"

"I was at the police department and he came into Marly Toups's office. His teenage daughter is missing."

"Oh, no."

"I saw her yesterday when Keely and I were on the way to Mr. B's to meet you and Tal."

"You saw his daughter?"

"Sounds incredible, doesn't it?"

"Yes, it does. But how did you know? You could hardly have recognized her after five years."

"He had a picture." Tessa reached into her handbag and pulled it out. "He wanted Jerry to enter it into the computer and pass it around to the mobile units. He seemed pretty desperate."

Stephanie studied the photo for a moment before looking up. "Tell me again how you came to spend the afternoon with him?"

"When I said I'd seen Teddy, he insisted on coming with me to look for her. So..." she shrugged "...he came with me."

"That's some coincidence, Tee."

"Uh-huh." Tessa looked at Teddy's face in the picture. The child had her father's strong chin and direct gaze. And the same silver-clear eyes. "She was with a pregnant girl who may show up here. I told them about the clinic. Would you keep an eye out for her? Alert the other staff? I know you don't post anything on the bulletin board in case it scares off the kids, but she's so young, Steph.''

''And you feel responsible.''

Tessa ignored that. ''If she does show up, do everything you can to keep her here, please. If Marly's not available, call me.''

''It'll take you forty minutes to get here from across the lake, Tee.''

''Just call me, Steph.''

Stephanie studied her. ''Do I sense a tiny crack in your resolve never to get personally involved?''

''No!'' Tessa recalled the bleak look in Dan Kendrick's eyes when he spoke his daughter's name. ''It's the little girl I'm worried about. I don't care what Kendrick says. I'm not responsible for the disaster he's made of his life.''

''He accused you of being responsible?''

''Yeah. I know it's dumb, but I feel I ought to go the extra mile on this one.''

''You help him find his little girl and that should square things?'' Stephanie studied the picture thoughtfully. ''Maybe. And maybe not. He'll always have that vile accusation hanging over him.''

''I can't do anything about that,'' Tessa said shortly.

''As you say, this is about Teddy, not her father.'' As Stephanie got to her feet, she smoothed both hands down the front of her dress, outlining the swell of her abdomen. She was pregnant again. T.J., the child who had brought her and Dr. Talbot Robichaux together, was now two years old. ''And now I've got to go.''

Her eyes danced as she looked at her sister. "Sure you don't want to visit that cemetery with us?"

"I'm sure," Tessa said, managing a smile.

"I'll post this." Stephanie waved the photo. "And don't beat up on yourself over this one, Tee. You can't save all the runaways in the world."

"And you can't save all the babies. 'Bye, Steph." Scooping up her purse, Tessa walked out the door.

DANIEL DROVE UP the lane that led to the farmhouse, using the sweep of his headlights to look for any sign of movement on the grounds. But there was nothing. The house was dark, meaning that Teddy wasn't waiting inside. He sat for a second, feeling tension still coiled like a snake in his belly. Even had Teddy managed to find his place this far out in the country, he wouldn't have been able to let her stay. He knew that and she knew that, but neither Teddy nor Joey had ever truly understood why. And he couldn't bring himself to tell them. Wiping his hand over his face wearily, he got out of the car.

He hadn't driven home when Tessa Hamilton left him. He'd turned his pickup around and headed back into the Quarter, where he'd spent the rest of the day and half the night looking high and low for his daughter. He'd seen dozens of kids, kids he'd known were not tourists, but he hadn't found Teddy. Nor had he spotted the group Tessa had described.

As he shoved his key in the door, he sensed movement on his left. The leap of his heart calmed when he heard a raspy *meeoww.*

"Hey, Cat." He pushed the door open and the striped tomcat darted past Daniel and streaked down the hall, heading for the kitchen. Daniel tossed his keys onto the table and closed the door, then followed the cat and snapped on the kitchen light.

The cat was on the counter, waiting calmly.

"What do you want, as if I didn't know?"

The cat gave him an unblinking stare. It was a familiar routine, one he and his cantankerous pet enacted at mealtime.

"A Mexican standoff, huh, buddy?"

The cat remained mute and still.

Daniel found a can of cat food and opened it. Not bothering to spoon it into a dish, he set the can on the floor and watched the cat leap gracefully off the counter, settle in front of the cat food, and without any particular haste, begin to eat. Wet and starving, the cat had appeared one rainy night as Daniel worked to restore an antique armoire in the barn. He'd offered half a discarded tuna fish sandwich, but the cat had eyed him suspiciously and kept his distance. Only when Daniel locked up, leaving a window cracked open, did the cat venture over to the food. The next morning he again appeared to watch Daniel work, and every morning since. He was still suspicious of strangers, but he would now allow Daniel to scratch behind his ears, although picking him up and stroking him was out of the question.

Daniel didn't know what kind of abuse the cat had escaped to wind up on his doorstep, but considering the animal's deep distrust of humans, it wasn't difficult to imagine. Sometimes Daniel thought the two of them had a lot in common.

While the cat ate, Daniel eyed the phone. Now that he had a lead on Teddy's whereabouts, he was honor-bound to call Beth. Unconventional though she was as a mother, she had to have some concern about Teddy. She was as capable as Daniel of imagining the terrifying situations their daughter could get into before she was found and safely back in New York.

His hand clamped to the back of his neck, he looked through the window into bleak darkness and tried to think of another option for Teddy, assuming of course that they found her. If she'd run away once, she might do so again. There were no other relatives who might offer her a home. Both he and Beth had only distant family, and no one who would happily take on a thirteen-year-old girl. God, he felt so powerless. It was unnatural for a father to stand by and do nothing like this.

He took the receiver and punched in Beth's number. After half a dozen rings, she answered, her voice thick and confused.

"Beth, it's me."

No reply came for a few seconds. "Daniel? What— Why— Do you know what time it is?"

Only then did Daniel glance at the clock over the stove. Three-fifteen. But damned if he'd apologize. "I just got home, Beth. I've spent the day and half the night searching for Teddy."

"She's not at your place, is she?" Her voice heightened with suspicion.

"No, but it seems you were right in thinking she was headed this way. She was spotted in the French Quarter Sunday afternoon by a woman who runs a shelter for runaways. I went looking for her, but it's easy for these kids to avoid adults if they want to.

Mostly I hoped word would get out that I'm looking for her and that maybe she'd try to contact me.''

"Don't count on it, Daniel. She's in such a silly, rebellious mood right now.''

"She's confused and troubled, Beth. Think of it. She has no money and no place to live. Even an adult would be terrified in those circumstances. Tessa said she looked scared, and scared kids are vulnerable on the street.''

"Who's Tessa?''

"Tessa Hamilton is the woman who runs the shelter.''

"Not the Tessa Hamilton who testified at our custody hearing?'' she asked with astonishment.

"Yeah, that Tessa Hamilton.'' Daniel bent his head, pinching the bridge of his nose. He didn't know why he'd told Beth that. It was simply more ammunition to lambaste him with.

He heard the rustle of bedclothes and knew she was sitting up now, giving him her full attention. "Maybe Teddy will show up on her doorstep. The way she talks, all kids would be better off in her care than with their own kin. To hear her tell it, she knows everything there is to know about raising kids properly,'' Beth said, then added maliciously, "And she doesn't hesitate to lecture anybody who doesn't measure up to her standards.''

Daniel frowned at the numbers on the keypad. "Do I detect a note of personal spite, Beth? Which would be odd. You wouldn't have custody of Teddy and Joey without Ms. Hamilton.''

Beth huffed in disgust. "She was Ms. Know-it-all during the sessions with the judge. You weren't around then, so you don't know how she questioned every word I said. If it hadn't been for my lawyer, I—''

"I didn't know you'd had any contact with Tessa," Daniel interrupted sharply. "When was this?"

"Oh, those tiresome conferences in the judge's chambers while we were discussing her testimony about the girl you molested."

"I didn't molest that girl, Beth."

"Oh, please." Beth blew out a long sigh. "Don't lct's argue over that again tonight, Daniel."

He was frowning in thought. "She must have been thinking my kids were doomed no matter which way the court decided," he murmured.

"What?"

"Nothing." He straightened. "Look, I'm ringing off now. I just called to tell you Teddy has been seen here and there's a good chance we might be able to find her if she doesn't take it into her head to run again."

"When you find her, send her straight back here on the first flight, Daniel. The next two weeks are terribly tight for me. I have commissions for three pieces to show in a spring fete. I don't need these distractions."

"Our daughter has run away, Beth. That's more than a distraction. You should be praying to avoid a tragedy."

Beth sighed again. "Oh, Daniel. It's not hard to see where Teddy gets her wild ideas. The two of you continually overreact."

"Overreact? Teddy's lost, Beth. She's somewhere in the back alleys of one of the most hedonistic cities in the world. She's in danger, for God's sake! Can't you get that through your head?''

"Just keep me posted, Daniel, you hear me?"

He stared at his shoes. "I hear you, Beth."

"Because she can't stay with you. I don't care how many times you deny doing anything wrong. I have custody and nothing's going to change that. Besides, if you had her you'd cater to these ridiculous moods of hers. We've been through all this—"

Daniel gently replaced the receiver, cutting Beth's tirade off in midsentence. Still frowning, he went to the back door and gazed through the glass panes. Had Tessa Hamilton had reservations about Beth getting custody of his children? Until tonight, he'd never even suspected that there had been contact between Beth and Tessa. Had the judge wanted Tessa's opinion of Beth? Had the judge sensed Beth's immaturity and selfishness? Had Tessa? And why hadn't his lawyer known about the goings-on in the judge's chambers? Why hadn't Daniel been informed?

Bottom line: would it have mattered? If all their concerns had been true, they would still have been in a bind. Because nothing would have been worse than turning Teddy and Joey over to a child molester.

CHAPTER FOUR

TEDDY HUDDLED in the corner and tried to keep her thoughts busy with something besides the noises coming from the couple on the foam mattress across the room. They'd been doing that for hours, it seemed, kissing and stuff. So far they hadn't actually done the Big Number, as Brian called it, but if they kept doing what they were doing much longer, it just might happen. Ugh, gross. She did not want to be in the room when two people did that.

To tell the truth, she didn't want to be in this room at all anymore. She wanted to get away from here and find her dad and live with him, but when she told Brian a little about her situation, he'd said if there was some legal reason why her dad hadn't let her and Joey live with him before, unless something had changed, her dad wouldn't be able to let her stay now. No matter how much she wanted to. The cops would just bust him and take her back to New York. One thing she was going to do for sure was ask her dad to tell her why, once and for all. But for right now, she didn't know what to do.

She shivered and curled into a ball, pulling her jacket over her as much as possible. It had turned chilly for New Orleans, so she was forced to sleep in her sweats, and tomorrow she wouldn't have any more clean clothes to change into. Her jeans were filthy, and so were all her shirts and underwear. Gosh, it would be nice to take a bath. She'd only had one since she got here. Shelly had sneaked her into a motel room when the paying customers had checked out and before the maids got there to clean up. Brian and Shelly knew lots of ways to get along like that. She'd felt guilty, sort of, but she'd wanted that bath real bad.

Glancing around at the dingy room, she wondered how much longer she could stand living like this. They'd been in this abandoned shop on the lower end of St. Peter Street for two days. When Brian located it, he'd sprung the lock on the back door and they had all been sort of camping out ever since. They were real careful not to use any light, such as candles or matches or anything, because if they were spotted, they'd be hustled out and maybe have to sleep outside again. She'd done that only once—the first night she'd been in the Quarter. But Brian had found her and brought her to be with these kids and she was really thankful. Running away had been pretty dopey, but it was too late to think about that now.

The problem now was to figure out a way to get to her dad's and stay there without getting him into trouble.

She tensed suddenly as the door opened. Brian and Shelly came inside smelling like the inside of a restaurant where they fried seafood. He tossed her a paper sack and she took it eagerly. She was so hungry she didn't care what was in it.

"Knock it off, you guys," Brian said, kicking at the couple on the mattress. "Teddy's a little kid, for cripes sake." He went to the front window, making sure nobody was looking, then came over and dropped down beside Teddy. "How ya doin', brat?"

"I'm okay." She sank her teeth into an egg roll. It was cold and greasy, but delicious. She'd never complain about what she ate again. Being hungry was awful.

"Your dad's been making the rounds in the Quarter looking for you, Teddy."

Her eyes flew to his. "Really?"

"Really."

"He's everywhere," Shelly said, rolling her eyes. She rubbed the small of her back and sank down on the mattress. "Sooner or later, he's gonna find you. Or find one of us, and then the shit's gonna hit the fan."

"Shut up, Shel." Brian took the empty sack and crumpled it into a ball. "You remember that lady who stopped us a couple of days ago? She wanted Shelly to see a doctor. Remember her?"

"Uh-huh." She'd seemed nice, Teddy thought. She still had her card stashed in her backpack.

"She was with your dad today, then he spent the rest of the night on his own combing every freakin' nook and cranny of the Quarter. Man, he don't seem to know how to give up."

Teddy wiped her hands on a discarded McDonald's napkin. "He's probably worried about me."

Brian nodded. "He's definitely worried."

"He's like on a mission," Shelly said, grimacing.

"Well, maybe I should let him know I'm okay."

"Didn't you say it's a legal thing you can't live with him?"

"I think so."

"Then the minute you show up, the cops're gonna be right there. They'll wanna know where you been, who you been with, then next thing you know we'll all be busted and forced into some kind of military-style day care."

"I wouldn't tell, Brian. Honest."

"She wouldn't tell, Brian. Honest," Shelly mimicked in a singsong voice.

"You might not mean to, brat, but you would. Those guys have ways." He reached over and fluffed her hair. "Better stick with us."

Teddy stared at the egg roll, but she wasn't hungry anymore.

TESSA CLAPPED HER HANDS to try to bring some order to the table. "Okay, gang, listen up. We've only got three weeks until the open house, and we want this place to look so spiffy that no prospective donor will leave without promising a six-figure endowment." She sat down and flipped open a notebook. "That means we'll all have to pitch in. There's painting, yard work, general housecleaning, plus we're going to do some of the cooking and serving ourselves that day. The budget does not stretch to full catering."

"I bet you want the girls to do the cooking, right?" Maggie May Greely said. Fourteen and the oldest of six siblings, she'd been substituting for her absentee mom since she was eight years old. "I hate cooking!"

"Rachel likes to cook," Tessa said, giving a questioning look to the dark-haired girl on her right.

"Sure," Rachel said quietly. Amber-eyed with a passion for music, Rachel had been abandoned to the foster system at age three. Her third offense for shoplifting CDs in a music store had resulted in a suspended sentence and six months at Sojourn.

"She can choose three deputies. Volunteers?" She gazed around the table again.

"Me, I guess," said Lisa.

"Anybody else?" When no others spoke, Tessa said, "Okay, Brett and Renée."

"I can't cook!" Renée complained.

"So wash dishes," Maggie May said, free with the advice now that she'd escaped kitchen duty.

Brett, who sported tattoos and spiked hair, looked sullenly at Tessa. "I'm a vegetarian. Why should I have to cook?"

Rachel, who seldom entered into the free-for-alls that sometimes ensued at the roundtable discussions, gave Brett a disgusted look. "You think a salad or cheese or bread or pasta just happens in thin air, Brett? You can fix the veggie trays. And make the tea and coffee."

"Hey, way to go, Rachel!" Leon Bennett did a rat-a-tat on the table with his knuckles, then grinned at Tessa. "She can be deputy open-house director, she gives orders so good, Ms. Tessa."

"What about you, Leon?" Tessa asked. "The grounds are a priority, considering how important first impressions are for our first-time visitors."

"Yeah, you gonna mow, Leon?" Curtis Jackson asked. "'Cause I mowed las' time and I wanna whack weeds. That lawn mower keeps goin' on the blink."

Tessa sighed. "We do need a new mower, and since the grounds are so huge, I'd hoped the parish would be able to find the money for a riding model, but…" she turned a page in the notebook "…it doesn't look good."

"No problemo, Ms. Tessa." Leon studied his nails confidently. "I can fix that puppy, you jest wait."

She smiled and made a check mark beside that task. "Thanks, Leon. That job is now assigned to you and Curtis."

Jake Raymond, chief psychologist for Sojourn, tapped his pen on a stack of juvenile files. "Did you ever get the parish to ante up for the new bookshelves, Tessa? We'd look so much more organized if we had more shelves. We have books, files and paper stacked everywhere."

Leon wiggled his eyebrows. "Yeah, we need to look *organized.*"

She shook her head. "Like the riding mower, that problem's on hold, Jake. There's just no money in the budget for anything that requires a skilled craftsman—in this case a good carpenter."

"Same song, second verse," Jake said, scratching his cheek. He looked almost young enough to be one of the kids at Sojourn. Idealistic and sensitive, he was sometimes less in charge than the kids he counseled. "Unfortunately, I'm not too good with a hammer and a saw."

"No joke." Leon rolled his eyes.

"Leon," Tessa said in a warning tone.

"I used to help my dad build things," Jacky Pinchot said, pushing shaggy bangs from her vivid blue eyes. "And I helped paint stuff when he finished it." Everyone at the table looked startled. A runaway, Jacky had been at Sojourn two months and had never volunteered any information about herself.

"That's good to know, Jacky," Tessa said, smiling. Mentioning her background was the first step to trusting. "If we could find someone to build some bookshelves at a reasonable price, we could save the cost of painting if we did it ourselves."

"But first we gotta find a carpenter," Leon said, looking morose.

"Okay, you found him."

All eyes went to the door. Tessa felt a small shock as she recognized Daniel Kendrick.

She stood up slowly. "Mr. Kendrick. This is a surprise."

He spread his hands, smiling. "I thought I'd take you up on your invitation to visit Sojourn."

Leon groaned. "Aw, man, I bet he's another shrink."

"No, like I said, a carpenter," Daniel replied before Tessa could speak. "And from what I heard outside the door, you folks need one."

"You volunteering to do carpenter work for us?" Leon asked, still suspicious.

Daniel moved toward the group, taking in the curious faces around the table. "It's no big deal, putting up a few shelves. I have the equipment and I think I might have some lumber already on hand. You did say bookshelves?" He looked at Jake Raymond.

"Sure did." Jake stood, reaching across the table to shake Daniel's hand. "I'm Jake Raymond, resident shrink with no woodworking skills," he said with a self-deprecating smile.

"Daniel Kendrick. Ms. Hamilton and I met yesterday at NOPD."

"No *shit!*" Leon looked at Daniel with open curiosity.

"Leon, one more step out of line and you're out of here." After giving him a second to decide, Tessa turned to Daniel. Was he really volunteering? As desperate as they were for help, she didn't think Daniel Kendrick was the answer to their problem. "We appreciate your offer, Mr. Kendrick, but it's not necessary. Although we don't have the money in the budget this quarter, I'm sure the funds will be allocated next quarter."

"You've been hoping for those allocations for over a year, Tessa," Jake Raymond reminded her.

"I could get started today," Daniel said. Tessa glanced at the faces of her charges. Everyone was looking at Daniel, who had his hands in his back pockets, a quintessentially male stance. She opened her mouth, ready to send him on his way, when another boy spoke.

"I took wood shop in school last semester," Greg Sanders said. "We built some shelves."

"Great," Daniel said. "I'll need a couple of helpers."

"I could help, too, Mr. Kendrick," Jacky said, tucking her silky hair behind one ear. "I'm going to be an architect. Well, I am!" She sent a fierce look toward Leon and Curtis, who'd snickered at her announcement. "My father's AIA certified."

"He's what?" Curtis was clearly skeptical.

"It means American Institute of Architects," Daniel explained. "After passing rigorous tests, an architect is certified to practise his profession." He smiled at Jacky. "That's an ambitious goal. Good luck."

Jacky flushed with pleasure, then asked shyly, "Are you an architect?"

"No, just a pretty good carpenter."

Tessa noticed his hands were callused and marked with several nicks and scratches. Oddly, she remembered his hands during the custody hearing, long-fingered, expressive, unmarked. Still well shaped and now even darker tanned, they were proof that whatever he did, he worked with his hands.

"So, how are you with lawn mowers?" Leon asked, jiggling his knee beneath the table. Tessa had long since given up trying to restrain his excessive energy.

"Sorry." Daniel chuckled, shaking his head. "I'm not good with lawn mowers, fixing them or pushing them."

The kids laughed. She realized they'd shifted to give him a seat at the table and everyone's attention was focused on him. Next thing, he'd commandeer the whole meeting. She met Jake Raymond's eyes and he winked. Anyone who could communicate with these kids was more than welcome in Jake's opinion. He was twice as welcome if he was volunteering to build bookshelves.

She studied Daniel as he chatted with Rachel—quiet-as-a-mouse Rachel! All it would take to send him on his way was to reveal his history. Jake would immediately become the professional psychologist, the kids would reject him, and Daniel wouldn't be able to get within a mile of Sojourn until Jake was satisfied he posed no threat to anybody. The chances of that with Daniel's history were slim to none. So why didn't she simply say it? Steph was right. Tessa felt responsible for what had happened after she testified. Daniel's firm insistence that he wasn't guilty was reopening doubts about her part in what happened five years ago.

Tessa clicked and reclicked the point of her pen as her thoughts raced. There had been good reason for her doubt, she recalled, studying the cover of her notebook. Before that court appearance, Daniel Kendrick had enjoyed a spotless reputation as a high school principal. He'd been considered a model citizen, husband and father. It had taken only one accusation by a young girl to wreck the reputation he'd built over fifteen years in that small Florida town.

"Ms. Hamilton?"

She blinked and looked into Daniel's silver eyes. "What?"

"I wondered if you'd thought to pass around my daughter's photo here."

The man was a master manipulator. She had planned to do just that, but in her own time, not Kendrick's. With a sigh, Tessa pulled an envelope from the pages of her notebook and addressed the group.

"Mr. Kendrick is the father of a thirteen-year-old girl who lives in New York. She's been missing for about a week." She held up Teddy's photo. "We think she may be in the New Orleans area. If you recognize her, it would be helpful to let us know before she gets into trouble out there. I don't have to tell anybody at this table what could happen to a naive young girl. Here, pass it around, Rachel."

Rachel studied it, shrugged and handed it to Leon. Tessa glanced at Daniel and found him intently watching the expressions on the kids' faces as the photo was passed around the table. It was probably a waste of time. Of the dozen there, only one had arrived recently enough to have seen Teddy in the Quarter. But she frowned as fourteen-year-old Greg Sanders took the picture. Greg was spending six months at Sojourn after being apprehended in a stolen vehicle with three older youths. All but Greg had been arrested and tried as adults, but Marly Toups and Jake Raymond had believed Greg when he said he didn't know the car was stolen when he'd accepted a ride from three strangers.

Greg had been in the foster-care system most of his life, bounced from family to family, but Jake believed he was still salvageable. Then, a week ago, he had simply walked out of Sojourn, disappointing Jake, Marly and Tessa. But just as casually as he'd walked off, five days later he had returned, explaining that he'd left to check on his elderly grandmother—the only constant presence in his life—who'd called him from the hospital after suffering a heart attack. He'd hung out in the Quarter for a few days and decided life was better at Sojourn than on the street. He could have seen Teddy in the five days he'd just spent in the Quarter, but it was a long shot.

Tessa watched him study the picture, then place it flat on the table and shove it along to Jacky. Tessa glanced at Daniel. Like her, he'd seen a quickly masked reaction on Greg's face. Tessa guessed the boy had recognized Teddy. "How about it, Greg? Does she look familiar?"

He shrugged. "Nope."

He was lying, but experience told her no amount of pressure would pull any information from him that

he wasn't ready to give. She turned to Daniel, expecting to find him ready to push Greg for a more
truthful answer, but he was silent, not even looking
at the boy. She'd dealt with many harried parents in
his situation, all of them clamoring for the tiniest clue
to their children's whereabouts. But she'd forgotten
about Daniel's profession. As a high school principal,
he was familiar with the tactics of teenagers reluctant
to impart information.

She took the photo as it finished the rounds. "I'm
going to post this on the bulletin board, guys. If anybody thinks of anything that might help Mr. Kendrick
in his search, I'm sure he would be grateful." She
picked up her notebook, holding it against her chest.
"Okay, about the open house. We've all got our as-
signments. I'll see each of you separately sometime
today and we'll discuss the details. For now, back to
your regular chores."

She waited until Jake and the last of the teens had
left the room, then turned to Daniel. "Mr. Kendrick—"

"Okay, Ms. Hamilton, I can see you're itching to
let me have it."

"But not here." Tessa turned on her heel and
marched out of the room. Her office was a quick minute's walk down the hall from the front of the big
Victorian-style house that served as Sojourn's main
building. She stepped inside, waited for Daniel to follow, then closed the door with a click.

Still standing, she turned to him fiercely. "That
was unforgivable, what you just did. How would you
like it if I crashed a staff meeting at your school and
calmly took over?"

"I'm the first to say I wouldn't tolerate it, Ms. Hamilton, and I apologize. But I'm desperate." He hesitated, but before Tessa could go on the attack again, he said, "My daughter's life is at stake. You know it would have been hopeless to ask your permission to spend some time at Sojourn. With my history very much in your mind, I had a snowball's chance in hell of getting it."

"What makes you think your chances are any better now that you've muscled your way in anyway, Mr. Kendrick?"

"I'm counting on your good heart. And on the fact that you met Teddy and saw firsthand how young and ill-equipped she is to be on the street. I'm also betting that you see so many runaways and at-risk kids that you'll do what you can to help me rescue my daughter before it's too late."

"You don't have to be here making bookshelves for me to do that. I'll help you try to find Teddy any way I can."

He clamped a hand behind his neck. "That's just not good enough, Ms. Hamilton."

"You think that being the resident carpenter gives you an excuse to spend unlimited time at Sojourn? What's your plan? To quiz these kids about the underground network in New Orleans?"

"Can you think of a better one?"

No. And she had to hand it to him for seizing a golden opportunity when it was presented. "Mr. Kendrick." She paused, rubbing a spot between her eyes. "There are sixteen young girls at Sojourn. Knowing the circumstances of your past as I do... You know you're asking the impossible."

"Why? The sheriff and his deputy know the details of my custody battle. Any right to privacy I may have had is gone, thanks to my ex-wife. While I'm at Sojourn, I'll be watched closer than a monkey with the Ebola virus."

"Ugh, what a rotten analogy."

"But apt." His mouth twisted bitterly. "You try living with a label like *child abuser*."

A person would have to be heartless indeed not to see his point. Tessa crossed her arms over her middle. "And you honestly believe your best chance to find Teddy can be found here?"

"I honestly believe that kid with the red hair and Dead Head tattooed on his knuckles recognized her picture."

Tessa nodded. "Yes, I noticed."

"Who is he?"

"Greg Sanders. He spent most of this past week in the Quarter?"

"Then he could have seen Teddy?"

"Yes, but you won't get anything out of him unless he volunteers it. These kids don't trust adults, no matter how they schmooze them up."

He laughed shortly. "Remember me? In my past life I was a high school principal, Ms. Hamilton."

"Yes, I know. I'm just reminding you so that you don't try any hard-discipline stuff, or worse yet, demand he tell you things against his will. You'll be out of here before you can say 'Ebola.'"

Hope and uncertainty made him frown ferociously. "Does this mean you've reconsidered?"

Tessa sighed. She was crazy. She must be to even consider letting this man invade Sojourn. She had no *proof* that he was innocent. She met his gaze, disconcerted by the unwavering intensity in his eyes.

"Ms. Hamilton, I give you my word that no child here, or anywhere else, for that matter, is in any jeopardy from me. I swear it on my daughter's life."

Yes, she was nuts, all right. And of course Kendrick was right. He'd be watched as closely as a serial killer every minute he was at Sojourn. And maybe he would pick up something useful to help him find his daughter. Who knew? Then he'd go away. Tessa looked beyond him through the window behind her desk. Marly Toups and Sheriff Walker Wade would wonder about her capacity to manage Sojourn if they knew what she was about to do. She drew in a deep breath. "When would you be able to start the bookshelves?"

There was an instant of silence. "Right away," he said gruffly, then cleared his throat. For a second Tessa thought there was a hint of tears in his eyes. He turned from her, reaching for the doorknob, and spoke without looking at her. "Maybe you could give me some idea what you have in mind. I'll just make a few notes, take some measurements."

Tears? Must have been a trick of the light. Daniel Kendrick had been to hell and back. He was too tough to cry.

THE PHONE WAS RINGING when Daniel got home about midday. He dropped his car keys into a tray, tossed the mail—mostly junk—and the unopened newspaper on a table, and with his heart hammering, reached to answer it. He didn't expect news of Teddy, but he couldn't help wishing for it with all his might.

"Hello?"

"Dad? It's me, Joey."

"Joey!" Daniel dropped into a chair. "What's up, son? Aren't you supposed to be in school today?"

"It's a teacher's training day and we're off."

"Does your mother know you're making this call?"

"Nah, she's gone to some lunch thing, and Mrs. Kowalski watches TV all day, which is good, because it gives me a chance to call you." Before Daniel could reply, he rushed on. "Dad, it's lucky I was here, because Teddy phoned."

Fear and relief rose up simultaneously. "Where is she, Joey?"

"She's in New Orleans, just like we thought."

"Are you sure? Where? Why hasn't she called me?"

"She's scared to, Dad. They told her if you weren't allowed to have your kids at your house, you could get in trouble if she just showed up, so she doesn't know what to do."

"Who? Who told her that?"

"These people she knows." Joey's voice was high with childish anxiety. "Dad, what's gonna happen? She doesn't have any money left and she's staying with a bunch of people who don't take baths, and they eat stuff that restaurants pitch out or whatever they can find from I don't know where. Dad, you gotta do something!"

Daniel gripped the receiver hard. "Wait, son. Calm down for a minute and let me get this straight. Teddy called and told you she was staying with a bunch of people. Who are they and where can I find them?"

"She said she couldn't tell me that because it would get them in trouble and then she would be put in this place the police have for runaways."

Daniel rubbed his thigh with a balled fist. "She must have told you something about where she is, Joey. Think, son!"

"I don't want her to get in trouble with the police, Dad."

"She won't. I've found a place here where she can stay, but you have to help me find her."

The boy was silent for a few excruciating moments. "She said it's somewhere close to that big church where the artists paint your picture on the sidewalk."

"The Saint Louis Cathedral."

"I guess."

"What else?"

"They don't have beds, just a couple of air mattresses they take with them."

"Any address? Any street? Anything, Joey!"

"I'm sorry, Dad. She didn't tell me that stuff."

Daniel suppressed a frustrated groan. "How about getting back in touch with you? Did she leave word where or how? A phone number?" But he knew the answer before Joey gave it.

"No, Dad." Joey's voice caught on a sob. "But you gotta find her. She's scared but she doesn't know what to do. She said it was dumb to do what she did in case I was thinking about trying it, too."

"Don't, Joey!" Daniel said in a sharp tone. "Don't even think about doing something so dangerous. Listen, I don't know how I'm going to do this, but I promise you I'm going to find a way to bring you down here for a visit. Just hang in there, son, until we find Teddy, then we'll talk about some changes. Can you do that?''

"I guess so."

"And, Joey, tell your mother to call me the moment she gets home, okay?''

"Okay, Dad."

"I love you, son."

"I love you, too, Dad. And, Dad, Teddy's really in trouble. We gotta do something."

"We will, son. I promise."

CHAPTER FIVE

DANIEL LOCKED the end of his steel tape to a baseboard and zipped it up, marking a point with a pencil. Then, moving six feet to the left, he measured and marked a second point. "Hand me that one-by-six, Greg."

The order was issued to Greg Sanders, but Jacky Pinchot jumped to obey. Greg muscled her aside and took a long board from a stack of new lumber nearby. He passed it to Daniel, who fitted it to the wall, then stepped back to check it. "Looks about right, huh, guys?"

Two students passing the arched entrance to the room distracted Greg. When they high-fived him, Greg grinned.

"It's not exactly flush, Mr. Kendrick," Jacky said, ignoring the students. She carefully examined the tight fit between the board and brace. "There's some space here at the top of the wall, although it's nice and tight at the bottom."

Daniel inspected the joint, his fingers finding the crack Jacky spotted. "You're right, but we can't do a lot about it, Jacky. This is an old house and over the years there's been some settling. The walls aren't plumb."

Jacky looked at Greg. "That means the joints

throughout the house aren't perfectly square. They're cocked sideways, sort of.''

"I know what *plumb* means, Jacky," Greg said gruffly.

"You didn't seem to be paying attention," she said.

"We'll fill those cracks with caulking compound before we stain it," Daniel said, trying to head off another spat between his helpers. Jacky and Greg had started bickering from the moment they'd shown up to lend a hand. Knowing word would get back to the group, Jacky wanted to prove she hadn't just been bragging about knowing how to build things, and Greg was determined not to be outdone by a female in a job that, in his estimation, was best performed by men.

Meantime, Daniel was losing patience. The bookshelves were his ticket to hanging around Sojourn, but his purpose was to get information about Teddy. And Greg had that information. So far this morning Daniel hadn't had an opportunity to broach the subject of his daughter, mainly because he didn't want to spook Greg and lose the only real link—fragile as it was—to Teddy.

After the phone call from Joey, Daniel had driven to the French Quarter and spent the rest of the day and most of the night searching for Teddy, but he still hadn't uncovered a trace of his daughter or her new-found friends. Knowing they were probably hiding from cops out of necessity, he'd hesitated to seek help from NOPD, but out of desperation, that was where he'd wound up. It was almost dawn when he'd given up in defeat. If he was going to find his daughter, it looked as if his best bet was Sojourn—and Tessa Hamilton.

"Here, Jacky, hold this end of the plank where I've marked it while I nail it to the wall."

Greg shouldered her aside. "I'll do it."

Jacky shoved him. "He told me!"

The board fell with a loud clatter. Daniel rammed his hammer into the leather loop on his belt and faced them. "Okay, you two...time out!" When they continued to glare at each other, he repeated, "Time out, I said, or I'm out of here to ask Ms. Hamilton to send me two people who can work without the aid of a referee."

Reluctantly they subsided, Jacky with her arms crossed and her mouth set in a mulish pout, Greg with cocked hips, gazing at the ceiling. Daniel leaned against the partially constructed shelves, surveying both of them. Coming on like a prison warden wouldn't gain him any points with these two. "Okay, listen up, guys. I need help building these shelves, but so far you've both been more of a hindrance. Jacky, you weren't bragging when you said you knew about building, information I assume you picked up from your father. And Greg, that shop class taught you a lot. You might think about an apprentice program offered at your high school even before you graduate. But right now, I need you both to work with me as a team, not squabble and bicker over every nail and board."

Neither of them said a word, but stood gazing in opposite directions.

"Hello, am I talking to myself here?"

Still no response.

Daniel sighed, shaking his head. "Look, have you two ever seen that show on TV where this couple—a man and a woman—tackle all sorts of projects around the house?"

"I guess," Greg said.

"Uh-huh," Jacky said.

"They work as a team, they don't fight over who does what."

With her hands on her hips, Jacky turned to Greg. "Did you hear that? She's a woman and she does everything he does, and she's just as good at it as he is."

Greg rolled his eyes. "She's on that show because they have to pretend that women can do the same things as men do. They can't, I don't care what you say."

"They can, too!" Jacky said, outraged. "And sometimes they do it a lot better!"

"Oh yeah?" Greg said. "Just try picking up six two-by-fours at once. You'd fall on your face."

"I won't have to pick up two-by-fours. I'd have a few stupid men like you around to do it for me!"

Wwhhheeet! With two fingers in his mouth, Daniel whistled shrilly. "Knock it off, you two!" He took each by the arm and hauled them across to the worktable, shoved them into chairs opposite each other, then sat down between them. "The point I was trying to make," he said with measured patience, "is that those two people work together to get a job done. One measures, another saws, one caulks, another paints. When a job requires one to help the other, it's done without arguing. You see what I'm saying here?"

He paused, waiting to see whether he was wasting

his breath. Jacky mumbled something and Greg gave a curt nod. A moment passed while Daniel thought about how to reach them. "It seems that threats aren't doing much to curb the hostility between you, so maybe we can try something a little more radical. What do you say?"

"What?" Greg asked suspiciously.

"I'm not the hostile one," Jacky objected, glaring at Greg, "he is."

Daniel held both hands up, palms out. "Doesn't anybody want to hear my radical idea?"

"I'm trying to, but she keeps mouthing off," Greg said, jerking a thumb in Jacky's direction.

"Because you're such a male chauvinist!"

Daniel almost smiled. Until today, he'd nearly forgotten how trying teenagers could be. He actually began to feel at home. "My idea is this. Communication. We're going to discuss why we can't get anything done because neither of you can resist zinging the other. I'd hoped that building the bookshelves would be an opportunity for both of you to learn something about woodworking, but—"

"It's a man's job," Greg said. "Women should stick to what they do best."

Jacky sneered. "I guess that means cleaning the house, cooking and having babies, huh?"

"Yeah, that's what it means."

"You are *so* stupid! Women have just the same brains as men and if they want to be cops or soldiers or...or architects, then they can!"

Greg leaned across the table, his nose almost touching hers. "And if women stayed at home where they belonged, the world wouldn't be such a rotten place."

Her mouth fell open. "How, I'd like to know?"

"Kids would be taken care of and meals cooked and men would want to come home."

"Uh-huh, oh, sure." Jacky was nodding with sarcasm. "Just like in my house when my mom did all that and my dad still got the hots for his secretary, so he just took off and we haven't seen him in a year. Yeah, well, my mom would have something to say about what you think's right for women, Greg."

Silenced, Greg looked away from Jacky's flashing eyes, glanced uneasily to Daniel, then stared at his own hands. "At least you've got a father," he mumbled.

"I *had* a father," Jacky said.

Greg was cracking his knuckles, one by one. "What about your mom?"

"She's too busy hating my father to miss me."

"So you just walked out, thinking the streets would be better than living with a mom and no dad?" Greg slouched back in his chair, his disgust evident. "Wow, and you called me stupid."

Jacky's temper flared again. "I guess I could've ripped off somebody's car and *driven* myself."

"I didn't know that car was stolen! I was just hitching a ride!"

"Like you didn't know those two lowlifes you were hitching with weren't lowlifes."

"I made a mistake, okay?"

Jacky assumed a look of astonishment. "What? The wise know-it-all Greg admits he made a mistake?" She put a hand on her chest. "Heavens! My heart's going pitty-pat."

Greg scowled darkly. "Yeah, well, sounds to me

like you've never had to figure out a way to get from *A* to *B* on your own, Miss Smart-mouth, but some of us don't have *architects* for fathers.'' He hunched forward, clutching the table with both hands. ''Here's how I define stupid. Stupid's running out on people like a spoiled brat. I bet your mom's worried sick about you!''

''Oh, now you're concerned about worried parents?'' Jacky hitched a thumb in Daniel's direction. ''If you suddenly care so much about parents, why don't you admit you recognized Mr. Kendrick's little girl? Why won't you tell him where she's at if you're so nice?''

Greg darted a look at Daniel, then began cracking his knuckles again. ''I couldn't be sure about that.''

Daniel studied the boy, almost holding his breath. ''You think you recognized Teddy, Greg?''

''It could've been her. I didn't stick around. They were all crowded in a dirty old store, no beds, no bathroom.'' His glance flashed to Jacky with defiance. ''Some of us don't have to be hit over the head to appreciate the difference between being here or safe at home and living like animals on the street.''

''What store was that, Greg?'' Daniel asked quietly.

Greg shrugged. ''A little hole in the wall on St. Peter. Used to be a souvenir shop.'' He met Daniel's eyes. ''They'd see you coming, Mr. Kendrick. You wouldn't be able to get close before they'd all run. They keep a lookout all the time.''

Daniel drove his hand through his hair in frustration.

Jacky traced a pattern on the tabletop with her finger. "You could go, Greg. They'd let you get close. You could tell Teddy her dad wants to see her."

"I don't know about that." He shrugged again. "She sticks so close to Brian she's practically joined at the hip with him."

"Brian?" Daniel's eyes narrowed.

"Yeah, he's sort of the main man in the group, you know what I mean?"

"Hey, I've got an idea." Jacky pulled her chair closer, her eyes sparkling. "We could both go, Greg, me and you. We could sort of infiltrate the group by pretending to be runaways."

"Yeah, you're good at that, all right."

She inhaled slowly. "Hear me out, please. We could befriend Teddy, sort of. Then when we got a chance, we could lure her away for a few minutes to a place where Mr. Kendrick and Ms. Hamilton were waiting in a car and kidnap her!"

Daniel smiled. "Well, that's a plan, Jacky. But if Teddy is hanging out with these kids and Greg can tell us the location, I don't think we'll have to resort to such dramatic measures."

"Could I see that picture again?" Greg asked.

Daniel slipped it from his shirt pocket and handed it over. He watched Greg study it much more intently than he'd done in the meeting the day before.

The boy nodded. "It's her, all right. She's looking a little ratty now, but the street does that."

Daniel stood up. "I appreciate your telling me, Greg."

The boy shrugged. "Aw, it's okay. I like doing the bookshelves. It's neat."

"Me, too." Not to be excluded, Jacky moved to

stand beside Daniel. "Are we gonna finish, or did you just come to get information about Teddy?"

"I always finish what I start, so I'll be back tomorrow." He started to put his arm around her shoulders for a reassuring squeeze, but caught himself in time.

"Hey, okaaay!" Greg grinned.

"So, are you guys ready to call a truce?"

"We'll be good," Jacky promised, looking at Greg to be sure she wasn't the only one. Greg punched her playfully on the arm and she kicked him on the knee. Before they got into a tussle that might turn real, Daniel broke them up, then looked at them soberly.

"Do you know what I noticed in our little session a few minutes ago when you were both going at each other like two cats in a sack?" They waited with sheepish expressions. "Could it be you guys aren't really mad at each other but at circumstances you can't control in your lives, that you're just taking it out on each other?"

"Like how?" Jacky wanted to know. Greg simply gave another shrug.

"It's probably difficult for Greg to understand why you'd leave a real home when he's never had one, Jacky. On the other hand, Greg, Jacky can't accept your readiness to confine women to traditional roles. Look what happened to her mom."

He gave them a moment, then added, "How about you spend some time thinking it over and then maybe both of you could work on that with Ms. Hamilton or Mr. Raymond?"

He got no promise from either of them on that, but he felt he'd planted a seed. "And meantime, I still need my two helpers tomorrow morning bright and early. Eight sharp."

TESSA STOOD at the doorway, arms crossed over her chest, and watched Daniel stack the unused lumber against the wall and gather his tools to take with him.

"Well done, Mr. Kendrick."

"Did you hear what Greg told me?" he asked, tossing a scrap board into the corner. "He knows where Teddy's staying."

"I heard, and I also heard the way you let them vent their anger and then set them to thinking about why they're angry."

He smiled. "Elementary, Ms. Hamilton."

She smiled, albeit reluctantly. The man had a strong ego in spite of the public humiliation he'd suffered. She had to admire that kind of strength. "Once a high school principal, always a high school principal, right?"

"Wrong." His smile vanished. "I'll never be that again."

Thanks to you. He didn't say it, but the words were there between them, harsh and unforgiving. And true.

"What do you want to do about finding Teddy?" she asked, unwilling to get into another futile exchange over his situation.

He frowned. "I'm not sure."

"Marly could be down there in fifteen minutes. One phone call from you and she'll have Teddy in custody within the hour."

"And on a plane to New York by nightfall," Daniel said shortly.

"Surely you want her to go back home?"

"Not before I see her," he said, looking at her steadily. "And you know what the chances of that will be if I call Marly Toups."

"Then what are you suggesting, Mr. Kendrick?"

"I think you know, Ms. Hamilton." He slid his hands into his pockets, holding her eyes with his laser-sharp stare. "I want us, you and I, to find her, and I want to bring her here to Sojourn."

"Mr. Kendrick—"

"Just for a few days, Ms. Hamilton, and you can keep an eye on us the whole time. What could it hurt?"

"What could it hurt?" she repeated, shaking her head at his audacity.

"What could it hurt? If you just think about Teddy and forget the B.S. of a system gone haywire, what could it hurt to allow her a few hours with her father?"

"You don't realize what you're asking. If I do something like that, it could jeopardize the whole Sojourn project." She looked away. "With your history—"

"My history's bullshit, too! You know I never tried to seduce that girl in Florida. You had doubts even then, Ms. Hamilton. I saw it in your eyes in the courtroom. Deny that if you can."

She didn't deny it. Couldn't.

He caught her arm and forced her to look at him. "Well, now you can make it up to me. You can give me some time with my daughter and then we'll call her mother and tell her to come get her."

"It's not that simple, Mr. Kendrick. I wish it were. You may be innocent, but—"

"I *am* innocent, goddamn it!"

She drew a deep breath. "Nevertheless, there are other considerations. First of all, there's the law. What you want to do is illegal. Someday you may be in a better position to change things, but until then you shouldn't react in a way that would jeopardize that opportunity. Grabbing Teddy does just that. And if that doesn't bother you, then think of it strictly from my position. The perception that I'm opening the doors to Sojourn to a man stamped with the stigma of child abuse would be the height of irresponsibility on my part."

He looked away, his features set bitterly. "So what's my option here? Putting her on a plane by herself? After she's risked her life to get here, I should just sit by and watch her fly back to New York?" He faced her. "Don't ask me to do that, Tessa. I want a chance to hug her and tell her I love her and Joey. I want to see her for breakfast, lunch and dinner for a couple of days, not a couple of hours. For God's sake, is that too much? I can't stand it any more—having a bunch of bureaucrats who don't know me or Teddy denying me and my kids even a semblance of normalcy in our lives."

Tessa felt his fury and pain with every word. She knew well how it felt to lose a child. She knew how it felt to be unworthy to even have a child. Still, she was honor-bound to obey the law. But how had he known about her doubts when she had been so careful to keep them to herself? So careful to disguise her dismay when she'd considered the import of the judge's decision?

Closing her eyes, she nodded. "I may regret this,

but okay, we'll go together and I'll bring Teddy here to Sojourn. Then we'll call Marly. Maybe I can persuade her to let Teddy stay a couple of days.''

"Are you sure?"

No, of course not. Far from it. But she felt morally bound to try to do something—not that she was going to tell him that. As desperate as he was, he wouldn't hesitate to pounce on any perceived weakness in her. "I'm sure I'll try, but I can't promise more than that."

Daniel rubbed an unsteady hand over his mouth. "Thank you, Ms. Hamilton. I swear you won't be sorry."

She laughed softly, shaking her head. "For heaven's sake, stop with the Ms. Hamilton. Call me Tessa."

AFTER ANOTHER conversation with Greg Sanders, Tessa felt confident that she knew where the empty shop was located. Teddy would be safe at Sojourn by nightfall, she assured Daniel, if the group was still holed up there. Tessa barely had time to tell Jake Raymond where they were headed before Daniel was out of her office and headed for his vehicle. Grabbing her shoulder bag, Tessa had to jog to keep up with him.

"There's no reason to take two cars," she said, dodging Leon and Curtis, who were tinkering with the lawn mower. "Besides, if they've been aware of your search, they surely know what you drive. Let's take my car."

He hesitated at the door of his battered pickup. "Mine's new," she told him, giving his arm an impatient tug. "That thing looks like it has seen better days. What if it breaks down halfway across the Causeway?"

"It won't." But he followed her to a sleek new sports model, black and shining in the sun. "That doesn't look like something you would choose."

"I didn't." Using the remote on her key chain, she unlocked the car with an electronic chirp. "It's Keely's choice."

"Mind if I drive?" He was eyeing the dash and sports options on the console with typical male appreciation.

Hiding a smile, she tossed him the keys. But before getting in, he escorted her around to the passenger side and opened the door for her. Even in his anxiety over Teddy, he didn't forget that small courtesy. A gentlemanly gesture, all too rare nowadays. He had been embroiled in divorce proceedings before the scandal broke, she recalled, and for a moment wondered about the reasons.

Once behind the wheel, he started the engine. "I'm in a hurry," he warned her. "Teddy was hanging out with these kids two days ago, but there's no guarantee she's still with them. Every second counts." And before she could reply, he had pulled away from Sojourn, as comfortable with the car as if he owned it. In minutes, they passed through the Causeway tollgates, and in complete disregard of the speed limit and the fact that two patrol cars were parked nearby, Daniel floored the accelerator.

Tessa bent to check that her seat belt was securely fastened. "You're doing eighty-five miles an hour,

Daniel," she murmured, watching the bridge stanchions whizzing by at breathtaking speed.

"I told you I was in a hurry," he said.

"They patrol this Causeway pretty closely."

"You can tell them we're on the trail of a runaway if they stop us," he said without missing a beat. After a second, he glanced at her. "You have some ID, right?"

"Yes." She studied the glistening surface of Lake Pontchartrain. "Which might work *if* we survive the crash."

He chuckled, a soft, deep rumble that made her turn and look at him. "Okay, I'll cool it."

Glancing at the dash, she realized he'd slowed to seventy-five. "I'm so relieved."

Daniel fumbled in his shirt pocket and found his sunglasses. "How'd you get into this business?" he asked.

"I was a runaway once myself."

He glanced at her in surprise. With good reason, Tessa thought. She had surprised herself, telling him that. She never told anybody else.

"Why?"

"Why did I run away?" she asked, squinting at gulls riding the wind above the lake. "Believe me, you don't want to know."

"Meaning you don't want to tell me."

She sighed and turned to look at him. "My sister and I were foster kids, Mr. Kendrick. We—"

"It's Daniel," he said.

After a second, she nodded. "Daniel. Our mother was...troubled and we never knew our father. Although some foster homes can be good, and some foster parents truly excellent, we weren't so lucky. We were both fourteen when we decided we were better off on the streets than in that house.''

"I could say it must have been pretty bad to make you choose such a risky life-style, but after Teddy, I'm not so quick to make those assumptions.''

She looked at him. "But you don't really know why Teddy ran away yet, do you?''

"No.''

"So you can't assume it wasn't something intolerable.''

"Did you run from something intolerable?''

"I'll just say that at the time we felt anything was better than staying with those people," Tessa said.

"You said you were both fourteen. Does that mean you have a twin?''

"Uh-huh. Stephanie lives in New Orleans.'' Thinking of her sister helped to push the disturbing past back into the dark hole where it belonged. "She and Tal have a baby boy, Talbot Jean-Claude Robichaux. He's almost two.''

"Are you identical twins?''

"Yes.''

"So is it true that twins have a sort of ESP? Do you and Stephanie share something like that?''

Tessa thought of the years apart from her twin and the ever present ache in her heart that had eased only after she and Steph were reunited. She thought of the months she'd lain sleepless and filled with anguish while Steph was enduring a painful divorce even though she had been alienated from her for years. She thought of the joy in her own heart when Steph and

Talbot Robichaux fell in love. "I guess we share something like that," she said, smiling faintly.

He studied her with interest. "Do you actually feel something when she's hurt?"

"It happens."

"That's amazing."

"Not so amazing when you think that we were conceived together, existed in utero for nine months together, spent babyhood and childhood together. If you'd had that much togetherness with anybody else, you'd probably share something like that, too."

"I assume you think alike as well."

Her amusement faded. "No. We're actually nothing alike."

"What does she do? I mean, besides being a wife and mother?"

"She's a physician and very active in the free clinic sponsored by Women's Hospital. In fact, she started their program for unwed teenage mothers. Most of them are still children themselves and have no idea how to be a parent."

"Babies having babies?"

"Yes."

"And you counsel troubled teens. Sounds like the two of you are very much alike."

"Only on the surface." From the time they were able to make choices without the interference of the state, Stephanie had made all the right ones and Tessa had made all the wrong ones. It had taken years of pain and a tragic mistake before Tessa had managed to pull herself together.

The chirp of her cellular phone was a welcome interruption. Reaching for her handbag, she pulled the phone out and answered it. "It's my sister," she told Daniel. "What's up, Steph?"

"I'm at the clinic, Tessa. We've just had a visit by a pregnant teenage girl and her boyfriend. I think they could be the two you mentioned when we talked last."

"Oh, lucky break. Were you able—"

"They were here for help, Tessa. They came to dump one of their own. It's the young girl you're looking for, I think. She's sick and hardly recognizable as the pretty child in the photo, but the likeness is there."

"Teddy?" Tessa repeated. "You think it's Teddy?"

The car swerved slightly as Daniel turned to look at her. Tessa put up a hand to caution him. "What's wrong with her?"

"Hard to tell just yet. Nausea and vomiting, which we now have under control. We've got her hooked up to an IV and she's resting. She's pale as milk and dehydrated, very weak, but her vitals are stable. Tal's here this afternoon and he's looked her over, too. We think she'll be all right."

"Is it drugs, Steph?"

"The kids who brought her say no. She started throwing up and couldn't seem to stop. At least they had the foresight to bring her here."

With one eye on the road and the other on Tessa, Daniel made a grab for the phone. "Let me talk to her!"

"Just drive!" she ordered in a fierce whisper. "Steph, what do you think is wrong?"

"Best guess is food poisoning. These kids are often

careless about what they eat. They don't realize how quickly food that isn't refrigerated can grow botulism or something equally deadly.''

"It could be that," Tessa said, moving back out of Daniel's reach when he persisted. "And don't give me that explosive look, Daniel. You're driving like a maniac as it is. Stephanie won't be able to tell you anything she can't tell me."

"I want to hear it firsthand, damn it!"

"And I want to survive this road trip!"

"What on earth's going on, Tessa? Who's with you?" Stephanie's voice was sharp with concern.

"It's Teddy's father—Daniel."

"Teddy's father? You're in the car with Daniel What's-his-name?"

"One of the kids gave us a lead on Teddy's whereabouts. We were on our way to try to find her and bring her back to Sojourn. We're on the Causeway about twenty minutes from you right now." She could hear Stephanie's thoughts as clearly as if she spoke them. "It's okay, Steph."

"We'll discuss it when you get here, Tessa."

Tessa sighed. "I know. Look, Steph… If Teddy's conscious, tell her her dad's on his way, will you?" She met Daniel's eyes. "And that he loves her."

She broke the connection, and without looking at Daniel, dropped the phone back into her handbag. "I know you're concerned, but it won't help if you land us in Lake Pontchartrain before you get to see your daughter."

"She's sure it's Teddy?" His hands gripped the wheel and he was hunched forward as if his own energy could propel the car faster.

"She thinks so. Don't panic, Daniel. She's in good hands. Steph's the best and Tal's there this afternoon as well."

"Tal?"

"Dr. Talbot Robichaux. Steph's husband is a physician, too."

"What's wrong with Teddy?" He forced himself back into his seat. "I heard you. It can't be drugs. Teddy wouldn't."

"Steph's not sure, but she suspects food poisoning. Teddy's dehydrated, but they've got an IV going. She'll be okay, Daniel."

"We're taking her back with us," he said flatly.

"We'll see," Tessa said just as flatly.

He gave her one last hard look and turned his attention back to the road. Tessa glanced at the advancing needle on the speedometer and sighed. If it had been Keely... She decided to say no more.

CHAPTER SIX

THE FREE CLINIC was located in a neighborhood where nobody felt safe after dark. And, like the neighborhood, the building had seen better days. A small yachting business, now long defunct, had flourished there in the thirties and forties. The panes on the windows were painted a muddy green to block out Louisiana's merciless heat. Noting their grimy surface, Daniel guessed no window cleaner had been near the building since the factory's heyday. He hoped it was only the look of the facility that was dilapidated. His daughter was somewhere inside. And sick.

His features were stern as he followed Tessa through double glass doors. They, at least, were clean. As was the newly renovated waiting room. A clerk stationed behind a desk littered with forms looked up with a harried expression. "Oh, hi, Ms. Hamilton. Dr. Stephanie said when you got here to go back to number six."

"Thanks, Cissy. Busy day?"

Cissy rolled her eyes. "Aren't they all?"

Smiling, Tessa walked past the desk and headed down the hall, motioning for Daniel to follow. The clinic was laid out much like any other emergency medical facility. Examining rooms on each side were half solid wall, half glass, every one occupied. He noted the numbers as they passed. Even numbers on the right. Two. Four. Six. With his heart banging in his chest, he looked through the glass and, for the first time in more than three months, saw the face of his daughter.

She was lying on an examining table covered in some kind of white woven blanket stamped with the clinic's name in faded black letters. Her left arm lay straight by her side, uncovered. An IV was taped to the back of her hand, the plastic cord snaking up to a plastic bag half filled with a clear liquid that was hooked to a metal pole. He swallowed once, hard. Her face was pale and still, her eyes closed. From where he stood, she looked tiny and helpless—her diminutive stature made to seem even smaller by the array of gadgets and medical paraphernalia packed into the cramped cubicle. A woman moved to intercept them—Tessa's twin. He noted the startling resemblance somewhere in the back of his mind.

With her finger to her lips, she headed Daniel off before he made it to Teddy's side. "Please, she's resting just now." She spoke softly, nudging him back from the door. "I thought we could talk before you wake her."

Daniel craned his neck to get a better look. "She's so still. Is she—"

"She's fine. She's been calling for you from the moment she got here...Mr. Kendrick, isn't it?" At his nod, Stephanie smiled, shifting the chart in her hand to pull the door almost closed. "She told us where to contact you, but there was no answer at the number she gave."

"I was at Sojourn," Daniel said, unable to take his

eyes off Teddy through the glass. "What happened? Why the IV? Does she need to be in a hospital?"

"Daniel." Tessa touched his arm. "One question at a time."

Stephanie consulted the chart. "It's food poisoning, probably botulism, but it's impossible to tell which of the foods she's eaten in the past twelve hours was contaminated. She ingested an egg roll, a hot dog, a packaged chicken salad sandwich which had an expired date. My best guess is that's the culprit."

"Will she be all right?" Daniel asked, still watching Teddy.

"Yes. The IV is replacing lost fluids. That's the third bag, and it'll be dripped in another half hour. She should be okay in a couple of days, but she'll be weak and she should stay quiet." Her gaze rested on Teddy. "She tells me she doesn't live with you, but that's where she would like to go." She turned to Daniel. "Tessa told me about Teddy a few days ago, Mr. Kendrick. Ordinarily I would call Social Services in a case like this, but because Tessa asked and because I trust her judgment, I haven't called Marly Toups." Her troubled gaze settled back on the sleeping girl. "I won't deny that I'm very concerned, however."

Daniel looked at Tessa, bracing himself. Would she honor her promise to take Teddy back to Sojourn? It was damn clear what her sister thought she should do. Jaw tight, he watched Tessa studying Teddy's face and waited for the words that would once more entangle him and his daughter in endless red tape and bureaucratic indifference.

Tessa read the notations on the chart herself. At

another time Daniel might have been interested in her astonishing likeness to her sister, but his mind was too taken up with the fear of having Teddy shipped off to a hospital, or worse—a foster home—where he would again be denied anything except supervised visitations. He crammed both hands into his pockets and watched his daughter sleep. If only he had found her last night before this happened. If only she had called him before leaving New York. If only... If only... God, his whole life was made up of "if only's."

Tessa handed the chart back to her sister. "Steph, as soon as she's awake I'm going to take her to Sojourn. She can rest as well there as someplace picked by Social Services."

Stephanie's gaze shot to Daniel, then back to her twin. She nodded slowly, studying Tessa's face. "You know what you're doing?"

Tessa laughed shortly. "Meaning if you were in my place you wouldn't get involved."

"Meaning I would be thinking about the kids at Sojourn and how one bad decision could jeopardize the whole project."

Stephanie looked directly at Daniel. "Do you understand what's at stake here, Mr. Kendrick? Do you realize what could happen if Social Services decides to make things difficult for Tessa? There are people who don't want a facility like Sojourn to succeed. Both Tessa and I have been targets of people who don't like to be reminded of the troubled kids in our midst or the expense involved in caring for them. They'll use any weapon that pops up to discredit our motives. I wouldn't like it if anything you did became a weapon to be used against Tessa.''

"Threats, Doctor?''

"A friendly warning, Mr. Kendrick. Tessa thinks she had something to do with you losing custody of your children, but she's wrong. She did her job. No more, no less. The *court* made that decision. If you were falsely accused, maybe she thinks she can make it up to you by helping you spend some time with Teddy. However, as I see it, nothing yet has proven you innocent.''

"She knows I'm innocent,'' Daniel said, stiff with resentment.

"She doesn't know it. And if it should turn out that you are, then I'll beg your pardon. Tessa's taking a huge risk. I'm simply reminding you so you'll know what's at stake here.''

"Don't worry, Tessa's reputation is safe with me.''

Tessa touched her sister's hand. "Could I get a word in here?'' When Daniel and Stephanie both looked at her, she said, "I'm aware of the risks and I take full responsibility. To set your mind at ease, Steph, I'd planned to see Marly and persuade her to assign Teddy to Sojourn rather than placing her in foster care or whatever Social Services decides until she's reunited with her mother in New York.''

"Well...'' Impulsively, Stephanie hugged her sister, whispering in her ear, "Be careful, you hear me?''

"I will.''

Daniel stood battling an exhilaration he hadn't felt in years. Not since he'd been hounded out of his job and home had his word been accepted as his bond.

Tessa's trust touched him as nothing had in a long time. She had promised him this time with Teddy, and not even her sister's well-placed concern had shaken her.

"May I see my daughter now?"

Still looking doubtful, Stephanie stepped aside and put out a hand. "Be my guest."

Tessa waited just inside the door of the examining room as Daniel went to Teddy's bedside. His daughter was very like him, Tessa thought, the same silky dark hair and sculpted cheekbones. Even her small firm chin was Daniel's in miniature. He didn't touch her at first, but stood and simply gazed at her. Then he stroked her cheek with his finger. Her lashes fluttered and she opened her eyes. His hand cupped her face and he tucked her hair behind her ear. She blinked once or twice, as if making sure he was real. Her eyes—the same silver gray of her father's—filled with tears.

"Hi, baby," Daniel said softly, his smile unsteady.

"Daddy, Daddy, you found me!" Heedless of the cord tethering her to the IV, she rose from the pillow, reaching for him. Daniel scooped her into his arms, cupping her dark head in one hand and holding her tightly against him as she broke into stormy sobs.

"Daddy, I kn-knew you would f-find me. I *prayed* so hard every night."

"And it worked, Teddy-bear," he whispered gruffly. "Here I am."

With her nose pressed to his chest, Teddy clutched his shirt in both fists. "I w-was so scared. I w-wanted to c-call you, but they said no. There was no place to st-stay and no food and I r-ran out of m-money in only th-three *days,* Daddy!''

"I know, I know, baby. It's okay. Daddy's got you now.'' With his eyes closed in painful relief, Daniel comforted her with soft words, rubbing her back and skinny shoulders, rocking her in the manner of any loving parent whose lost child has been found.

"Then I got sick, Daddy.'' Teddy's words were muffled in his shirt. "It was *awful!* I threw up and threw up. I b-begged them to do something, to call you, but B-Brian brought me here instead.''

"He did the right thing, honey.''

Quieting now, Teddy nestled in a spot beneath Daniel's chin. "When I got here, I told them your n-number, but the doctor said nobody answered.'' Her eyes overflowed again. "I was afraid you'd g-gone somewhere and maybe not told us. What if you'd moved, Daddy?''

Pulling back, Daniel cupped her face in his hands and looked deep into her eyes. "I would never go someplace and not tell you and Joey where to find me, Teddy. You'll always know where I am, because no matter what happens or where I live, I'll always be your father.''

"I know that's what you always say, but—'' Teddy sniffed and rubbed her nose with her right hand. "Sometimes it's so hard because we...Joey and me...we want to be with you.''

"But running away was not the way, Teddy-bear.''

"I'm sorry, but I just couldn't think of anything else to do.'' As she settled back against the pillow, Teddy's chin wobbled and her eyes filled again. "I guess I messed up, huh?''

Daniel rubbed his thumb over her chin. "Well, you gave us all a scare, baby."

"Does that mean you're gonna send me back?"

He brushed her silky bangs from her eyes. "Maybe not, at least, not just yet."

Her eyes widened and her mouth formed an O. "Really? Really and truly? I can stay? You're going to let me come and live with you? And Joey, too?"

"Whoa...not so fast. No, you can't live with me, but you're going to stay at a special place near me."

Her joy faded. "I can't stay with you?"

"You know you can't, honey. But you'll like it at this place. It's called Sojourn, and there are lots of kids your age to keep you company. I'm building some shelves for them, so I'll be there every day and we can see each other."

She frowned with wary suspicion. "Sojourn. That sounds like some kind of...of... Oh, I don't know. A place for bad kids. Mom's always saying she's going to send me away if I don't act right. Did Mom tell you to send me there?"

He took her hand and placed it on his heart. "You aren't a bad kid, Teddy. You're good and fine, a kid any parent would be proud to love. Your mother knows nothing about Sojourn. My friend helped me work out this plan so that you and I can be together for a little while."

"And I won't have to go back to New York?"

"Not right away, but eventually, yes. That's where you live, Teddy."

"No!" She snatched her hand away. "I won't go back there, Daddy! Mom hates me. She hates being my mom. Ask Joey. She hates us both. She only cares about her painting. If you'll just try, you can talk her into letting us live with you. She won't care if we leave, you'll see.'' Her face crumpled and tears spilled onto her cheeks. ''Nobody wants us. Not you or Mom or anybody! Me and Joey know that, but it…it hurts so much, Daddy.''

Daniel pulled Teddy back into his embrace and looked at Tessa. For a moment, he seemed as much in need of comfort and reassurance as his daughter, and Tessa found herself wishing she could offer it. But wishing couldn't fix what was wrong in Daniel Kendrick's family. This was no simple custody dispute between two people with children who'd discovered their marriage had been a mistake. It was going to take far more than wishes to make things right.

WHILE DANIEL CALMED Teddy down and talked her into lying quietly until the last of the fluids in the IV were gone, Tessa called Marly Toups to persuade her to release Teddy into her custody. It hadn't been easy. Impossible without the permission of the custodial parent, Marly had told them at first.

''But what if Beth Kendrick says it's okay?'' Tessa argued. ''I've met her, Marly. I testified at the custody hearing. She knows I have the welfare of her children at heart. Just let me try, okay?''

Once the connection was broken, Tessa stood staring at the telephone. It was an indication of the extent of overload in the system that Marly hadn't demanded details of Tessa's testimony, which would surely have given her second thoughts. If Tessa called Beth Kendrick and talked her into letting Teddy stay at Sojourn for a few days and something went wrong, depending on the size of the scandal, the media would have a field day. Sojourn would be destroyed by the scandal along with Tessa's reputation, and it would possibly cost Marly her job.

Tessa rubbed one throbbing temple. Weighed against the risks she took if she went ahead was the heartbreak and pain of two children. It followed that Daniel's son was as bewildered and hurt as Teddy. Tessa couldn't do anything. But how could she allow the good of the whole program to ride on the welfare of two kids? And Marly... Still standing at the phone, Tessa closed her eyes. The enormity of the risk made her tremble.

She'd worked so diligently to make Sojourn a haven for forgotten kids, kids the system wouldn't otherwise recognize. Didn't that describe Daniel's children? And didn't she have some responsibility for their situation? And wasn't she honor-bound to at least try to do something when, by a curious stroke of fate, she was the only one who could? Finally, it came down to one simple thing. Either she believed in Daniel's innocence or she didn't.

"You'd better not let me down, Daniel Kendrick," she muttered, turning to leave the room. She drew back in surprise to find Daniel standing just behind her.

"I won't let you down," he said, glancing at the telephone. "Is everything fixed?"

"Not quite. I was just on my way to see you. I need your wife's phone number."

"Ex-wife." He pulled his wallet from the back pocket of his jeans and slipped a business card from the tri-fold. "This one's a business number and this is her apartment. It's almost six there, so she should be at home." As Tessa took the card, his gaze was intense on her face. "You didn't tell Marly the details of your testimony at the custody hearing. Why, Tessa?"

She sank onto the side of the desk, rubbing a spot between her eyes. "Don't ask me. Maybe Stephanie's right, maybe I'm trying to ease a guilty conscience."

"In spite of my bellyaching, there's no need for you to have a guilty conscience."

"I know. But after listening to Teddy weeping her heart out, convinced her mother doesn't love her and that you don't want her or her brother, I find I'm rethinking everything that happened five years ago. I just don't want to believe I had any part in setting such a fiasco into motion."

"You did your duty. Both you and your sister are right about that."

"But maybe I should have asked a few more questions," Tessa said, rubbing a spot on the tile floor with the tip of her shoe.

Casually, Daniel sat down beside her, one hip on the desktop. "Maybe we're being given a second chance to try to fix it."

Tessa gave him a sidelong look and found him watching her. A little shiver slid up her spine. She moved a shoulder to try to block the feeling. There was no place in her life for that. Especially not with this man.

She stood up and pulled the phone around to dial. "Here goes." She waited through three rings, conscious of Daniel standing close—tall, just a bit tense as he waited, but utterly male. She turned slightly so that he wasn't in the range of her vision and mentally urged Beth Kendrick to pick up the damn phone.

"Hello?"

"Mrs. Kendrick?" When Daniel touched her face to draw her eyes to his, she nearly lost her train of thought.

"She's Beth Carson, not Kendrick. She doesn't use my name."

"Ah, Ms. Carson? Beth Carson?"

"Yes, this is she." Her voice was sharp, laced with irritation.

"This is Tessa Hamilton, Ms. Carson. You may not remember me, but I—"

"I remember you, Ms. Hamilton. Tessa." There was no surprised pleasure at hearing from the single most important witness involved in her custody case against Daniel. And no curiosity, just the cool, courteous acknowledgment of a distant connection.

"I'm at a clinic in New Orleans, ah…Beth. Teddy's here."

"A clinic? As in medical clinic?"

"Yes, that's right. Teddy—"

"Is she sick? Has she had an accident?" Finally her tone reflected a stirring of concern.

"She's okay. She's been staying with some homeless teenagers in the French Quarter, and they—"

"That little idiot!" Exasperation mixed with renewed irritation. "I *knew* it would be something like this. I hope you're not going to tell me there's a boy involved."

Tessa met Daniel's eyes. "No, Beth, there are no boys involved. Apparently she got hold of some tainted food and her friends became concerned when she couldn't stop vomiting. They took her to the free clinic. She's dehydrated, but—''

"What kind of free clinic?" Suspicion sharpened her tone.

Tessa hesitated. "It's affiliated with Women's Hospital."

"For the indigent, I assume."

"Well…yes."

A large gusty sigh. "Wouldn't you know it?"

Tessa frowned. "I beg your pardon?"

"My daughter has been nothing but trouble for the past year, Tessa. Puberty, I suppose. Or maybe just sheer stubbornness, a trait she inherited from her father, which you may not know now, but if you spend any time with him, you soon will. And speaking of Daniel, I thought she'd go straight to him and of course he'd take her in and probably never even call me to tell me she was safe. Now you say she's in a charity clinic alongside who knows what kind of vagrants or druggies, upchucking because she's been eating garbage." She released another large sigh. "Well, it's enough to drive me around the bend, Tessa. Is she well enough to travel? Not that I'm flying down yet. I'm in the throes of a very important event here with commitments I simply can't just set aside. I can't possibly hop a plane, not for a few days."

What kind of commitments outweighed the woman's duty to her child? Tessa wondered, then shied away from that thought. What right had she, of all people, to criticize Beth Carson? At least she was there for her kids.

Beth's tone suddenly brightened. "Oh, you know

what, Tessa? Since Daniel's there, why don't you call him and have him pick her up, take her to his place—he's always nagging me about wanting her and Joey with him. Well, here's his chance. That'll work temporarily, won't it?''

Daniel could hear her, Tessa realized from the look on his face. He stood with his arms folded, his jaw clenched with fury. Tessa rubbed the spot between her eyes again. ''Beth, what about the allegations revealed at the custody hearing? Are you saying you don't object to Teddy's staying with her father?''

Beth huffed with impatience. ''What choice do I have, I'd like to know? I'm here, Teddy's there. Daniel's her father. Let him try to cope with her for a change.''

''You called the sheriff's office when you decided she was missing and told them you suspected Daniel was behind her disappearance. At that time you wanted him arrested if she was there. Now you've changed your mind?''

''I'm simply in a bind, and Daniel's the logical person to step into the breach. Is that so complicated? He's her father, for God's sake!''

Tessa drew a deep breath, trying not to show her disgust. ''Whether he's her father or not, by law he's allowed only supervised visitation with his children. It may be convenient for you to disregard that at the moment, Beth, but I'm afraid the sheriff and the juvenile officer in the parish won't.''

Beth gave a little scream of irritation. ''Oh, this is so stupid! I mean it, I can't come down there right now.''

''I have a suggestion, Beth.''

A heartbeat of silence. "What is it?"

"I'm the administrator of Sojourn, a juvenile refuge. We offer temporary shelter and counseling for runaway teens, among others. Teddy would fall into that category. I've spoken to the juvenile officer at NOPD, who has agreed that Teddy can recuperate there for a few days. She'll be released in my custody, and naturally I will take full responsibility for her safety and welfare while she's at Sojourn. I believe this will solve the problem, at least temporarily." Tessa met Daniel's eyes for a brief, intense moment. "Would you consider that?"

"Sojourn?" Beth said the name as if it were toxic waste. "It sounds like one of those places for battered wives."

"There are no adults at Sojourn except the staff."

"Criminals, then? What are the kids there for?"

"Various things, Beth. Nothing serious."

"Well, I don't know..."

"Teddy truly isn't strong enough to fly to New York on her own. If you don't approve of her staying at Sojourn, juvenile authorities will assign her to foster care until—"

"Foster care!" There was horror in her tone. "No. Absolutely not. Why can't Daniel—"

"Daniel is forbidden by the court to be with his children, Beth. You can't pick and choose when it's convenient to accept or reject that ruling." In her exasperation, Tessa turned to Daniel. His face was a rigid mask, but his eyes burned with a passion that matched her own outrage. "Look, Beth, I know how you must feel. Your child has run away. She's sick and stranded. Think of it this way. I, of all people, understand the dynamics of your divorce and the custody trial. Who better than me to care for Teddy until she can be with you again?''

"Well, I suppose I haven't much choice...."

Tessa glanced at the card from Daniel's wallet and saw a fax number. "I'll fax you some paperwork. All you have to do is sign it, fax it back to me, then pop the originals in the mail."

"This is so unnecessary," Beth grumbled. "If Teddy hadn't gone off half-cocked that way... You just tell her for me that I'll have a few things to say to her when she gets home. And...she's grounded for a month. I've just about had it, Tessa. I'm seriously considering boarding school. Tell her that, too. This better not *ever* happen again, or so help me—"

"I have another call, Beth," Tessa lied. "That fax'll be on the wire within the hour."

Tessa stayed for a moment with her hand on the receiver, then looked up and met Daniel's eyes. "Well, I think that went well, don't you?" she said brightly.

His gaze was locked on her face. "Thank you."

"She's not exactly...brimming with maternal concern, is she?"

"No."

She held up one finger. "Just don't do anything, Daniel—*anything*—to make me regret sticking my neck out."

"I've said I won't and my word is about all I've got left nowadays." He gave a short laugh. "Not that I'm ever offered an opportunity to prove it."

"Well, here's your chance."

He sank again to the edge of the desk, head down,

his hands resting on his thighs. "It's all so hopeless, isn't it? She'll never change."

"Like many women today, her career seems to demand so much of her life that there's not much left over for her children. Or for Teddy, at least."

"It's the same with Joey." He gazed at a crystal paperweight on Stephanie's desk. "Other women have careers without neglecting their children. Beth just doesn't want the hassle. She only fought for custody because she thought she should. The threat about boarding school isn't an empty one." He picked up the paperweight and stared at the colors inside.

Aware of her own shortcomings, Tessa knew people often had good reasons for bad behavior, although she'd yet to see any such trauma in Beth's life. On the contrary, the woman had seemed to have everything—two nice kids, a career, a lovely home and Daniel. Daniel. Again, she pushed that thought away. "Maybe there are things you don't know, Daniel."

"Such as?"

"Reasons for her behavior," Tessa said, unconvinced even as she said it. "Maybe what you see as neglect is something going on inside her that she feels unable to share with you."

Daniel set the paperweight aside. "Are you sure we're talking about the same person? Because if so, I can tell you after eight years of marriage to Beth that there's nothing that would justify her attitude toward Teddy and Joey. She's an egotistical, self-centered person whose art is the single most important thing in her life—other than keeping up appearances. It's nice of you to suggest that there could be mitigating circumstances, but you're wrong."

Trapped in the deep silver of his gaze, Tessa didn't

argue. But her heart jumped when he cupped her face in one hand. "I'm not so sure about you," he added, lazily rubbing a thumb over her cheekbone. "Why would you feel a need to defend Beth? Guilt? Forget it. I've already conceded you were only doing your duty in testifying."

Tessa couldn't believe she was standing here enthralled by a man's touch. She hadn't felt this way in—oh, since God knew. Maybe never. Her blossoming sexuality had been brutally arrested in a dark barn on a stormy afternoon in Arkansas. "I always try to see the other person's point of view," she said, wrapping her fingers around his wrist.

He held her a second longer, refusing to let her look away in spite of her hold on his wrist. "Very commendable."

But his eyes were full of speculation. Fine, let him speculate. This was about him and his problems, not hers. He let her go when she moved, and she released him, too. But her fingers tingled from the warmth of his skin and the feel of the strength in his hard, male wrist. "I think we should check on Teddy. She's probably awake now."

Daniel nodded. "You're probably right."

Tessa headed for the examining room, aware of him close behind her with every step. He was a dangerous man. Somehow in the past few moments his interest had shifted away from his ex-wife and focused on her. He sensed something personal in her defense of Beth. Tessa suspected he was the kind of man who would try again to pry her secrets from her. She hated the very thought. If he ever found out, he would probably think his kids were lucky to have Beth and not a woman like Tessa for a mother.

CHAPTER SEVEN

IT WAS LATE when Daniel and Tessa finally headed back to Sojourn with Teddy asleep in the back seat of the car. As Daniel turned into the curved driveway, the young girl stirred and sat up, blinking sleepily. "Are we here?"

"We're here." He got out and opened the back door, but when he started to lift Teddy into his arms, she resisted. Puzzled, he saw that she was looking at Sojourn's wide front porch where half a dozen teenagers stood watching.

"I'm okay, Daddy. You don't have to carry me."

Daniel sought Tessa's opinion with a questioning look. "I'll just walk along beside Teddy," Tessa said, handing him a gym bag stuffed with a few clothes and necessities hastily purchased for Teddy before they left the city. "If you'll carry her things, we'll get her settled before you have to leave."

Still pale and shaky, Teddy clung to Daniel's hand. "Daddy, you're staying with me, aren't you?"

"I can't, honey. No parents allowed at Sojourn overnight. But I'll be back tomorrow morning and every morning for a few days to work on some bookshelves, so we'll have lots of time together."

"Well…"

Tessa slipped an arm around the girl's waist.

"Teddy, come and meet some of the people you're going to be staying with for the next few days. And then we'll get you settled."

Before they'd taken three steps, Leon tripped down the porch stairs, eyebrows pumping up and down. "Ho, Ms. Tessa, did you notice them grounds? Me and Curtis did some big-time mowin' and weed-eatin' today."

"From what I can see, you've made a good start, Leon. Remind me to order some mulch for the beds."

"Mulch!" He rolled his eyes. "You mean we ain't finished?"

"Aren't finished."

"That's what I'm askin'."

"We'll discuss it tomorrow, Leon." Supporting Teddy, who was wobbling with weakness, Tessa climbed the porch steps slowly. When they reached the top, Jacky, looking pleased with herself, sidled close to Daniel.

"I painted the bookshelves, Mr. Kendrick," she said, sporting a paint-spattered T-shirt.

"I told her they weren't ready to paint, Mr. Kendrick," Greg said. "But she wouldn't listen."

Jacky glared at him. "I only painted the ones that were finished," she said.

"Yeah, and what if they were supposed to be stained, not painted?" Greg demanded.

"Ms. Tessa already told me what color they'd be—white!"

"Enough, you two." Daniel silenced them with a look. "We'll discuss it tomorrow."

"Welcome home," Tessa muttered.

"Hey, Mom. I was just about to give you up."

"Keely!" Tessa's irritation fled at the sight of her daughter. "I didn't know you were coming this weekend. Is Alison with you?"

"No, she has some kind of college prep tea tomorrow, and since I wanted to spend the weekend, she sent greetings instead."

"Well, I'm glad you could make it. I'm short two female counselors this weekend."

"No problem." Keely gave Teddy a smile. "Hi. I'm Keely Hamilton, my mom's kid. And you are...?"

"Teddy Kendrick," she said shyly. "This is my dad."

"Mr. Kendrick, I presume." Keely stuck out her hand. "Keely Hamilton, sir."

Daniel smiled, shifting Teddy's bag to take her hand. "Daniel Kendrick. And I would have guessed Tessa to be your mother."

"It's the eyes, and..." Keely grinned "...the smile, right?"

"All of the above, right. Do you live around here?"

"I'm a student at Tulane. Premed."

He glanced at Tessa. "Uh-huh. I could have guessed that, too."

"Who's the little chick?" Curtis asked, openly studying Teddy.

"My daughter, Teddy," Daniel said, touching Teddy's dark hair. "This is Curtis, Leon, Greg, Jacky...hmm, Rachel, right?"

Rachel smiled. "Right. Hi, Teddy"

"Hi."

Tessa urged Teddy gently past the crowd at the

front door. "Teddy's had a big day, gang, so we'll save the conversation until tomorrow. Right now I think we'd better get her inside and tucked in. Otis, Bill..." She singled out the two Sojourn counselors who sat apart on the oak swing at the edge of the porch. "Time for the guys to head for the garçonnière."

With a chorus of moans and groans, the boys trouped down the porch steps at the urging of Otis and Bill. Keeping to a brick path that led to a smaller dwelling barely visible from the porch, they soon disappeared beneath the deep shadows of two huge live oaks.

"Keely, if you'll settle the girls into their rooms, I'll meet you in the kitchen as soon as I get Teddy tucked in."

"Garçonnière?" Daniel repeated with amusement, following Tessa and Teddy up the curving staircase.

"What's a garçonnière?" Teddy asked, craning her neck at a hexagonal window on the first landing to try to catch another glimpse of the boys.

"Bachelor quarters," Tessa replied. "Southern aristocrats often housed their unmarried sons separately from their unmarried daughters. The garçonnière was always situated far enough away so as not to shock their sisters by any unseemly bachelor behavior."

Teddy wrinkled her nose. "That's weird."

"Can't see you and Joey living like that, huh, baby?" Daniel said, still smiling.

"Uh-uh. No way."

He tugged at her hair. "Luckily, you're living in the 1990s, not the 1850s."

"It sounds unfair to me."

"Boys had different rules from girls in those days," Tessa said.

"Social norms of the 1850s might be ridiculed today, but their architecture is still a marvel," Daniel said, admiring the beauty of an elaborate medallion on the ceiling. "This is a wonderful old place."

"I think so, too." Tessa touched the satiny surface of the stair railing. "We're lucky to be here. Sojourn was originally the summer dwelling for a wealthy New Orleans sugar planter. There was no sugar cane on the north shore of Lake Pontchartrain, but many well-to-do families spent the hot summer months away from their swampy plantations and their town houses in the city proper."

"The privileged aristocracy," Daniel said dryly.

"Yes. Fortunately Sojourn survived the Civil War intact, as well as the lean years that followed. It was badly damaged in a fire in 1950, and the owners considered it too expensive to restore, so they donated it to a charitable group, who later leased it to Women's Hospital after they promised to renovate it. I have custodial responsibility as long as it's used for charitable purposes. My quarters are on the third floor."

"Wow, three floors!" Teddy's knees were wobbling.

"That's where we're headed. Can you make it?"

"C'mere, Teddy-bear." Daniel handed the gym bag to Tessa and swung his daughter up into his arms, where she wilted against him like a sick kitten. "Another few minutes and we'll have you all tucked in snug as a bug," he said, brushing a kiss on the top of her head.

"What about Keely, Ms. Hamilton?"

"Keely has her own room next to yours. I'm putting you in the room Alison uses when she's here."

"Who's Alison?"

"My sister's stepdaughter. She's a senior in high school this year." They had reached the third floor. Tessa opened a door. "And here we are."

She hurried across the floor to remove the white eyelet coverlet from the tester bed and turn down the linens, then, while Daniel eased Teddy down onto the bed, she opened the gym bag. "Sleep shirt and toothbrush are inside, Teddy." She nodded toward a door connecting the bedroom with Keely's. "The bathroom's there. Do you need any help changing?"

"I'm okay." She pulled Daniel down to kiss him good-night. "Promise you'll come back tomorrow morning, Daddy?"

He cupped her face in one hand. "Promise. And you show Ms. Hamilton what a good girl you are by settling down and going right to sleep. We want to let her know how much we appreciate being able to stay here."

"Okay." Teddy tilted her head to nuzzle his hand. "I wish Joey could be with us, Daddy."

"I wish that, too, baby."

"Will you call him and tell him where we are and that we're okay?"

"First thing when I get home."

"Mom will probably be there when you call."

"Um-hmm, probably."

"She's gonna try to make you send me back right away."

"And she has the right to do that, remember?"

She made a face and picked at the lace trim on the sheet. "Those stupid rules."

He tugged a strand of her hair. "Maybe we can talk your mom into bending them a little this time, what do you think?"

Her head came up. "Really?"

"No promises, Teddy-bear, but I'm going to try."

TESSA'S DAUGHTER was waiting in the foyer when Daniel got downstairs. "Your mom's checking on the girls," he told her, moving toward a library table at the front door. "I left some papers here. Do you know where they are?" They were copies of the documents Tessa was faxing to Beth, but before she signed them, he needed to read them to be sure there wasn't a provision that would prevent his visits to Sojourn to see Teddy.

Keely motioned for him to follow her. "They're in the kitchen with your jacket. This way. I've made tea," she said, urging him past the room where he'd begun building the shelves into a big old-fashioned kitchen.

She gave him a minute to look over the papers, then pulled out a chair at the table. "You can sit there," she said. A pretty teapot and three designer mugs were arranged beside a small plate piled high with brownies. "Mom's probably making a bed check on the second floor, but not in the sense you're thinking. Last thing every night she lets each girl know she's there if needed. For anything. Same for me when I'm here. We always have a chat over tea before we go to bed."

She grinned as she began pouring from the teapot. "Mom has a weakness for brownies."

He took the filled mug from her, unable to resist a chance to get to know Tessa's daughter better. "Brownies, hmm? I'll keep that in mind, although Tessa doesn't look like her weakness has done any harm."

Keely smiled into her tea. "She is gorgeous, isn't she?"

"Very attractive." Daniel reached for a brownie.

"'Very attractive.'" She wrinkled her nose. "That's it?"

Daniel chuckled softly, thinking what her mother would say if she heard this conversation. "Okay, she's gorgeous." Keely was a pretty charmer and wise beyond her years. He guessed her to be eighteen or nineteen, a couple of years older than the charmer who'd burned him in his past life. He glanced warily at the door and suddenly wished Tessa would hurry.

Cupping her mug with both hands, Keely looked at him. "I heard you volunteered to put in the bookshelves at Sojourn. How did that happen?"

"I was looking for Teddy at NOPD, which seemed a good place to start at the time, and ran into your mother. Tessa recognized her from the photo I had with me."

"Fate."

He looked into her eyes—so like her mother's. "Some people might think so."

"But not you."

"I don't know what to think, to tell you the truth, Keely. Call it fate. Or coincidence. Call it whatever you like, but it was the first lucky break I'd had in the search for my daughter. I thought a cop might recognize Teddy from her picture, but it was your mother who made the connection and went with me to try to find her."

"It must have been a real disappointment when you didn't find her right away, but those kids she was running with are experts at avoiding cops and anxious parents." She frowned, thinking. "In fact, the kids here might have given you some tips. They know the streets better than any cop or my Mom. Did you think of that?"

"Actually, I did."

"Wait a minute." Her expression changed. "That's why you were building those shelves." Keely set her mug down carefully. "Cool. So, now you've found her. Didn't she want to go home with you?"

"Keely, Mr. Kendrick's had a long day and I'm sure he's tired. He doesn't need a third degree."

"Oh, hi, Mom." Keely pushed a mug toward her. "Take a seat. Darjeeling and your favorite—brownies loaded with nuts."

Daniel partially rose from his chair. "Did Teddy settle down okay?"

Tessa nodded, waving him down, then slipped into the place across from him. "She was asleep before you reached the second-floor landing. Don't worry about her. I'll check on her during the night, but she seems fine. Steph wouldn't have released her otherwise."

Keely put a brownie on a napkin and passed it to Tessa. "Mom, I forgot to tell you when you first came in, but that reporter Pete Veillon called while you were out.''

Tessa paused in the act of breaking the brownie in half. "Did he say what he wanted?"

"An interview." Keely balled up a napkin and aimed it at a trash can beside the stove. "He said he'd been trying for days to reach you but you never returned his calls. I took his number and made no promises.''

"Good."

Pete Veillon. Daniel knew the name, an investigative reporter on one of the local TV stations. Veillon was famous for sensational exposés. "Channel Two's Pete Veillon?" he asked. "The guy who blew the whistle on the state's health-care scandal?"

"The same," Keely said.

Tessa pushed the brownie aside untouched. "He's been trying to get inside Sojourn for some time now to do a feature.''

"Maybe you should just give him the interview, Mom. He's not going to stop trying. Let him come for the open house, see what Sojourn's about. What harm can it do? You run this place like a church, it's so squeaky clean.''

Tessa sighed. "I'll think about it."

Keely grinned at Daniel. "She's very protective about Sojourn. You'd think it was consecrated ground or something.''

Maybe not consecrated ground, Daniel thought, studying Tessa as she sipped her tea. But Tessa took Sojourn very seriously. Which made him even more amazed that she was opening its doors to him and his daughter.

In that moment, the enormity of the risk she was taking suddenly dawned on him. Not only would Sojourn be jeopardized if something went wrong, but her own personal reputation would be destroyed. *Admiration* and *gratitude* were words too weak to describe what he felt. He'd almost forgotten there were people in the world like Tessa, people willing to give and give for a cause bigger than themselves. Willing to take a risk for a troubled young girl. Willing to trust a man with a tainted reputation. He moved restlessly, sloshing his tea. It wouldn't take much for something to go wrong.

But it wouldn't go wrong, he vowed. If she gave him this chance, he would see to it Sojourn didn't suffer. That Tessa wouldn't suffer.

"Your mother should be proud." Although he spoke to Keely, Daniel was looking into Tessa's eyes. "A cause like this takes time and energy and commitment."

"Yep, that's my mom," Keely said, still teasing her mother playfully. Unabashed by Tessa's self-conscious dismay, she added, "I don't know why Teddy's not going home with you, Daniel, but staying here with my mom at Sojourn's the next best thing."

"Keely, for heaven's sake!" Tessa shook her head helplessly.

Daniel pushed his chair back, glancing at his watch. "I'd better go since it's an hour later in New York and I still have to call my son to let him know his sister's okay. If Teddy wakes up and seems unduly upset, Tessa, will you call me? I can come right over."

"In the middle of the night? I don't think so."

"Then just give me a call. That's not against the rules, is it?''

Still unsettled, Tessa began collecting spoons from the table. "And if it were?''

"I'd want to talk to her anyway, Tessa," he explained patiently. "Wouldn't you if it were Keely?''

Tessa stopped and looked directly at him. "I understand and sympathize with your situation as Teddy's father, Daniel, but I'm not tempting fate by bending any more rules.''

Keely was watching, bright-eyed with curiosity. "Has she been this testy all day, Daniel? She does that sometimes when one of her little lambs goes astray.''

"Teddy's not one of my little lambs, Keely, and she's only here for a few days." She grabbed her tea, sloshing some onto the table. "She has to go back to New York.''

"New York.'' Jumping on this new fact, Keely studied Daniel thoughtfully. "The kids told me you have a woodworking business, so I assume you live here. New York's a long way from Louisiana, Dad.''

"About eighteen hundred miles.''

"Divorced and Mom has custody, huh? So that's why you can't take her to your place?''

"Keely!'' Tessa set her mug down with a thump. "Daniel's private life is none of our business.''

Keely shrugged. "Sorry, Daniel. No offense intended, okay?''

"None taken,'' Daniel said, smiling faintly.

Keely glanced at her mother. "I was with Mom in the Quarter last weekend when we spotted Teddy with that scuzzy group. Lucky you found her when you did. New Orleans's streets can be really bad, Daniel. I don't think she's tough enough to have survived very long without big-time damage.''

Daniel drained the last of his tea. "Is any thirteen-year-old girl that tough?''

"A few." Keely tipped back on the legs of her chair and gave her mother a secret smile. "And some even survive it to go on to happiness ever after. Right, Mom?''

"Daniel's right." Tessa stood up abruptly, looking at her watch. "It's late.''

He was no mind reader, but it didn't take one to pick up on some unspoken exchange between mother and daughter. Intrigued now, Daniel tucked the discovery in the back of his mind to explore another time. "Thanks for the nightcap, Keely." He stood, brushing crumbs from his lap. "And for the brownie.''

"Anytime.''

"Walk me to my car, Tessa?''

Keely smiled and then winked at him.

"I have something for Teddy in my pickup," he explained quickly. The little minx!

"Go ahead, Mom. I'll finish up here. And Daniel..." She waited while he shrugged into his jacket. "Don't forget your papers.''

DANIEL HELD THE front door for Tessa, who sailed through at an agitated pace. "Your daughter is an extraordinary young woman, Tessa.''

"Thanks, I think.''

"She's obviously a big fan of yours.''

Her reply was an exasperated sound, something between a strangled croak and a moan, making the corner of Daniel's mouth hike up with amusement. "Most moms would be over the moon to have a teenage daughter who showed that much open affection."

"She was…was…" Words failed Tessa.

"Vetting me?" Daniel supplied smoothly.

"It's ridiculous!" Already Tessa was having trouble justifying her decision to allow a man like Daniel on the premises of Sojourn. And then to have Keely misinterpreting the situation as…as…something personal was just too much.

"You must be very proud of her."

She hesitated, thinking how she was going to lambaste her cheeky daughter when she got back inside, then relaxed with a helpless laugh. "There aren't enough words," she said simply. "Although sometimes I'd like to try to find the right ones so I can occasionally get the last one. Daniel, please disregard whatever she thought she was doing just now. I'm so embarrassed!"

"You're overreacting, Tessa. She's a delightful girl. Or am I allowed to say something like that considering my history?" he added quietly.

"You're allowed, because if I thought you meant anything more, I'd have to kill you."

He chuckled again. "Thank you."

At the corner of the brick walkway, they turned and headed for Daniel's vehicle. Behind them, the big house was dark except for the soft glow in the front foyer and the light at Keely's upstairs window. A night owl, she sometimes read until all hours.

"She's a good student?"

Tessa smiled. "Excellent."

"And she seems completely supportive of your work here at Sojourn."

"Completely. If I died tomorrow, she could step into my shoes and probably do a better job. But medicine's her true calling."

They had reached his pickup. The legal papers were rolled into a cylinder which he bumped against his thigh. "I'm jealous."

"Jealous?"

"Yeah. Of your relationship with your daughter. Of the childhood years you've shared. You'll always have that, you and Keely."

Tessa caught her breath. Held it. Daniel's assumption of her role in Keely's childhood was so wildly off the mark that she almost laughed.

He glanced up. A full moon hung heavy and round over the tops of the trees. "I worry that when my kids finally grow up and have a chance to make their own choices there'll be nothing left between us. That it'll be too late."

With her arms wrapped around her middle, Tessa wondered what he would think if he knew the truth. She didn't want to be reminded of her past tonight, of the horrendous mistakes that were like ugly milestones along the road her life had taken, but it always intruded. She'd spent the day doing what she did best—tracing the path of a lost child. This man's child. Rescuing and reassuring, uniting a family. It was a way of making amends, as if her work to ease the pain of the shattered families she encountered in her job could somehow diminish the size and scope of her own transgressions. She was used to basking in the goodness of that feeling when she rescued a child, not coming up hard against the reality of her past.

"There was something you wanted to get from your pickup," she reminded him, blocking out the black thoughts. "Something for Teddy?"

"Oh, yeah." He reached past her, opened the door and pulled out a shopping bag. "It's a stationery box, a replica of the boxes used by ladies in the nineteenth century when correspondence was an art."

"No telephones or E-mail," Tessa murmured, rubbing the satiny finish.

"She's good about writing me, but I worry now that she's a teenager other things will...push me out of her thoughts."

"If her reaction when she saw you this afternoon at the clinic is any indication, I don't think you have anything to worry about."

"Yeah, well. We both know how constant is a teenager's loyalty."

No argument there. "Did you make this?"

"Yeah. I admire the workmanship used back then. It's a challenge trying to copy it. And it passes the time."

His face in the moonlight was all sharp angles and planes, severe and yet... She couldn't quite describe it. She bundled up the box in the bag and began to back away. "Speaking of time, I really must get back to the girls."

"And I still have to make that call to Joey."

"Good night."

"See you tomorrow, Tessa."

His voice had roughened. The sound of it stirred something deep inside her. She hurried away, the gift to his daughter held tight against her.

CHAPTER EIGHT

SHE WAS A WOMAN with secrets, Tessa Hamilton. A couple of times now Daniel had noticed a look in her eye, a tone of voice—a word—that warned him off. The more he was with her, the more convinced he was that he'd only encountered the tip of the iceberg in the woman who was Keely's mother, Stephanie's twin, rescuer of lost kids and foster parent to the misfits at Sojourn.

He drove the dark, winding lane away from Sojourn thinking of her. There'd been no need for Keely to emphasize her mother's appeal. He'd been uneasily aware of it almost from the get-go. And considering their history, she was absolutely the last woman he should be fantasizing about. Even so, there was something about Tessa Hamilton. He'd noticed her looking…wary sometimes. Fearful. But what would a woman like Tessa have to be wary about? Or fearful?

He approached the stop sign at the end of Sojourn Lane. Fate had brought Tessa Hamilton back into his life, and his situation with Teddy made it necessary to deal with her, but secrets made Daniel uncomfortable. There had been enough of the unexpected and the unforeseen in the past five years to last him a lifetime. At the stop sign, he considered taking a right turn and heading to the lake. When he was troubled, he liked to walk the sandy shoreline. Staring at the murky surface seemed to help him sort out his thoughts. But after a moment, he decided it was a luxury he couldn't take time for tonight.

He turned left while his mind continued to consider the problem of Tessa Hamilton. Idly he touched the rearview mirror to deflect the glare of headlights behind him. He tried to recall if he'd ever heard any mention of Tessa's ex-husband, Keely's father. Maybe that's where the mystery was, although it was difficult to picture Tessa being browbeaten by an exhusband. By anyone, for that matter.

If it wasn't Tessa's personal life putting that look in her eyes, then could it be worry about Sojourn? He could imagine her fearful and concerned about the shelter. Sojourn was almost an obsession with her. From a public standpoint, if that's what was bothering her, she was worrying needlessly. In spite of the perceived threat from a nosy media, saving "throwaway" kids was the kind of thing people would rally to defend. It would take a scandal of major proportions to undermine Sojourn.

He was startled by a sudden blast of sound. Behind him blue lights were flashing and a siren screamed. Police. His stomach lurched, and he swore softly. Foot on the brake, he swerved to the roadside and stopped. Braced, he watched through his rearview as the police car hit the shoulder and slid on the gravel to within an inch of his bumper. The shrill pulsing halted as the driver killed the engine.

In the dead silence that followed, Daniel drew a deep breath, his hands gripping the wheel, and wondered why he was being stopped. Maybe it was the traffic sign at the end of the lane. He couldn't recall whether he'd come to a full stop. But where the hell had the cruiser been? He could have sworn there was nothing alive at that intersection with the possible exception of bullfrogs and armadillos. With a sigh, he opened the door and got out of the pickup.

The cruiser's headlights were set on bright, blinding him. Unable to see a face, Daniel stood waiting for the uniformed lawman to materialize out of the darkness, but a moment before the officer stepped into the glare of the headlights, Daniel recognized the thick body and swaggering gait of Dwayne Duplantis.

With a creak of spit-shined leather, Duplantis sauntered up to him and stopped. "Out pretty late, aren't you, Mr. Kendrick?"

"I don't have a curfew, Deputy."

"Maybe not, but what I'm trying to figure out is why a man like you would be on this particular deserted road at this hour of the night."

It's a free country. None of your goddamn business. Daniel's mind cranked out half a dozen smart-ass responses, but what he said was, "I sometimes drive down to the lake at night. It's peaceful. Even 'a man like me' has a right to relax."

"You doin' something makes you need to relax?"

"It beats sitting around doing nothing, Deputy."

"I'm gonna want to see your license."

Daniel reached into his back pocket and pulled out his wallet. Handing it over, he asked, "What's the problem?"

Duplantis said nothing as he pulled his flashlight from a holder at his waist and trained the beam on the license. Taking his time, he studied it at length.

Off to the side in a stand of cattails, a bullfrog croaked a message. Daniel fixed his gaze on the fence line across the road and waited out Duplantis's little exercise in intimidation.

Using his flashlight, the deputy pushed the bill of his cap up a scant half inch and then aimed it into the interior of Daniel's pickup. "Step back, Kendrick."

Daniel knew better than to argue. He watched Duplantis flash the beam over the dash, then down on the floorboard. "Are you searching for something in particular?"

"You'll know if I find it." Duplantis grunted, spotting a small box tucked beneath the passenger seat. Checking to see that Daniel was standing well back, he pulled the box out and opened it. The gleam of his flashlight reflected off a collection of small hand tools—a good pair of pliers, a monkey wrench, two screw drivers, a roll of electrical tape and a roll of duct tape, all standard items for a man who drove an aging automobile. Without bothering with the lid, Duplantis tossed the box onto the seat.

"I try to be prepared," Daniel explained, deadpan.

"A regular Boy Scout, are you?" With a snort, Duplantis stepped to the side of the pickup and lifted the bin. After a quick flash with his light, he dropped the lid and walked to the rear, sweeping the beam of his flashlight over the empty surface. He walked back to Daniel and handed him his license. "You see anybody on this road within the last hour?"

"No."

The deputy eyed him suspiciously. "Nobody?"

"I tend to mind my own business, Deputy. If there was any traffic, I didn't notice."

With the light now trained on Daniel's face, Duplantis studied him in silence. A full thirty seconds ticked by before he said, "Had a robbery at a convenience store about an hour ago. Two thugs wearing stockings over their faces took a few dollars from the cash drawer and stole a weapon. Pistol-whipped the woman clerk when she told them she didn't have the combination to the safe in the back."

Daniel listened, his features revealing none of the turmoil in his chest. Did Duplantis suspect he had anything to do with the robbery?

"What exactly does this have to do with me?"

"They drove a pickup truck."

"What make and model?"

"Witnesses were two kids, all shook up and couldn't be sure. Seemed to think it was dark, in pretty sad shape." He flicked a glance at Daniel's Chevy.

"I haven't been shopping tonight." Or breaking the law.

"Like I said, witnesses couldn't be sure."

Daniel drew in a long breath. "Are you suggesting I might have been involved in an armed robbery, Deputy Duplantis?"

Duplantis leaned over to spit a few inches from Daniel's shoe. "I'm not suggesting anything, Kendrick. We've got men out all over this part of the parish trying to flush these two out. I find you pokin' along this deserted stretch of highway and my instincts tell me you aren't out cleansin' your soul or meditatin', you get my drift?"

"I get it. And I'm telling you I was doing nothing illegal when you spotted me and I haven't been anywhere near a convenience store in more than a week. You're going to have to come up with something more substantial than innuendo, Deputy, or I'm going to get in my vehicle and go home.''

Without haste, Duplantis settled his cap firmly on his head. He used his flashlight to inspect Daniel again, sweeping the beam from head to foot. ''There's nothing out this way except the lakeshore. I don't see any sand on your shoes, which leads me to think you haven't been walking the beach.''

Daniel hesitated, trying to decide how much to admit. This joker would love to make something of the fact that a man like Daniel was hanging around a facility sheltering troubled teenage girls.

''I probably don't have to tell you that that winding road leads to Sojourn, Kendrick. You know about Sojourn?''

''I've been in touch with Juvenile at NOPD. They mentioned the shelter.''

''Bunch of runaways and such hang out there, did they tell you that?''

''As I understand it, they shelter runaways and kids whose behavior doesn't warrant incarceration in a jail cell.''

''Sweet young things, the way I hear it,'' Duplantis said, watching slyly as Daniel drew in a sharp breath. ''Soft, sweet little girls. What's the problem, Kendrick. I hit a nerve?''

Sickened, Daniel said nothing.

Duplantis adjusted his visor with his hand, keeping the beam of his flashlight trained on Daniel. ''I took it upon myself to look into your case, Kendrick. You ought to know that.''

Daniel was unsurprised, but what did catch him off guard was the force of black fury that rose in him at the thought of this Neanderthal riffling through his private papers to ferret out the dark details of that time, enjoying the moment. He waited a beat or two until he'd mastered the rage that roared in his ears.

"Exactly which case was that, Deputy?" he asked evenly. "Because the only thing you would find in any court of law with my name on it would be my divorce decree. Anything else, such as the records of the custody hearing in Florida, are sealed in that state by order of the court." His tone dropped as he added, "You wouldn't have had access to that, at least, not legally."

Duplantis spat again in the grass. "You know, that's somethin' I guess I'll never understand, the way the court helps you perverts by sealin' documents."

"I'm hiding nothing, Deputy."

"Yeah, well, that remains to be seen." He clicked off his flashlight and lowered but didn't holster it. Instead, he stood bumping it against a thick thigh. "Just remember this, Kendrick, in case you're thinkin' to go to Miz Hamilton to help you locate your little girl. A man like you's got no business goin' near a place like that. Now me, I'd throw you right out of the parish if it was my decision, but seein' as my hands are tied, I thought I'd just let you know this." He stopped. Waited. "I can't keep you away from Sojourn, Kendrick, but I'm gonna be watching you. I'm gonna stick closer to you than white on rice." He holstered his flashlight with a hard shove. "And don't forget it."

DANIEL FLUNG HIS KEYS at the table and slung his jacket in the vicinity of the coatrack. When he failed to greet Cat, the animal meowed and leaped onto the back of a chair, then sat warily. With his hand pressed to the back of his neck, Daniel stood surveying the room and cursing Dwayne Duplantis. Stung by the deputy's baiting, he had driven away with fury and sickness churning in his gut. He'd spent five years trying to come to terms with the filthy label stuck on him by the court, but it never got any easier. Then, like tonight, something happened and he was reminded that he was always fair game, always suspect.

God, for the first time in five years, he could spend some time with Teddy, and he meant to do just that. The devil with Duplantis and his ilk. There was no legal basis for Duplantis to dog his every move, but Daniel hadn't survived the past five years as a transient without learning something about cops. The deputy didn't like him. He could make his life a misery. He could harass him over every crime committed in the parish even though he wasn't remotely involved. Tonight's episode could be just the beginning. And there wasn't a hell of a lot Daniel could do about it.

Worse than that, Duplantis posed a threat to Tessa, as well. Now that his attention was fixed on Daniel, it was just a matter of time before he realized Daniel was visiting Sojourn regularly. Duplantis wouldn't miss a chance to make mischief with that. Feeling weary beyond belief, Daniel resolved to tell Tessa about tonight's encounter first thing tomorrow.

Rubbing at tense neck muscles, he headed for the telephone. He still had to make the call to New York. He owed it to Beth to give her a firsthand report on

Teddy, but before he dialed her number, he noticed that his answering machine was blinking and punched the button to pick it up.

As the tape rewound, he leaned against the counter, surveying his family room. Family room, indeed. No family of his had ever been inside the house. And no family would feel at home here. The place was furnished with almost spartan restraint. The small things that made a house into a home were missing—knick-knacks, art, keepsakes. The only reminder of his past life was a picture of Teddy and Joey on the door of the refrigerator.

Joey's voice on tape stopped his thoughts abruptly. "Hi, Dad, this is Joey. Mom just told me you found Teddy and she's staying with you for a few days. Dad, I thought you said we weren't allowed to stay with you, so how can Teddy do that? But if she can, then so can I, right? School's out now and I don't have to be back for ten weeks, Dad. Please let me come, too. Please, Dad. I could catch a plane and I could be there tomorrow. I'm not scared to fly alone. Please, please, you gotta let me come, too, Dad."

A catch in the boy's voice sent a pain through Daniel's chest. Head bent, he pinched the bridge of his nose and waited for the tape to end. He heard Joey sniff, then the boy said, "I thought running away was dumb when Teddy did it, Dad, but it got her to New Orleans and now she's with you and I'm here. And I'm thinkin', which one of us is dumb now?" After a pause, Joey added, "I'll see you soon, Dad."

"Damn," Daniel breathed, snatching up the phone. He punched the number for the New York apartment and waited through several rings, cursing when he heard the machine kick in. "Hi, this is Beth. Sorry I can't take your call, but if you leave your name and number, I'll get back to you." *Bee-ee-p.*

Daniel resisted the urge to slam the receiver down. Where the hell was she at this hour? And so much for setting her mind at ease over Teddy. "Beth, this is Daniel. It's almost midnight and I've just returned from settling Teddy in at the shelter under Tessa Hamilton's care. The IV replenished the fluids she lost and she seems okay. She was sleeping when I left. I'll be keeping a close watch on her for the next week or so and will keep you posted."

He paused, searching for words to convey his unease over Joey, but he didn't want Joey picking up the message. If the boy wasn't signaling that he planned to try what Teddy had done, he didn't want to put the idea into his head. "Call me when you pick this up, Beth, no matter what time it is. We need to talk. And tell Joey I'll call him first thing tomorrow. I—"

"Dad? This is Joey, Dad."

"Joey? Son, it's the middle of the night. Where's your mother?"

"I don't know. Out somewhere. Who cares?"

Another wrench to Daniel's heart. "Who's with you, son? You're not alone, are you?"

"No, Mrs. Kowalski's here. She fell asleep in front of the television. Forget all that, Dad. What's with Teddy? Is she, like, okay? You weren't just saying that, right, Dad?"

"She's fine, Joey. She was sick after eating some food that was spoiled, but she was taken to a medical clinic and got treatment. She'll be at a shelter for a few days.''

"So she's not staying with you, Dad?"

"No, nothing's changed even though Teddy's here in Louisiana, Joey. She can't stay in my house, and if you were down here, you wouldn't be able to stay here, either.''

"But she gets to see you every day, I bet," Joey said sullenly.

Daniel tipped his head back, sighing. "I told you I'd see whether I could arrange to get you down here for a visit, Joey. I haven't forgotten that promise. Be patient, son.''

"But Mom's gonna say no!" Joey cried. "I know she is!''

"Just give me a few days, Joey," Daniel begged. "I'm going to try my best to work something out. You've got to trust me on this, son. I want you down here as much as you want to come.''

"I don't care about coming down there, Dad. I just want to be with you.''

"And you will, Joey. You will.''

After he hung up, Daniel stepped out onto the back porch, letting the screen door close softly behind him. The night was quiet, yet alive with the sounds of nocturnal creatures. Dark clouds were building in the sky above the trees, edging over the surface of the moon. A quick flicker, then a jagged neon light arced across the black horizon. Cat meowed irritably at being shut inside.

Daniel pushed the door open a crack to let him out, and the cat rubbed against his leg to remind Daniel that he hadn't been fed. Daniel bent and scratched him behind his ears. Beth claimed to be allergic to cats, and although Daniel had never seen any evidence that she was, she'd forbidden all pets when Teddy and Joey begged for one. Another in a long list of deprivations his children had suffered.

"To hell with the law," he muttered, looking Cat in the eye. "To hell with stupid-ass courts and shortsighted judges. To hell with the whole frigged-up system!" He stood and headed back inside, vowing to do something to ease his kids' misery, even if it was wrong. Cat trotted happily beside him.

IN THE NEXT three days Daniel spent more quality time with his daughter than in the past three years combined. Since his divorce, he'd visited New York often, and Beth had accompanied Teddy and Joey to New Orleans a couple of times, but they'd always stayed in a hotel. Having Teddy near him for three whole days might seem unremarkable to other dads, but to him it was time to be treasured.

Although Teddy never expressed any interest in helping, she seemed content to watch him work on the bookshelves. After a couple of days, he worried that she was unnaturally quiet, almost sullen. He intended to ask Tessa to arrange some time for him to talk with her about why she ran away. But as long as they had an audience, Teddy wasn't about to reveal her private thoughts.

It no longer surprised him how naturally he turned to Tessa to help him smooth the way to a better relationship with his daughter. With each passing day, he was more and more indebted to her. And with each passing day, he came to a greater appreciation for her work at Sojourn. He held his breath that he wouldn't be the cause of any problem at the shelter. He'd told Tessa about meeting Duplantis at the end of Sojourn Lane. She had been concerned, but after studying the problem in the quiet of her office, she'd searched him out and told him she didn't believe in borrowing trouble. They'd deal with any garbage stirred up by Duplantis if and when it happened.

The woman was amazing.

A flash of movement at the door caught his eye. But it wasn't Tessa who entered the room, it was Keely hauling an overflowing laundry basket.

"Hi, gang." Keely set the basket on the floor and flashed a smile at everyone. "Teddy. How's it goin'?"

"Okay." Teddy sat on a tall stool, her feet locked around the rungs, eating an apple. Across the room, Daniel worked with Greg fitting doors on a closed cabinet beneath the shelves.

"Hi, Keely." Daniel motioned to Greg to hold a door in place while he secured a hinge. "You wouldn't happen to have anything of a chocolate nature in that basket, would you?"

"Sorry. You and Mom will have to get your chocolate fix some other way. There's a ton of dirty laundry that isn't going to wash itself."

Jacky looked up, stirring a can of paint. "You're not looking for me, are you? It's not my turn. I'm on for Friday."

Leon appeared with a stack of molding balanced on one shoulder. "It ain't my day, either. Check the chart, you don't believe me."

"Chill out, both of you. Teddy's the lucky individual today.'' Keely heaved an exaggerated sigh. ''The honeymoon's over, kiddo.''

Teddy eyed her suspiciously over the remains of the apple. ''What's that supposed to mean?''

''Just what it sounds like, Teddy-bear.'' Keely reached out and plucked the apple from her hand, then tossed it into a trash can. She pointed to the basket. ''Mondays, Wednesdays and Fridays we do the laundry around here. Those nice fresh sheets and towels you use don't wash and dry themselves, honey bun. Not to *mention* your Skivvies.''

Teddy got off the stool. ''You mean you want me to wash clothes and stuff?''

Keely gave the group a pleased look. ''You hear that, gang? She's quick!''

''I don't want to do laundry,'' Teddy said with a look of distaste.

''Hey, I'm with you on that one,'' Keely said cheerfully. ''Not a lot of fun mucking around with other people's dirty clothes. No, indeed!'' She clicked her tongue and wagged her head. ''It's a dirty job, all right, but somebody's got to do it. Unfortunately for you and me, today it's us.''

Teddy gave Daniel a distressed look. ''Daddy, did you hear her?''

''I heard her, honey.'' Daniel reached for his screwdriver. ''Around here everyone pitches in to do the chores. You want a clean towel when you take a bath, don't you?''

''But I've never had to wash clothes, Daddy. I don't know how.''

''Lucky for you, the Maytag's easily mastered,'' Keely said, shoving the overflowing basket toward

Teddy with her foot. "You take that one to the laundry room while I go upstairs and get the other one."

"No." Teddy folded her arms. "I don't want to and you can't make me. You're not in charge around here."

"Teddy!" Daniel straightened with a frown, setting his tool aside.

"Oooh, Daddy's girl doesn't want dishpan hands," Leon said, wriggling the fingers of both hands at Teddy.

"If she bitches at doing the laundry, wait'll she has to do bathroom duty," Jacky said.

"I'm not doing any stupid chores!" Teddy cried, her arms stiff at her sides. "I'm not like the rest of you. I'm here because my dad's here, not because I broke the law or anything like that."

"Truancy is against the law," Greg said quietly.

"Vagrancy, too, last time I looked," Leon said.

"Panhandling, likewise." Jacky dipped a brush into white paint.

Keely made a clicking sound. "Too bad rudeness isn't."

"Not against the law, no," Daniel said, taking Teddy by the arm. "But it's against the rules in our family. Teddy, you owe everyone here an apology."

Teddy jerked to free herself. "What family? Don't try to pretend we're like a normal family, Dad, because we're not and you know it."

Daniel let her go, but looked at her sternly. "I want you to go with Keely now and do as she asks after you apologize. The reason you're at Sojourn is irrelevant. You still have to do your fair share."

"Oh, yeah? Just what exactly is the reason I'm at

Sojourn? You've got a perfectly good house, haven't you? Shouldn't I be staying there?'' She looked at him stubbornly, but her eyes were bright with tears.

''We'll discuss this in private, Teddy.''

''In private? When, I'd like to know.'' She dashed angrily at the tears. ''You haven't spent one minute alone with me—just me by myself—since I've been here. Every second you're building those stupid shelves or sawing or hammering or talking with all these other people. So when will you have a free minute to talk to just me, Dad?''

''Hey, knock it off, Teddy-bear.'' Leon slouched against the wall, his thumbs hooked in the loops on his jeans, his look reproachful. ''This is our main man you're raggin' on.''

''Shut up!'' Teddy cried. ''I'm not talking to you!''

''Well, 'scuse me.'' Leon shook one hand as though he'd touched something hot.

''And he's not your main man,'' Teddy said. ''He never even knew any of you until a week ago.''

''What's going on here?'' Tessa stood at the door, frowning.

Daniel studied his daughter with concern. ''Just a little misunderstanding, Tessa. Teddy's going to lend Keely a hand with the laundry. Right, Teddy?''

Teddy stared stubbornly at the floor and remained silent.

Daniel took a step forward. ''Listen to me, young lady, just because—''

Tessa interrupted smoothly. ''Keely, take the basket to the laundry room. Daniel and Teddy, come with me to my study, please. The rest of you...'' She looked at Daniel's three helpers. ''Daniel will be tied up for a while. Is it all right for them to work without supervision, Daniel?''

He nodded. ''Yeah, except for the doors. Don't try to fit them until I get back, Greg. Jacky, Leon, remember to protect the floors when you paint that molding.''

''Gotcha covered, man,'' Leon said. Greg nodded.

''What about the apology?'' Jacky asked.

Daniel turned to his daughter with a severe look.

''Sorry,'' Teddy muttered, but her gray eyes flashed with resentment.

''Oh, yeah, I believe that,'' Jacky said.

''My office,'' Tessa repeated, nailing Daniel, then Teddy, with a look he guessed proved very effective with unruly teenagers. It was one he had used himself many times. If he hadn't been so irate over Teddy's behavior, he might have found it amusing.

He followed Tessa out of the room, nudging Teddy along. No small feat. She moved as if they were headed for a trip to the woodshed. He had seldom seen her show less cooperation. But then, he'd never seen her behave as she had a few minutes before, either. She'd sounded like a spoiled brat, a snob. He remembered the sunny eight-year-old he'd been forced to abandon five years before and felt bewilderment added to his guilt and loss.

Tessa didn't take the seat behind her desk. Instead, she went to a pretty blue-checked armchair and gestured for Daniel and Teddy to sit on the sofa against the wall. Daniel waited for Teddy, who finally flounced down but refused to look at either of the adults.

Tessa leaned forward slightly. ''Teddy, I take it

you were upset just now in the games room. Do you want to tell me about it?"

"No." After one quick, defiant look, Teddy went back to studying her hands.

Daniel stirred, ready to explode. "Teddy, I've had just about—"

"Daniel." Tessa silenced him with one look. "Please. Now, Teddy, let's go back a moment. Something upset you in the games room. What was it?"

"I don't have to talk to you."

"Actually, you do, Teddy. Unless you want to talk to Marly Toups instead."

Teddy's expression changed to puzzlement. "Who's that?"

"The juvenile officer who allowed you to come to Sojourn instead of sending you into foster care until your mother can come and take you home to New York."

Teddy turned to Daniel in distress. "That's not true, is it, Daddy? You wouldn't let them put me in a foster home when you live right here."

"The choice wasn't mine to make, Teddy. When you ran away, you automatically became a part of the legal system."

"I didn't really run away," Teddy argued. "I bought a bus ticket like any other person and I came down to be with my father." Her mouth twisted bitterly. "I didn't know you didn't want me and I'd wind up in a place like this."

"It's not that I don't want you, Teddy. I've told you that over and over again. It's a legal thing, honey."

"What kind of legal thing, Daddy? You never tell us."

No, he never told them because it was beyond him. How could he tell his children something so ugly? But when they talked about coming to visit him, he always found an excuse to change the subject. Now Teddy had reached an age where she wasn't going to be put off. Daniel looked helplessly at Tessa.

"Is that what the scene in the games room was all about, Teddy?" Tessa asked with sympathy. "You feel resentful because you believe your father doesn't want you?"

Teddy set her face in a dark scowl. "I know he doesn't. If he did, I'd be at his house, not here."

"You don't believe him when he says he can't have you at his house because of certain legal problems?"

"Legal means court stuff and judges, right?"

"That's right."

"What kind of judge would keep kids from going to visit their own father?"

Tessa felt Daniel's eyes on her, but her gaze stayed on Teddy. She searched for the right words. "Sometimes there are circumstances that make judges decide these things in a way that seems unfair."

"What circumstances? And don't say I'm too young to understand. That's what Dad always says."

Tessa did glance at Daniel then. There was irony in his embittered gaze. How many times must he have reached this point in trying to explain to his children why he couldn't have them in his home?

"Your father loves you, Teddy. Never doubt that."

"Well, he sure doesn't act like it."

Frantically Tessa racked her brain for a way out. "Do you understand what this statement means, Teddy? A man is innocent until proven guilty?"

Teddy shrugged with bewilderment. "I guess. Like if a person is accused of something, you aren't supposed to believe he did it until he's had a trial and everybody knows he did it." She looked uncertain. "Is that right?"

"Yes, and sometimes people are accused but there's no trial. There's no jury of twelve people to weigh the evidence and come to the correct conclusion." Tessa realized she was treading deep water trying to explain to this child her father's neglect for the past five years. She looked at Daniel and saw his gaze was fixed on her intently. He was on his feet, his fists driven deep in his pockets. She waited, giving him time to tell her to stop, but he stayed silent.

She swallowed and prayed for the right words. "That's what happened to your father, Teddy. When people divorce and there are children, the future of the children is decided at a custody hearing. You understand that, don't you?"

"I think so. Mom got custody of Joey and me, not Dad."

Tessa nodded. "And the reason that happened is because a person made some serious accusations about your dad. The judge then had to decide whether they were true or not. Remember, there was no jury to help the judge make that decision."

"Are you saying somebody said bad things about Dad?"

"Yes."

"What kind of bad things?"

Tessa looked again for guidance from Daniel and he gave her a nod, one quick movement, but it was enough. "A sixteen-year-old girl at the high school where your father was principal accused Daniel of making improper advances to her."

Teddy's face darkened in a frown and her mouth opened in astonishment. "You mean like sex stuff?"

"Sexual advances, yes."

"That's crazy! That's pure bogus! My dad would never do anything like that. She had to be lying, Ms. Tessa, right?" She looked at Daniel. "Right, Dad?"

"Right, honey."

"Yes," Tessa said. "Your father claimed all along that she lied."

Teddy was nodding. "Because my dad's a good person. He's like...really sincere, you know? And he seems sad sometimes because he's not around to be a full-time dad for us. He's a lot more patient than Mom and he tries to be a good father, even though sometimes it has to be done on the telephone." She gave them a bewildered look. "How could anybody believe bad stuff like that? Joey and I wouldn't want to live with him if he was that kind of person."

A faint smile curved Tessa's lips. "I can see that, Teddy."

"I wish the judge had talked to me," Teddy said, looking thoughtful. "And Joey. We could have told our side of the story."

"Unfortunately, judges don't always get to talk to the kids," Tessa replied. "Even though it's the kids who can sometimes give the most accurate picture of a parent."

"This isn't fair." Teddy's mouth trembled. "For

five years we haven't had a dad just because a judge believed lies from some stupid girl.''

"Judges are human like the rest of us, Teddy. This person said what she said and...and there were other people who backed up her story.''

Springing up from the sofa, Teddy burst into tears and ran to Daniel. "But they were all lying! Doesn't that count for anything?''

Daniel held her fast, stroking her hair. "It seems wrong to us because it's caused us so much unhappiness, but we didn't have any choice back then, and we still don't now. The law's the law. We just have to make the best of a bad situation, sweetheart. Running away was a dangerous thing to do, but luckily it's opened a way for us to spend some time together. We owe Tessa for fixing it so that you could be at Sojourn, which means you and I get to be together, even if only for a little while. You see that, don't you, Teddy?''

"I guess,'' Teddy murmured, her arms tight around Daniel's waist.

He kissed the top of her head. "And you'll be a good girl, okay?''

"You mean help with the laundry and stuff?''

He met Tessa's gaze over Teddy's head. "That's what I mean. You help with the chores, the same as everybody else.''

"Okay.''

He gave her a squeeze. "That's my Teddy-bear.''

Teddy stayed where she was for a moment, her face still buried in Daniel's shirt. Then she nodded and pulled back. Wiping her nose with her hand, she looked at her father with a stubborn expression very like the one Tessa had seen more than once on Daniel's face. "Dad, I think we ought to try to find that girl who told those lies and see if she'll take it all back."

Tessa looked at Daniel. "I think you're right, Teddy."

CHAPTER NINE

AFTER DANIEL AND TEDDY left her study, Tessa spent a few minutes trying to clear up some paperwork, but she couldn't settle down to it. Her thoughts kept returning to a time five years ago and the part she'd played in the tragedy that was Daniel Kendrick's family today. With her hands idle on the desk, she thought of the sixteen-year-old who'd made the charges against Daniel. Judy. Judy Lovell. In spite of the hundreds of troubled teenage girls she'd worked with over the years, she had no trouble recalling Judy's name. But the chances of finding her, as Teddy suggested, and having her retract her accusations seemed remote indeed. In fact, slim to none.

Untrue accusations, Tessa now firmly believed. When Judy had tearfully revealed the details of her seduction, Tessa had given her the benefit of the doubt, but at the time, Tessa hadn't met Daniel and knew nothing about him. She was convinced that Judy had been sexually traumatized. All the signs were there. And the girl was adamant that it had been Daniel Kendrick who'd done it.

Daniel had claimed that he was never alone with her, although he admitted giving special attention to the girl. He'd insisted it was because he knew she was troubled and confused and seeking a father figure. The girl's parents were having marital problems, and much of the responsibility for her younger siblings had fallen to Judy. According to Daniel, she was desperately seeking a way out of an unbearable situation at home when she had taken refuge at Tessa's shelter.

But why accuse Daniel? It was a question Tessa had often pondered.

If Judy's accusations were true, she would hardly welcome anyone uncovering memories of a terrible time in her life. And if Judy had lied about Daniel, she would hardly admit it now. Facing disapproval and outrage if she had her life together again could be as traumatic as the molestation itself had been.

Tessa stood up abruptly and walked to the window. She had pondered all these questions agonizingly five years ago. It hadn't been a casual decision to get involved in a case that could separate a father from his children for all their childhood. Upon meeting Daniel Kendrick then, and learning about his position and reputation, she had tried to figure out why he would have been driven to seduce a teenage girl.

She recalled her rationalizations at the time: Kendrick was in the midst of a divorce. The emotional upheaval could have made him vulnerable. Having the adoration of a teenage girl could have soothed his damaged ego after learning that his wife was having an affair with another man.

But in the end, none of that excused what he'd done.

And Judy had been so insistent.

But Tessa's doubts had been strong even then. Now that she'd spent some time with Daniel, she was more than ever convinced that something else had been going on in the girl's life at the time. Something that had nothing to do with Daniel.

And if she'd been lying... Tessa shuddered at the thought. Judy *had* been lying, and the result was Teddy's heartbreak and Joey's bewilderment. And Daniel robbed of five years from his children's childhood. A lifetime.

"Hi." Daniel rapped softly on the open door. "Can I have a minute?"

Tessa turned, blinking to banish the shadows of that time. "Oh, okay." She waved with distraction at the chair, swallowing an ache in her throat. "Have a seat."

"Everything okay?"

"Uh-huh." She cleared her throat.

He took a few steps into the room but didn't sit down. With an uncertain half smile, he shifted from one foot to the other. "Ah, I was wondering... Have you made any plans for lunch today?"

She shrugged with confusion. "I have lunch here every day, you know that."

"Yeah, well, is that something you have to do? I mean..." He gave a wry chuckle. "Do you ever play hooky?"

"Sometimes."

"Then how about today? I'd like to treat you to lunch."

"I don't know, Daniel. I—"

"Come on, it'll be a nice break. Besides, I'd like to thank you."

She frowned. "Thank me? For what?"

"For what you did today. For stepping in at just

the right moment and then for reassuring Teddy. The situation was spiraling out of control. You saved the day."

"Hardly. And you don't have to thank me. After working with kids for so long, I've discovered that a stranger can sometimes say things that would be rejected outright if they were said by a parent."

The intent look in his silver eyes made her heart stumble. "But we're not strangers, are we, Tessa?"

She moved to the security of her desk, sat down and picked up a pen. But he loomed taller and more disturbing from that angle, so she stood up again. "Practically speaking, we are."

"Okay, if you say so. But would you have lunch with me?"

She sighed. "I don't think that would be a good idea, Daniel."

"Why not?"

"Because...because..."

With that half smile on his face again, he folded his arms. "Uh-huh. Because...?"

"Oh, I suppose it's okay." She tossed the pen down. "What time did you want to go?"

"Now."

"Now?"

"It's nearly one o'clock."

She looked at her watch. "I hadn't realized."

He shifted so that his weight was on one hip. "So, do you need to tell anybody?"

Her own sense of humor kicked in then. "Why? You're not planning to abduct me, are you?" She bent to rummage in her desk drawer, hunting for her purse.

"I wish," he murmured.

Purse in hand, she looked up, startled. "What?"

He moved to the door without answering. "I told Keely we'd be gone an hour or so. She's going to keep my crew in line until we get back."

Tessa slipped past him, telling herself the breathless feeling meant nothing. She was having lunch with the father of one of her kids. Nothing more, nothing less.

"Is COFFEE RANI OKAY?"

"Sure, they have a fabulous lunch menu." Tessa allowed Daniel to help her down from the pickup. The parking lot was clearing somewhat, and, for the most part, the usual business lunch crowd had come and gone.

They went into the trendy deli and ordered at the counter. Daniel suggested that they take their food to the tables outside, and Tessa did so willingly. It had nothing to do with the enhanced privacy outdoors, she told herself.

She bit into a piece of grilled chicken and gave a pleasurable hum. "This is delicious. How's yours?"

"Great. But I'm so famished that a Big Mac would have been just as good."

While he talked, she allowed herself to study him. He had the kind of face that aged well, but the mark of the past five years was stamped on it—around the eyes, in the brackets carved beside his mouth, in the set of his strong chin. He wore a stark white pullover that accented the depth of his tan and the width and power of his shoulders. She didn't remember him being so fit when he'd had a desk job. Plain carpentry wouldn't have put that strength in his upper body.

"Where did you go when you left Florida?" she asked, surprising herself almost as much as Daniel.

He finished the first half of his sandwich and washed it down with iced tea. "Anywhere. Nowhere."

"What did you do?"

"Meaning I couldn't get a job like the one I left?" Seeing her embarrassment, he looked across the lawn at a border of colorful petunias. "I wasted the first two years drifting, drinking, cursing fate, conjuring up ways to punish everybody who'd lied about me. What that accomplished mostly was to alienate myself from my kids even more than the people in the screwed-up system had."

"That would be me, I suppose," Tessa said, setting her fork aside.

"Among others." His smile was a bit off center. "But mostly I focused on Judy Lovell and my wife." His face changed, went cold. "The rest of them I now give the benefit of the doubt, but that kid and Beth knew the truth."

"I was thinking of Judy today."

"Why?"

"Teddy's remark about finding her, I suppose."

"Hoping she'll recant. Fat chance."

"She definitely won't if you don't ask her."

Daniel put both hands down beside his plate and looked directly at her. "Am I hearing this right, Tessa? You think I should make an effort to find Judy Lovell? And if I did locate her, you believe there's a chance in hell that she would admit she'd lied about me?"

"It's worth a try, isn't it?"

He leaned back, still studying her as if he'd never seen her before. Tessa picked up her fork to finish her salad. "Unless all your talk about your innocence is just that."

"You know it's not."

She looked at him. "Do I, Daniel?"

"You know you're having second thoughts about my guilt. You'd never have allowed me at Sojourn if you weren't."

She toyed with her salad. "Maybe. Yes."

"You don't sound totally convinced."

She darted a quick smile at him, watching as he picked up the second half of his sandwich and winked at her. "So I guess I'll have to get busy and do some more convincing."

Lord, he had a killer smile. She grabbed her iced tea and took a hasty gulp, which went down the wrong way. Fumbling for a napkin, she choked and coughed until he got up, laughing, and pounded her on the back. "I'm okay," she croaked, still hacking. "Daniel, stop."

"I hate it when that happens, don't you?" he said, dropping back into his chair.

"Yes."

"Sure you're okay?"

She cleared her throat and waved a hand. "I'm fine." It came out raspily.

"So, when can we start? What do we need to do first? I've got it!" He snapped his fingers. "I'll bet the records at Cypress House will have some information, such as her parents' address.''

"Social security number,'' Tessa managed to croak, still fighting the urge to cough.

"Social security number? Her parents' numbers?'' Daniel leaned forward intently.

"Not her parents', Judy's,'' Tessa said, finally able to speak. "She had a part-time job at the pizza shop. We might be able to trace her through that.''

"Tessa. I don't know what to say.'' Daniel shook his head, sat back. "I'm always thanking you, it seems. First, you help me find Teddy, then you welcome her to Sojourn at considerable risk to the program. Now you're willing to help me find this girl—no, woman. She'd be about twenty-one now.'' He smiled helplessly, shaking his head. "I'll be so beholden to you that I'll have to build a complete new wing at Sojourn. Otherwise you'll be soaking me for piddling stuff like bookshelves and kitchen cabinets from now till the year 2020.''

Her salad finished, she picked up her napkin. "Even if you find Judy Lovell, that's only the first step. She may hang with her story. Even if she lied, she may not be willing to admit it and suffer the public ridicule. There's a lot of bad sentiment nowadays about people who falsely accuse others. Remember that poor guy a year or so ago who was the suspect at the bombing during the Olympics in Atlanta? He didn't do it, but he and his mother lived through hell until he was eventually cleared.''

"Give me five minutes with Judy and I'll persuade her,'' Daniel said confidently. "They never granted me that request five years ago.''

"You tried to talk to her then?" Tessa asked.

Daniel gave a short laugh. "If you could call it that. I phoned her home several times but her folks flatly refused to let me see her. I was determined to try to reason with her, so I just drove over there one night." He was shaking his head. "Bad decision. She sort of cowered in the corner while her father ranted and raved. Bottom line is, he told me if I didn't leave her alone—leave *them* alone—he'd get a restraining order. Said his daughter had suffered enough from what I'd done."

He sat back with a wry look. "Like I said, give me five minutes with Judy—alone—and I'll persuade her."

"You'll work the same magic as you did this morning with your daughter, I assume?"

Daniel had the grace to shrug. "Okay, I screwed up there. Give me five minutes with Judy and *you* in the room, then."

"I can just picture that scene," Tessa said dryly.

Daniel reached for her hand. "Me, too. I can see it, too."

Tessa looked at their clasped hands in alarm. "Daniel, I'm not sure what's going on here. I didn't mean to imply anything...personal by suggesting you look for your accuser. And there's nothing personal in letting Teddy stay at Sojourn. I shouldn't even be having lunch with you. I always strive to keep my personal life and Sojourn separate."

"What personal life? From what the kids say, you don't do anything that doesn't link in some way to Sojourn."

"That's not true. What about Keely? What about

my sister in New Orleans? I have a very full personal life."

He let her hand go. "I had the idea you were talking about personal as in a man in your life."

"I suppose I was. I am."

"So is there one?"

She closed her eyes. "Daniel, please—" Tessa broke off as a uniformed police officer stopped at their table.

"Well, Kendrick, you sure do turn up in some unexpected places." Dwayne Duplantis hitched at the leather holstering the weapon at his side. "Business falling off that you got time for a social lunch?"

"Business is fine," Daniel snapped.

"Deputy Duplantis," Tessa said, wondering how much he'd heard.

He tipped his hat. "Miz Hamilton, you know this guy?"

"I don't usually have lunch with people I don't know, Deputy."

Duplantis turned his reptilian gaze back to Daniel. "This lady's a little old for you, isn't she, Kendrick?"

Daniel stood abruptly, sending his chair back against the wall with a crash. "Daniel!" Tessa said, reaching to touch his arm. "Don't. It's not worth it."

"Lotta young girls at Sojourn, right, Kendrick?" Duplantis's grin was all teeth. "Tender young things."

Daniel's jaw was so rigid it could have been chiseled in marble. He reached into his wallet and threw a twenty on the table. "Tessa, if you've finished..."

"I have." She tossed her napkin on the table and scooped up her purse.

Duplantis stepped back, his meaty hands propped on his hips. "Y'all still having that open house thing next weekend?"

"We are," Tessa snapped.

"Open to the public, is it?"

"It is."

He gave Daniel a sneering appraisal before looking again at Tessa. "I'd be careful if I was you. 'Course that's your decision."

Daniel touched her elbow. "Come on, Tessa."

"Right." Without looking back at Duplantis, she walked away with Daniel.

DANIEL CONTROLLED the urge to slam the pickup into gear, then roar out of the parking lot in a squeal of tires, but he knew Duplantis would like nothing better than to stop him and ticket him for reckless driving. Clamping his jaw, he pulled out onto the main street gently and merged into the traffic, fighting his instincts.

"I see what you mean, Daniel."

"What?"

"If that was an example of the way he treated you that night when he stopped you on Sojourn Lane, it's no wonder you were alarmed." She shuddered. "He's a vile man. A snake."

Daniel drove a hand through his hair. "He's on my case, Tessa. He's not the first cop with an attitude I've encountered in the past five years and he won't be the last. I can handle it."

"He seemed to know your personal history."

"He was the one who showed up at my place last week to tell me Teddy was missing and that my ex-wife said she'd better not be staying with me or she'd see to it I was arrested."

"Beautiful."

"Duplantis took great pleasure in passing that along."

"I can imagine."

"And Beth must have taken great pleasure in making the call to the sheriff's office."

She touched his arm. "I'm sorry, Daniel."

He shrugged her off. He always felt dirty when this happened. Soiled. "Yeah, well. It's not as if it hasn't happened before."

She was quiet a full minute. "I wonder if Sheriff Wade is aware of Duplantis's special interest in you?"

"I don't know, but even if he were, I can't see the sheriff worrying about a little harassment being directed at a sex offender."

"Stop saying that, Daniel!" Tessa looked at him sternly, then hastily buckled her seat belt as she noticed the speed at which he was driving. "And it is harassment. There's a law against that."

"Yeah, well, you get used to it." He glanced down and saw he was going eighty-five miles an hour. Muttering an oath, he forced himself to ease off the gas. When he spoke, pain and frustration and regret mixed together in his voice. "He's bad news, Tessa. He's gonna cause trouble for Sojourn, wait and see."

She settled back. "Then we'll deal with it."

"I LIKE HIM, MOM."

Tessa pulled something from the laundry basket. "Look at my new shirt, Keely. It's ruined!" She shook the wrinkles from a yellow polo and held it up. "You forgot to wash it in cold water, didn't you? This shirt cost thirty-eight dollars! I'll bet you didn't shrink anything that belongs to you."

Keely grabbed the shirt. "That belongs to me. Yours is right here." She passed a neatly folded yellow polo to her mother. "And don't pretend you didn't hear me. Where has Daniel Kendrick been hiding, I'd like to know? The north shore's hardly big enough that you wouldn't notice a man like him."

"He lives out. On a farm."

Keely halted in the act of folding a pair of denim shorts. "A farm? I thought he was a carpenter or something."

"He is a carpenter. His shop equipment is set up in the barn."

"Uh-huh."

"He specializes in custom kitchens and the like." She reached for a pile of socks. "But he also does very nice reproductions of antiques. I saw a Victorian stationery box. It was lovely."

Keely watched Tessa match up the socks. "And his house? Nice, is it?"

Something in Keely's voice made Tessa look up. "I've never been out to his house, Keely."

Keely shrugged. "Well, you could have fooled me after that rundown of his résumé. But hey, Mom, as I said, I like him. Who wouldn't? He's gorgeous!"

"You should be careful judging a book by its cover."

"Oh, puh-leeze."

"Well, it's true." She placed the socks in Keely's

basket. "However, after having him underfoot for the past two weeks, I'd say he seems nice enough."

"Underfoot."

Tessa cleared her throat. "Well, highly visible. For two weeks. Of course, it's because of Teddy. He is a very concerned father."

"And he's only 'nice enough.'"

Tessa dropped the nightgown she was folding. "All right, Keely. I know you're on one of your fishing expeditions again. You're suggesting there's something going on between Daniel Kendrick and me, and you couldn't be more wrong. He's the father of a runaway. I operate a shelter for runaways. What could be more logical than for him to spend some time here?"

"Building bookshelves? Mentoring kids? With the occasional intimate lunch with you?"

"We were discussing his daughter!"

"You came home looking flustered."

Tessa frowned ferociously. "Did Stephanie put you up to this?"

Keely assumed a look of wide-eyed, wickedly amused innocence. "Wow, are you ever a suspicious person, Mom. And testy. Do you think your own sister would be sneaky enough to do something like that?"

"Yes," Tessa snapped. "She's been trying to fix me up with a man ever since she fell in love with Tal."

"Well, a man like Talbot Robichaux would be worth falling in love with. Good-looking, good job, good father. Uh-huh, he's definitely…nice enough."

"I'm not looking for a lover."

Keely's face softened. "No, Mom, but how about a husband? You'd make some lucky man a wonderful wife. And it's not too late to have a couple of little rug rats, either. Come on, you don't want me to be an only child."

Tessa grabbed another towel, but amusement made her mouth quirk. "This is a ridiculous conversation. How many mother-daughter talks sound like ours, I wonder?"

"That's right, change the subject. We weren't talking about you and me, we were discussing you and Daniel. You know..." Keely got a thoughtful look on her face. "There's something about the two of you when you're together. It's almost as if you've known each other before. You know how we used to talk a lot about fate and karma, Mom? Maybe you've known him in another time."

Yes, five years ago. "We're hardly soul mates, Keely."

"How do you know that?"

"Trust me," Tessa said dryly.

Keely ignored her. "He's interested in his kid, you're right about that, but he's interested in you, too. I can tell by the way he looks at you. Like he's tempted, but he's hanging back for some reason. That's why I think it's fated for the two of you to be here, Mom. You look the same. I catch you watching him with the same sort of...longing. As if you like him but you shouldn't touch. Like he's forbidden fruit." She handed over another of Tessa's shirts. "You know what I mean?"

"I certainly do not."

Keely nodded. "I thought you would."

Tessa laughed. "You're impossible, Keely. You are not going to manufacture a romance between Daniel and me, so give it a rest, girl. Besides, even if I were in the mood for love, it could hardly be with Daniel Kendrick. There's too much history. He—"

"History? What kind of history?"

"Oh, Keely, leave it alone, will you?"

"You *have* met him before!"

With dismay, Tessa saw Keely's quick mind sorting through the meager facts she knew about Daniel. "But where? How?" She thought a minute. "Was it when you were in foster care with Aunt Stephanie?"

"No!"

"I know you and Aunt Stephanie came to New Orleans when you were fourteen. Did you go to high school with him or something?" Her mouth fell open. "Mom, is he my father?"

"My God, Keely. No. You know who your father was." Tessa closed her eyes and rubbed her forehead. "I can't believe you said something like that."

"It was just a question, Mom. So if you don't want me bombarding you with more questions, tell me about you and Daniel Kendrick. Before two weeks ago, that is."

Tessa sighed. "It was a long time ago, Keely."

"When, exactly? And I know it's a long time since you were sexually active, Mom."

Tessa held a towel high, hiding her face. "You're doing it again, Keely. Barging into territory that other mothers and daughters tactfully shy away from."

Keely made a dismissive sound. "We're not like other mothers and daughters, Mom, so the rules don't apply. Now, tell me about Daniel Kendrick and you."

"It's not something I can reveal, Keely. There are legal issues involved." When Keely tried to argue, she added, "Besides, it's nothing like you think. It was not a romance."

"Swear to God?"

Tessa rolled her eyes to the ceiling. "Yes, for heaven's sake!"

"So *when* was it? You can *reveal* that, can't you?" She rolled her eyes, too.

"Five years ago."

"When he was in Florida."

Tessa frowned. "Yes, but how—?"

"He told me he used to be a high school principal."

"He told you that?"

"He told me, Mom."

Tessa grabbed another towel. "Well, it was during that time. Some of the girls at Cypress House were high school students, although so many of them were dropouts. But some were students, and naturally they were *his* students."

"This sounds like gobbledygook."

"You asked for generalities. That's what I'm giving you."

"I'm gonna ask Aunt Stephanie."

"No!"

"Why not?"

"She doesn't know much about me during that time, Keely."

"You were hiding."

"Yes." Tessa closed her eyes, letting the towel lie in her lap. She felt Keely's touch and looked up to find her daughter looking at her with love.

"It's okay, Mom. I know that was a bad time for you."

"For you, it was even worse. I can never make it up to you, Keely," she whispered.

"Mom." Keely tossed her clothes aside and got down on her haunches in front of her mother. She took Tessa's hands and squeezed them firmly. "We've been over this in therapy and in private. You had a miserable childhood. You were raped, Mom. You made some bad decisions, but you were—you *are* a good person. The best. You've got to forgive yourself and let this go. I have. I love you just as you are."

Tears filled Tessa's eyes as she reached for Keely and hugged her with all her might. "You are such a good daughter," she whispered. "I love you so much."

Keely laughed a little shakily. "Yeah, well, I love you, too. Even if you do tend to overreact."

Tessa turned her loose and gave her a playful shove, toppling Keely over on her backside. "Get back to those clothes, girl."

Keely picked up a T-shirt. "So tell me more about Daniel."

CHAPTER TEN

FOR THE TENTH TIME in an hour, the phone rang. And rang. Intent on the blinking cursor in front of her, Tessa tried to ignore the ringing. Keely had promised to man the phones while Tessa worked to finalize the details for the open house. Where was she? On the fifth ring, Tessa pushed away from her computer and grabbed the receiver.

"Sojourn, may I help you?" She shuffled through a stack of printouts, only partially aware of the caller. "Yes, this is Tessa Hamilton."

"Ms. Hamilton, you are one difficult lady to reach. This is Pete Veillon, WXNO-TV."

For a second Tessa toyed with the notion of hanging up on him, but he would only call back. She decided to deal with him head-on. "Mr. Veillon, first of all, I apologize for not having responded to your messages, but I'm terribly busy lately. As you know, we're having an open house on Saturday, and since that's only two days away, I simply don't have the time for an interview. After the open house, however, perhaps we could—"

"I'm planning to be at the open house, Ms. Hamilton," he interrupted smoothly. "I've got a full crew scheduled. And since the cameras will be everywhere, don't you think it's reasonable to add your own input to our feature?''

Eyes closed, Tessa propped her head on one hand. ''Mr. Veillon—''

''Pete. Call me Pete.''

''I can't devote the kind of time you'd need before the open house to do justice to Sojourn.''

''Actually, that's something you could have avoided. I've been trying to reach you for weeks.''

She sat back in her chair. ''What exactly is the focus of your feature?''

''We're not firm on that as of today, to tell the truth. Sojourn is appealing from a human-interest point of view, naturally, but the public's perception of teenage homeless and runaways opens the door for a more in-depth piece.''

Whatever that meant. Tessa reached with resignation for her datebook. ''How about next Wednesday, Mr. Veillon?''

''Pete. Well, hell, Tessa, that's after the open house. My producer's expecting the feature to be ready for the ten o'clock news Saturday night.''

''I thought you said the focus for the article wasn't yet decided. How can you finalize it by 10:00 p.m.?''

''The open house will be over well within time for me to make deadline, don't you worry.'' He chuckled heartily.

''I'm sorry. Wednesday at ten in the morning is the best I can do, Mr. Veillon.''

Tessa hung up and scribbled the date on the page. She'd rather have a root canal than talk to Pete Veillon, but the man wasn't going to give it a rest until he'd poked and pried into every corner at Sojourn.

She drew an elaborate box around the date, thinking. Until now, she'd resisted talking to the media for two reasons. First, because she feared the publicity might somehow have a negative spin. And second, because of her own spotty past. There might be no damage to Sojourn if the public knew all her secrets, but she was still ashamed of the way she'd wasted so many years. She had a right to shield herself from the often cruel spotlight of public opinion, didn't she?

It wasn't difficult to understand Daniel's defensiveness about his past. And he claimed to be innocent. She was guilty of the sins they might dig up.

She was once more at her PC when Keely poked her head around the door of her study with a look of distaste on her face. "Some guy from the sheriff's office is asking for you, Mom."

Tessa's hands paused on the keyboard. "The sheriff's office? Who is it, Keely?"

"It's me, Miz Hamilton. Dwayne Duplantis."

What else could go wrong this day? First Pete Veillon and now Deputy Duplantis. Without waiting for an invitation, the deputy moved into her study carrying a folded document in one hand. From its blue jacket, Tessa assumed it was some kind of legal document.

"Nice to see you again," he said, showing a lot of teeth in his smile.

Smarmy, Tessa thought. When he'd ruined her lunch with Daniel a few days ago, there had been none of the affability he exuded now.

"What can I do for you, Deputy Duplantis?" she asked coldly.

He glanced at Keely. "This one of your Sojourn kids?"

"This is my daughter. Keely, this is Deputy Dwayne Duplantis of the sheriff's office."

"Hey, sorry about that, hon," he said, favoring her with another smile.

"Keely," she said coolly.

"Say, what?"

"My name is Keely, not hon."

Clearing her throat, Tessa stood up. "Keely, would you check on that order of paper plates and utensils for the buffet? You can use the computer in Jake's office to get the vendor's name. Jake won't be back until four. And remember, we have to have everything in place Friday afternoon. Saturday morning, we'll be run ragged with last-minute details."

"Gotcha, Mom." Keely flicked another look at Duplantis, then turned on her heel, walking as if she'd caught a whiff of some foul odor in Tessa's study. Duplantis watched her leave, not bothering to disguise his admiration for the shape of her backside in snug jeans. Keely left the door open, but when she had disappeared beyond the winding staircase, Duplantis closed it, giving it a final tug to see that it was secure.

"Is this official business, Deputy?"

"Sure thing. I know you're a busy lady." Taking care with the sharp creases in his pants, Duplantis took a seat in the chair opposite her desk. Still maintaining his genial air, he gazed around at the decor in her study.

"Hey, this old place turned out real nice, didn't it? Considering its condition a few years back, I mean. I remember when we were kids, it stood empty I don't know how long and we used to come out here to do a little target practice. Place was full of squirrels, snakes, bats, you name it." He patted the Glock semi-automatic holstered in polished leather at his waist and grinned. "I started at the police academy, I didn't have any problem qualifying with this baby. All them hours at Sojourn paid off. Yes, sir. I was no more'n thirteen and I could shoot the...ah, eyeballs off a squirrel at fifty yards."

"Incredible."

"I guess it was." He was shaking his head, smiling at the memory.

"When we finally acquired the property, every single windowpane was destroyed. I guess you can take credit for a few of them."

He shrugged, unembarrassed. "More'n a few."

"The original handblown glass dated back to the Civil War. Did you know that?"

"No kidding?"

"But..." She shrugged. "As you say, it's all gone now."

"Yeah. Probably replaced it with stuff that's a lot better, huh?"

She picked up her pen. "What was it you needed to see me about, Deputy?"

He unfolded the blue-backed paper, smoothing a meaty palm over the creases to straighten it. "Well, I tell you...it's my nephew, Kyle Faciane. My sister's kid. He's fourteen." He shook his head with pained resignation. "That fool kid got involved in a little ruckus at a convenience store on the highway. Took some cash—not much—less than a hundred bucks." He drew in a heavy sigh. "And they got a little rough with the night clerk. Anyway, he's been before the judge now and you can see by his arrest record, he's probably going to be in hot water.'' He slid the paper across her desk.

"I read about that incident in the paper, Deputy. The clerk was seriously injured. It was a woman and she was pistol-whipped. The next update I caught said she was in the hospital in ICU with a severe concussion. What happened to the weapon they stole?"

"There was no weapon," he said. "You saw the arrest record. Besides, you know how the media tries to blow these things out of proportion."

And if there was a weapon, Tessa thought, Duplantis would have been shrewd enough to make sure his nephew and his partners in crime got rid of it. But she said nothing.

"The truth is, Miz Hamilton, this time the kid's screwed up." He tapped the document with a fat finger and pushed it across the desk within her reach. "Read that, you'll see a pattern I bet you're familiar with. His daddy run off when he was about two and my sister never quite got herself together afterward. Some women are like that, you know? A little problem, they fold, then the kids sorta self-destruct. I know shrinks take that kind of stuff into consideration now."

She scanned the document, not taking time to read it carefully, but picking out salient points. Name. Age. Multiple arrests for juvenile offenses, the most serious a charge for trafficking in stolen merchandise. Car theft, four counts. The words *just joy riding* had been written in by hand. Duplantis's effort to minimize a serious charge. Tessa pushed the document back to him.

Duplantis seemed to expect some response, and when she remained silent, some of his down-home friendliness faded. "Those shrinks don't like to put kids Kyle's age in with adult criminals, Miz Hamilton. I'm thinking you agree with that, seeing your mission here."

"I don't see how that's relevant to your problem with Kyle, Deputy. He isn't being incarcerated with adults. According to that document, the judge has placed him in juvenile detention until his trial. That's hardly Angola."

He shifted slightly forward, his meaty hands gripping the wooden chair arms. "Well, you see, Jolene—that's my sister—partic'larly asked me to keep him out of hot water if I could, you understand what I'm saying? He gets sent up for two years, he's in with a real bad element whether it's Angola or not. I don't have to tell you that. God knows what it might do to him being exposed to a bunch of scumbag juvies with arrest records for everything from drugs to prostitution. No telling what direction he'd go then."

Tessa glanced at the paperwork. "Your nephew's arrest record is pretty significant, Deputy. Even if you somehow suppress his involvement in the robbery and assault on that clerk at the convenience store, it's going to be difficult to intervene on his behalf. Public sentiment's against you, too. People have become less tolerant of violence perpetrated by youths."

He was nodding before she finished. "That's just why I'm here at Sojourn, Miz Hamilton. I know you take in a few boys here. They board in that building on the south side of the grounds, isn't that right?''

"We do have six boys here, Deputy, but they haven't committed the kinds of offenses your nephew has. Not even close. Some are runaways, some are incorrigibles who've had trouble in the foster-care system, some are simply homeless kids we try to help reunite with their parents.''

"Shoplifting's a crime same as ripping off a stereo.''

He must somehow have gained access to the records of Sojourn's current juveniles. She watched in repugnance as he stroked the Glock at his side.

"You think about it, Miz Hamilton. There's no difference…in principle. And when it's kids doing it, we gotta think of their future.''

Tessa wondered if he thought of the future of the youthful offenders he encountered in his daily patrols. She couldn't see Duplantis treating kids who weren't related to him with the same generosity of spirit he expected of her. She decided to get on with it.

"What was it you wanted to see me about, Deputy?''

"Hell, I thought you would have guessed by now. I want Kyle to stay here at Sojourn instead of at the parish juvy.''

She stared, not sure for a moment that he could be serious. "Deputy Duplantis, there's a big difference between shoplifting a CD in a music store and assault with intent to do bodily harm. Pistol-whipping a woman. Stealing the cash from a convenience store. Your nephew would be totally out of place at Sojourn.''

"He'd be fine here. He's a good kid."

"Pardon me, Deputy, but his rap sheet has no less than a dozen offenses on it. He's a budding young criminal. There's no place at Sojourn for someone like Kyle. We're simply not equipped. I'm sorry."

"He won't give you any trouble," Duplantis said, his jaw set stubbornly. "I've laid down the law to that kid."

Tessa sighed, wondering if he actually believed a stern lecture and the threat of who knows what from his uncle would deter a boy with a foot-long rap sheet. "It's no use, Deputy. I'm sorry."

He glared at her. "My nephew's not going through the system for this. I know some people. I'm bringing him to Sojourn instead."

Lacing her hands together, Tessa rested them on the mat in front of her. "And how do you plan to do that, sir? You can hardly drop him off and drive away. You need my concurrence before the authorities will allow it."

"And I'll get it, too." Duplantis stood up. "A lot of people are unhappy over having a place like Sojourn in this town. I don't think you want to risk having your public image damaged."

"Are you threatening me, sir?"

"No need to use that word, Miz Hamilton. I'm just telling you how it is. You expect home folks to stand by while you coddle a bunch of snot-nosed brats from all over the country, then when one of our own needs help, you suddenly don't have room."

"It's not that we don't have room, Deputy, we—" Tessa stopped as he leaned closer, his eyes narrowed to slits.

"There's lots of ways you're vulnerable running a place like Sojourn. I think you can find room for my nephew, if you get my drift."

"As I said, Deputy Duplantis, there is paperwork required before admitting juveniles to Sojourn. You can't just circumvent the system."

"You don't say." He eased back from her desk and headed toward the door. "It'd be interesting to see what kind of paperwork you have on the most recent kid you took in. Picked up a little runaway in the Quarter, I heard. Kid came all the way from New York City."

Shaken, Tessa got to her feet. How on earth had he discovered that Teddy was here? Her paperwork wasn't in the system. Had he found out through his persistent surveillance of Daniel? "I'm not at liberty to discuss personal details about the children at Sojourn."

"Yeah, I can sure understand you keeping a lid on that kid's 'personal details,' considering who her old man is. Word gets out, it would probably raise a few eyebrows around here."

If she hadn't understood the hint of a threat before, there was no mistaking Duplantis's intent now. Hoping he didn't notice the way her hands shook, she glanced at her watch. "I'm afraid I have a very busy schedule today, Deputy. So, if you have nothing further..."

He stopped at the door with his hand on the knob. "I think we understand each other, Miz Hamilton." He settled his hat on his head. "Oh, I nearly forgot. Me and my sister, Jolene, will probably be dropping in for the open house. She's real excited over Kyle staying here." He smiled. "See you Saturday."

DANIEL SAW THE SQUAD CAR parked at Sojourn when he arrived with a load of pine planks to repair the back porch. It wasn't unusual for a lawman from the three surrounding parishes to be at Sojourn, but as he drove closer, he recognized the insignia of the sheriff's department. Muttering an oath, he veered off the main drive to a side lane that led to the back of the big house and parked the pickup.

He told himself if it wasn't Duplantis, there could be good reasons for somebody else from Sheriff Wade's office being at Sojourn. But more than likely it was Duplantis. He'd been suspicious after spotting Daniel on the deserted road two weeks ago. Seeing him with Tessa at the deli was one coincidence too many for a man like Duplantis. Ten to one, he'd been digging up dirt on Daniel ever since.

Grim-faced, Daniel sat hunched behind the wheel. He was never going to be able to live a life without this kind of thing happening. If not here, then somewhere else. If not Duplantis, then some other overly aggressive cop would be pursuing him.

For such a heinous crime, a man was guilty until proved innocent.

He realized Keely was standing on the back steps looking anxious. As she hurried to meet him, he got out, frowning. "What's going on, Keely?"

"Daniel, I think you should go to Mom's study. She's in there with a sheriff's deputy—Duplantis is his name. He came about half an hour ago and made a big deal of closing the door behind him." Her blue eyes troubled, she turned to look at the door. "He obviously forgot the transoms over the doors. I heard most of what they said."

Daniel was on his way up the porch steps before Keely finished. She hurried beside him. "He was threatening her, Daniel. You won't believe what he said."

With his hand on the doorknob, Daniel stopped. "What kind of threat? What did he say?"

Before he could pull the door open, he felt it pushed from the opposite side. It was Tessa. "Daniel, I'm glad you're here. Dwayne Duplantis just left."

"Keely told me. It's one thing for that bastard to be riding me, but if he's threatened you, I'm taking it directly to the sheriff. I don't know whether Wade condones this kind of thing from his deputies, but it's still a free country. He—"

"Daniel, Daniel." She pulled him inside the kitchen. "Calm down. Keely, go back to Jake's office and finish checking the supplies for the buffet. We don't need last-minute glitches in things like supplies and deliveries for the open house. And stay on top of the phones. Pete Veillon called before Duplantis arrived and pinned me down for an interview."

"You were going to have to talk to Pete Veillon sooner or later, Mom," Keely said.

"Go, Keely." Tessa gave her a small shove toward the hall.

"What did he mean about Teddy, Mom?" she asked, resisting.

"Teddy?" Daniel felt dread unfurling inside him. If the bastard had somehow found out about Teddy,

Daniel wouldn't be the only person to suffer. "He knows about Teddy?"

"Why shouldn't he know about Teddy?" Keely asked with bewilderment. "Why is that a problem?"

Tessa touched her forehead. "One at a time, please. Keely, I'll explain everything to you later. For now, go check on those supplies and monitor the phones. Please."

"Everything?" she asked, looking skeptical.

Daniel touched the girl's arm. "Keely, do as your mom says for now, okay?"

Keely opened her mouth to argue, but something in his face stopped her. "Sure, okay." She started backing out of the room, her eyes on her mother. "But you don't have to take those threats, Mom. He's supposed to uphold the law, not trash it that way. He was definitely trying to intimidate you." She looked at Daniel. "Make her tell you everything, Daniel."

He was shaking his head and rubbing the back of his neck when Keely finally disappeared down the hall. "If Duplantis comes back, he'd better hope he doesn't run into Keely first. He'd never get past her to get to you again."

Tessa's mouth twisted. "I'd rather sic her on Pete Veillon."

Daniel cupped her cheek in one hand. "Poor Tessa. First Veillon and then Duplantis. This is shaping up to be a stressful day."

She sighed with the ridiculous urge to turn her face into his hand and then...and then just let her whole body follow suit. How would it feel to let herself be embraced and coddled for a while, just for a few precious minutes? Had there ever been anyone to lean on? With the exception of Stephanie and Keely, she couldn't recall anyone simply being there for her, accepting her. Loving her.

God, what was she thinking? She looked up, her thoughts clouding her eyes, clouding her reason. Daniel met her gaze, his own unreadable, but she felt the intensity of...something between them. Daniel Kendrick was the last person she should want to lean on.

"Tessa," he murmured, rubbing his thumb over her lips.

Her limbs felt as if they were weighted down. She found his wrist with her hand and curled her fingers around it. To make him move. Or to hold him in place and to hold on to the incredible rightness of his touch.

He brought his other hand up and cupped her whole face. His gaze was like a flame touching her eyes, her mouth. With her eyes wide on his, the sounds of Sojourn receded, the hum of the fridge, the sound of boards being unloaded on the other side of the door, a burst of music from Leon's boombox.

"This is no place, Tessa," he murmured, moving his thumb back and forth, back and forth.

"No."

"I want to be alone with you. Is that possible?"

"I... It's the middle of the day."

A smile touched his mouth. "Is that the only reason?"

"I don't know."

"Because if it isn't, then I can wait."

God, she had never anticipated this. What was happening? Why Daniel, of all people? Why now?

He removed his hands, leaving her feeling as if

she'd been close to the rim of an abyss and had barely missed falling. She forced her mind back to sanity.

"Duplantis." Saying the name steadied her. Without looking at Daniel, she dropped into a chair. "We have to think what to do, Daniel."

He hesitated for a moment, then took a seat across the table from her. "Tell me exactly what he said about Teddy."

"He let me know he knew who she was and that he'd seen her records."

"And he didn't threaten to take her in?"

"No, he found a better way to use her. She's leverage to get what he wants from me."

Instant fury flared in Daniel's eyes. "What the hell are you talking about?"

She realized he was thinking of sexual harassment. "It's not what you're imagining," she said dryly. "Keely's more to his taste."

"Keely?" His outrage was almost as strong.

"He likes the look of her in jeans," Tessa said. "No, there was nothing as harmless as sexual harassment on his mind today. If there had been, I would have ushered him out the door before he took a seat."

"Then what did he want?"

Halfway through the details of Duplantis's visit, Daniel was up and pacing. Anger radiated from him, showed in the way he clamped a hand to the back of his neck, in the frown darkening his features. He was swearing by the time she finished.

"That son of a bitch can't force you to open Sojourn to a violent adolescent, no matter who the kid's related to. I saw Duplantis the night it happened. He said the clerk had been pistol-whipped. That's assault with a deadly weapon. Having a kid capable of that on the premises would endanger everyone at Sojourn. And if an incident occurred, it would disrupt the whole program." He stopped abruptly, meeting her eyes. "From that look on your face, I see I'm preaching to the converted, right?"

"Right. I've no intention of accepting Kyle at Sojourn. And Duplantis will probably retaliate. That's what worries me."

"Which is why he mentioned Teddy."

"And you."

Daniel shoved his hands deep in his pockets. "Do you think he's just blowing smoke?"

She was shaking her head. "Who knows?"

He kicked at a raised seam in the wood floor before looking at her. "But we can't afford to take any chances, can we?"

We. How was it that he was identifying with Sojourn as if he cared? Teddy couldn't stay more than another week or two at the most, while the damage Duplantis might inflict could mean the end of the program altogether. And the end of her role as its administrator. The end of hope for the kids living here.

Daniel pulled out a chair and sat down again. "Do you think you can stall him until the open house on Saturday?"

"Probably. But why? What difference does it make?"

He glanced at the back door, where the kids were horsing around unloading the wood from his pickup. "I've still got a few little touch-up projects to get the place in good shape for Saturday. Meanwhile I'll call

Beth to come and get Teddy. She'll bitch, but she'll do it.''

It was the only logical solution. With Teddy gone and Daniel no longer on the premises, Duplantis had no leverage.

A few minutes later, Tessa watched Daniel directing Greg, Jacky and Leon in mending the porch floor. Eager for his approval, they responded quickly when he gave an order. It was incredible how much work Daniel got out of them. In a perfect world, she could imagine Daniel presiding over classes at Sojourn in woodworking and reading blueprints, teaching layout and design. In a perfect world.

Instead, by Saturday morning, Daniel and Teddy would be gone and things would be back to normal. *She* would be back to normal, and whatever it was that was happening between Daniel and herself would be over. Sojourn had to take precedence over her personal desires. She'd lived her life that way for years.

But still, she was surprised at the depth of her disappointment.

CHAPTER ELEVEN

EARLY ON THE DAY of the open house, Daniel got a call from Tessa. The contractor who'd promised to deliver eight long buffet tables had been rear-ended on the interstate. Only three of the tables survived the crash. Could Daniel hastily construct something before the guests arrived at two in the afternoon? As he loaded his pickup with the materials he would need, he told himself the anticipation he felt was brought on by the urgency he'd heard in Tessa's voice. But he was lying to himself.

Beth had been unable to fly to New Orleans yet, but Teddy was staying with Stephanie's housekeeper to keep her safe from prying reporters. So the anticipation had nothing to do with seeing his daughter. No, it was solely because he was going to see Tessa.

By 7:00 a.m., he was on the grounds, and with Greg, Jacky, Leon and Curtis helping, he began building five makeshift tables. The legs looked more like sawhorses than the spiffy caterer's models that Tessa had contracted for, but they did the job.

"These look great, Daniel."

Tessa, in a green T-shirt and white shorts that made her long legs seem endless, was coming across the lawn toward him. He removed his baseball cap and wiped sweat from his face with his sleeve, then wrenched his gaze from her to survey the crude tables critically. "I hope you have something to cover them. There's no time to paint them."

"I've got the tablecloths right here." She held a stack of white damask wrapped in plastic. Pressed for time, she hadn't bothered with makeup, and instead of the sleek, smooth hairdo she usually wore, her streaky blond hair was pulled up and away from her face and held in place with a clip. She looked even more beautiful to him. Desire rose in him, hot and hungry.

God, she was as gorgeous as he was a mess, he realized. After several hours working in the sun, he was rumpled and sweaty. He hadn't even taken the time to shave. And Leon had swiped him across the midriff with a board, ripping his shirt and plowing a furrow in his flesh with it. He rubbed his hand over it now and winced.

"What happened to you?" Full of concern, Tessa put the linens on the table and pushed his hand aside to take a look. "Oh, you've got a deep gash there, Daniel. It needs to be cleaned and bandaged."

"It's okay. I'm going home in a minute."

She looked up at him and for a heartbeat they were both silenced.

Up close, he could see a few freckles across her nose and felt a crazy urge to kiss them.

He was wrinkled and hot and he needed a shave, but she'd never seen a man look more desirable.

"I need to get out of here," he said gruffly, his eyes still on her face.

She nodded.

"Veillon's TV crew will probably arrive soon."

"Yes." Her gaze fell to his mouth, and it was all Daniel could do not to kiss her right then and there.

He looked away, focusing anywhere but on Tessa. Leon was tangling the extension cord, but Daniel let it go. "They'll need to set up before the action begins," he said. "All we need is for Veillon to see me and get curious."

There was nothing unusual about a man in work clothes helping set up for the open house, but they couldn't afford to take chances. He slapped his baseball cap against his thigh and clamped it on his head.

"I'm out of here as soon as I tidy up and collect my tools."

Tessa nodded, then gestured at the tables. "Thank you for doing this, Daniel. We were really in a bind."

"Forget it." He looked around, making sure his equipment was together. Jacky and Greg were picking up wood scraps and trying to collect some of the sawdust.

"Did you ever reach Beth?" Tessa asked.

He bent to pick up a hammer on the ground. "Yeah, finally. She's in New Mexico to do some research on Anasazi Indian artifacts." He tossed the hammer into the tool tray with a clang. "That's the direction she wants to go in the next phase of her work, she tells me, and she just couldn't pass up this opportunity when a couple of friends of hers were headed out there. Joey, of course, is left with the housekeeper." A box of nails landed beside the hammer. "Bottom line is, she can't come for Teddy until next week. I hope that doesn't screw up anything here, Tessa. But don't worry, I'll stay away."

"Yes. All right."

He looked at her intently. Teddy staying a few days longer at Sojourn meant it wasn't safe for him to be on the premises. He would miss his daughter, but he'd miss Tessa almost as much. Maybe even more. He was astonished how quickly she'd become important in his life.

"We can't afford to take chances with Duplantis nosing around," he said.

"I know."

They were again regarding each other in silence when a car approached on the gravel lane. Daniel turned as a Land Rover packed with passengers pulled into the parking area. He swore and set about packing the rest of his things in a rush.

"It's okay," Tessa said, stopping him with a touch on his shoulder. "It's Stephanie and Tal. And I think that's Travis driving."

"Who's Travis?"

"He's Tal's brother. Come on, I'll introduce you." She motioned for him to follow, talking over her shoulder. "He's president of the company that owns the Robichaux restaurants in New Orleans now that their parents are retired. Travis has been very supportive of Sojourn. One of his restaurants furnished some of the food today."

Daniel had seen pictures of Dr. Talbot Robichaux in the society pages of the *Times Picayune*, but he didn't recognize the brother. As he watched, a tall man got out of the Land Rover and waved at Tessa.

Tessa hugged Stephanie and greeted Tal and Travis, then scooped up a chubby toddler for a kiss. The boy ducked and giggled and squirmed to get down, but Tessa held him until he'd rubbed noses

with her, then, with an affectionate squeeze, she set
him on his feet and sent him off with a tap on his
backside. Squealing, he ran toward Keely, who was
waving from the steps of the big house and calling,
"T.J., come and give me a hug, too!"

"I swear that child never slows down," Tessa said,
pushing her hair from her face. They smiled watching
T.J. scramble up the stairs and fling his arms around
Keely's knees.

"A trait he inherited from his mother and his
aunt," Tal said, carrying a box. "I'm depending on
you to give your sister a lecture today, Tessa. She's
burning the candle again."

Tessa gave Stephanie a keen look. In a high-
waisted dress of soft yellow, her twin's pregnancy
was barely showing. Still, there was a gentle swell
below her waist and an air of quiet joy about her.

"You're not doing too much, are you, Steph? You
reduced your time at the clinic to two days a week,
right?"

"She did not," Tal said, giving his wife a chastis-
ing look. "But she promised me she would give notice first thing Monday morning."

"And I'm going to do it, so both of you give it a
rest." Slipping her arm through her husband's, she
gave him an affectionate hug and made an exasperated face at Tessa.

"We'll talk later," Tessa said, unintimidated.

Travis Robichaux caught up, carrying a box, which
he set on the end of a table before turning to kiss
Tessa. On the mouth. "Hi, pretty lady," he said, ex-
uding charm. "You're looking fabulous, as usual."

"And so are you," Tessa said after giving him a hug.

Hell, the guy looked like a male model in dazzling white polo and knife-sharp khakis, Daniel thought sourly. He looked down at his filthy hands and torn shirt. Beside Travis, Daniel felt like yesterday's dirty socks.

Wanting to hit something—someone?—he watched Travis pluck a decorative bag stuffed with tissue from the box and hand it to Tessa with a flourish. She gave a little squeal—a sound Daniel had never heard from Tessa before—and removed the tissue with a breathless look on her face. Her expression softened with wonder as she pulled out a single crystal wineglass. Delicate and lavishly etched, it was exquisitely beautiful.

"Oooh…" she said.

Not only did she look like a teenager today, now she sounded like one, Daniel thought.

"For your collection," Travis said, smiling, his hands behind his back. "And to commemorate Sojourn's open house."

"Travis! You keep doing this." She held the glass up to the sunlight, turning it this way and that. She turned impulsively to Daniel. "Travis and I share an appreciation for antique crystal and he knows I'm especially partial to wineglasses."

Daniel made a sound he hoped didn't sound too churlish.

She gave Travis another impulsive hug. "Oh, it's beautiful, Travis. Thank you."

"You're welcome." He grinned boyishly, enjoying her pleasure.

"But you shouldn't, Travis."

"Okay, no more. Not even if you beg me."

Everyone laughed at her expression. Except Daniel. Battling jealousy, he kept his eyes cool and blank as he watched the byplay between Tessa and Travis. He realized he had a death grip on a screwdriver and forced himself to place it quietly in the tray with his other tools. What did he expect when a woman was as warm and beautiful as Tessa? That other men wouldn't find her just as desirable as he did? Men like Travis Robichaux—successful, attractive, respectable. Men whose names were untarnished.

"The place is looking great, Tessa," Travis said, surveying the grounds. "You've really done wonderful things to this old place."

"I had help, as you well know." She turned to Daniel. "Travis has been one of our most enthusiastic supporters."

Daniel inclined his head. He'd heard that the first time she said it, damn it.

"He's a miracle worker when it comes to fundraising."

"You flatter me, darlin'," Travis murmured, looking anything but uncomfortable at her praise.

"It's true, isn't it, Steph? He smiles like that at those aging Southern ladies with tons of money, and before they have a chance to catch their breath, they're writing checks to Sojourn. Big checks!" She flashed him a grateful smile.

"So, when are you going to let me wine and dine you if I'm so wonderful?" he asked, his arms still folded over his chest.

"When you get the Hibernia Bank to cough up that

donation they promised for new air-conditioning in the garçonnière.''

Stephanie laughed. ''Gotcha,'' she said to Travis. Then, turning in a circle, she surveyed the grounds and the big house as he had done and shook her head with wonder. ''You really have done a wonderful job, Tee. The place hasn't looked this good in fifty years, I'll bet. Is everything ready for the festivities at two?''

''Yes, thanks to Daniel.'' Tessa smiled at him. ''Tal and Travis, you haven't met the man who saved our bacon yet. Daniel's a local cabinetmaker who volunteered to build those bookshelves we've needed for so long. But I don't think he realized what he was getting into. Daniel, this is Talbot Robichaux, Stephanie's husband, and his brother, Travis.'' She turned to the Robichaux men. ''Daniel Kendrick, guys.''

''Daniel, nice to meet you,'' Tal said, shaking hands.

''Same here,'' Travis said.

''Looks like you've been busy this morning,'' Tal observed, eyeing the tables. ''You just finishing up?''

''Yeah.'' Daniel ran a hand over the unsanded surface of the table. ''But don't get too close. They won't win any prizes for finish work.''

Travis frowned at Tessa. ''What happened to the supplier I recommended?''

''A mishap on the interstate,'' she explained. ''I called Daniel at 6:00 a.m., and fortunately he had enough material on hand to do this. He literally saved the day.''

''I had a little help from my friends,'' Daniel said, acknowledging the three teens who were clearing away the last of the debris.

"Ho, Mr. Robichaux," Leon said, high-fiving Travis. "Haven't seen you around in a while. Where you been, man?"

"Would you believe Houston?"

"Houston!" Leon made a comical face. "Man, what's in Houston you can't find right here in the Big Easy?"

"A site for a new Robichaux's. You need a job?"

Leon's eyes got big. "Man, you know I do. You offerin' one?"

"Get out of here, behave yourself, finish school and you've got it, Leon. You did a good job bussing tables for me last year."

"Yeah, but I don't know a soul in Houston, man."

"Do you know anybody on Chartres in the Quarter?"

Leon grinned. "Ever'body, man. I know ever'body down there."

Travis clapped him on the shoulder. "Okay, it's the Chartres location."

With a whoop, Leon gathered a load of wood scraps and headed toward the back of the big house with Greg, talking a mile a minute.

"Thanks, Travis," Tessa said. "Leon's going to need a part-time job to make it this time. His mother needs money and he has to help her out some. He won't disappoint you."

"I'm counting on it," Travis said.

Stephanie had been quietly observing Daniel. She spoke as he bent over to lift the tool tray. "Teddy is doing just fine, Daniel."

"Tessa took good care of her here at Sojourn." He straightened with the tool tray in his hand. "I never reached you to say thank you personally, but I'm grateful for what you did—what you're doing.''

"The flowers said it just as well. They were beautiful. Thank you." Stephanie smiled softly. "The gesture was unnecessary but appreciated."

Seeing Tessa's confusion, she explained. "Daniel sent flowers to the clinic—gorgeous yellow roses."

He turned to find Tessa studying him thoughtfully. "I'm going to hit the road, Tessa. If there's nothing else you need…"

"No. No, thanks, Daniel." Out of habit, one hand went up as if to sweep her hair back. Finding it clipped neatly, she clasped her hands together and glanced distractedly at the area where he'd been working. "Do you have everything?"

"Yeah." Daniel nodded curtly to the Robichaux men. "Nice meeting you." With a brief smile for Stephanie, he turned and strode off in the direction of his pickup.

"IF YOU WANTED publicity for Sojourn, you've certainly hit the jackpot today, Tee.''

Tessa gave her makeup a final critical look, then rose from the vanity stool in front of her mirror to see what Stephanie meant. She parted the blinds and looked down on the front lawn. It was a beehive of media activity. With less than an hour to go before the doors were opened to the public, Veillon's crews were already set up. TV wire was strung over the grass and up the stairs. Technical paraphernalia was spread with no regard for Tessa's careful arrangements to make the entrance to Sojourn attractive. And more equipment was being unloaded from the back of a van.

Tessa dropped the blinds with a snap. "He's ruining the look of the entrance, Steph! And after all our work to make a nice first impression when people entered the house. Those wires are everywhere. And those stupid light things are too close to the tall palms on the porch. They'll probably be damaged from the heat." She shoved her feet into the black patent pumps that matched her outfit. "I'm going down there and make him get rid of that stuff right now!"

Stephanie grabbed her arm. "No, you don't need to get yourself all worked up right before your guests arrive. Let me find Tal and he can do it. He knows Pete Veillon. He'll put it to him in a way that won't get his back up."

"Meaning I *would* get his back up?"

With her head to one side, Stephanie observed her twin. "Well, your hair is almost crackling with temper."

Tessa grinned reluctantly. "I was never famous for my tactful ways."

Stephanie grinned, too. "No, and it got both of us into trouble more times than I care to recall. Let's stay out of trouble today, what do you say?"

"Well, call him right now. Use the intercom." She pointed to the wall. "We're on the third floor, remember."

While Stephanie paged Tal on the intercom, Tessa surveyed herself in a framed mirror standing in the corner. When Stephanie finished, she twitched at her short yellow jacket. "How do I look?" she asked anxiously.

Stephanie ran a practiced eye over Tessa's outfit. "Yellow-and-black linen. Dramatic but tasteful. Professional but sexy."

"Sexy! I don't want to look sexy."

"According to Tal and Travis, you couldn't look any other way." She ran a hand over her tummy with chagrin. "Unfortunately, I haven't looked sexy in so long I've forgotten what it feels like."

"You look sexily pregnant." Tessa gave her a hug. "You're so lucky."

For a moment their eyes held. "You wish you were pregnant, Tee?"

"Of course not." Tessa turned to look for a piece of jewelry for her outfit. "I just meant you're lucky in your situation. You have Tal and T.J. and the new baby. Even Alison. How many teenage stepdaughters adore their stepmama? Your life is chock-full of love, Steph, and people. Whereas I've got Sojourn and not much else."

"You have Keely, Tee."

"Yes, and I adore her. I don't have to tell you that. But she's in college now, and soon it'll be med school. You know how demanding that'll be. There'll be weeks on end when I won't see her, nor would I expect to. So, sometimes..." Her gaze strayed to the window.

"It's Daniel, isn't it?"

Tessa swung around, her sleek hair following the movement. "Daniel? I've only known the man a couple of weeks, Steph." She busied herself again sifting through her jewelry.

"It took one night for me to fall in love with Tal."

"Then you were extremely foolish."

"Yes, Mother."

She found the pin and stuck herself trying to put it on. "Ouch!"

Stephanie took it from her and deftly pinned it in place. "Daniel seems extremely nice."

"That's not what you said two weeks ago."

"I was reserving judgment then. Now I've decided that he seems extremely nice. And I saw the way he looked at you this morning."

Tessa knew her heart was banging, but she hoped to fool Steph for once. Unfortunately, she felt color flooding her face, and when she spoke, her voice sounded as if a hand were squeezing her throat. "How did he look?"

"Jealous as hell."

Tessa's eyes widened. "Jealous? What…who…?"

"Jealous of Travis, you goose. Are you blind? And Travis, the devil, was well aware of it. I wanted to swat him."

"There's nothing like that between Travis and me. He's a good friend and that's all."

"Try convincing Daniel of that. He wanted to punch him out when you hugged him the second time."

Tessa put a hand to her cheek in confusion, while inside she felt thrilled. Flattered. Scared.

"Tessa. You've fallen in love with him, haven't you?"

For moments they studied each other's eyes.

There was no sidestepping her sister's question. "I don't know the answer to that, Steph. Where a man is concerned, I'm not even sure I know what love is."

"What about his past?"

"I don't believe Daniel is guilty of making sexual advances to a young girl. I think he's incapable of such an act. I've watched him dealing with the kids here. He's a natural teacher, he's sensitive, he's firm when necessary. He doesn't show partiality, even though I know he likes some kids better than others. There's no hint of anything sexual in his manner. I would sense it, I know I would, Steph." She moved across the floor in agitation. "Does that sound crazy?" she asked, turning to face her twin. "Have I totally lost any sense of perspective where Daniel's concerned?"

Stephanie gave a helpless shrug, her eyes dark with concern. "Only you can answer that, Tee. You've had a couple of weeks of pretty constant exposure to the man. You're a good judge of character. Your success with the kids here at Sojourn and in Florida is proof of that."

"If I'm such a good judge of character, how did I mess up so royally with Daniel and his accuser?"

"You didn't know either one of them, Tessa. You said that yourself. The girl sought refuge at Cypress House for one night. She was gone the next day. And you'd never met Daniel."

Tessa toyed with a small framed picture on a tiny table, picked up a letter opener, then put it down. Straightened a Limoges figurine Steph had given her for her birthday. "The custody hearing lasted two days," she said, her back to Steph. "I had doubts even then, but the girl was so convincing. It bothered me there was no medical exam. The abuse...the alleged abuse had occurred months before she said anything."

"Well, maybe it wasn't Daniel who did it, Tee."
When Tessa turned to look at her, Stephanie added,
"Maybe someone else did it. Fathers, uncles, close
friends—we know those are the most common offenders. Surely you thought of that at the time?"

"Actually, I did." Tessa sank down on the side of
her bed. "And I suggested to Daniel a couple of days
ago that we should try to locate his accuser. Try to
clear his name. He was ready to go right then. I don't
know how much luck we'd have, but it would be
worth a try."

"We?" Stephanie lifted an eyebrow.

Tessa looked at her. "Yes, we. Daniel and me."

"The old guilt's kicking in again, is it?"

"Well, it's the least I can do, since I certainly had
a hand in ruining his life."

"And if you can fix it, maybe then you'll admit
you're in love with him."

Tessa jumped to her feet. "Do you realize what
you're saying, Steph? Who's to say Daniel would
even want me if his name was cleared? There's a
lot—"

"Me! I'm saying it," Stephanie said with an outraged look. "And Tal would say it. And Travis and
anybody else who knows a thing about you. What the
heck are you talking about? Of course he'd want you.
Any man would."

"I've got some pretty heavy baggage, Steph. You
know that. I don't know if a man could forgive that.
I—"

"Forgive?" Steph was up and glaring, her hands
propped on her hips. "Forgive what? We were both
neglected kids, shunted around into a dozen foster

homes, ignored, overworked, humiliated. Then *you* were raped, for God's sake! And you want a man to forgive you?" She drew in a deep breath, shaking her head at Tessa.

"I'm going to forget you said something so wrong-headed, Tee, because you insult yourself after the long, hard, painful climb you made out of your past to become the woman you are today." Winding down, she gave a swipe at her hair, catching it and holding it off her neck. "God, I'm so hot and bothered I don't think I'm fit to go downstairs yet. I'm going to have to buzz Tal on that stupid intercom again and—"

She stopped after a glance at Tessa. "Oh, shit, oh, shit. Tee, I've made you cry." She went to Tessa's side and grabbed her hand, rubbing it against her own cheek. "I didn't mean to get all stirred up like that, Tee, but it just ticked me off to hear you put yourself down that way." She fumbled in the drawer of the bedside table and found a tissue. "Here now, mop up. Your makeup is ruined, damn it. You're going to have to redo it. I can't believe I did this!" she wailed when Tessa's shoulders began to shake.

Tessa put out a hand, waving blindly. "It's okay, Steph. Give me a minute."

Stephanie leaned back, frowning. "You're not crying now, you're laughing." She pulled Tessa's face around with a hand beneath her chin. Their eyes met and they burst into teary laughter.

"Remind me not to say anything like that to you again," Tessa said when she could speak. She grimaced, looking at the dark smudges from her eye makeup on the tissue. "Especially when I've got an open house scheduled in less than half an hour and three hundred guests to impress.''

Stephanie jumped up. "Then get a move on." She shoved Tessa toward her dressing table. "Repair the damage and I'll go downstairs and make sure Pete Veillon's crew has gotten the message.''

Tessa stood up and caught her sister's hand before she could get away. Smiling, she pulled her close and gave her a fervent hug. "Thanks, Steph.''

Stephanie's expression turned fierce again. "Just remember what I said, you hear me?''

Tessa gave her a shove. "Go.''

THE GROUP GATHERED in the kitchen at Sojourn gaped at the television set. "I can't believe this!" Keely exclaimed joyously as the credits for the late news scrolled past with, of all things, a shot of Sojourn in the background. "Mom, isn't it incredible? Wow, and we were worried Mr. Veillon was going to diss us.''

"Nice," Tal agreed, smiling at a dazed Tessa as he muted a commercial with the TV remote. "For once Veillon did a very balanced feature. And it doesn't hurt that some of the VIPs on hand were happy to praise Sojourn on camera.''

Stephanie bent to wipe cookie crumbs from T.J.'s sleepy face as he toddled by. "And don't forget that those VIPs were at the open house because of what Sojourn stands for. They didn't know Pete Veillon would be covering the opening.'' She blew a kiss to her sister. "A definite tribute to you, Tee. Congratulations!''

Tessa managed a smile, still not believing what

she'd seen on the news. "I just knew he would ruin it all somehow."

Keely swept T.J. up and playfully rubbed noses with him. "You always expect disaster, Mom. This time you were way off."

"We need to break out the champagne," Stephanie said, then added with a sigh, "Unfortunately, Tee won't drink it and I'm not allowed, so we'll have to make do with something nonalcoholic."

"I assume you want to make a toast," Tal said from the chair beside his wife. He smiled faintly as she leaned into his palm at the small of her back.

"Yes, but I don't have enough energy to stand up."

"You're not the only one." Tal watched T.J. yawn widely, then hoisted him onto his lap. "C'mere, buddy. You look as pooped as your mama."

Stephanie leaned over and stroked her small son's head, smiling as he crammed his thumb in his mouth. "Yes, but it was a fabulous day. A great success."

"I do think it went well," Tessa agreed, smiling.

Keely groaned. "That's my mom, the queen of understatement." She jumped up. "We've got something in the fridge, I think. Mom, can we use your special glasses?"

"That's what they're for." While Keely rummaged in the fridge, Tessa went into the dining room and took several of her precious wineglasses from an antique hutch. Then, before going back to the kitchen, she paused, reflecting on the day. There had been no reason for her anxiety about the presence of TV cameras.

Acquainting the public with Sojourn had been the

purpose of the open house in the first place. She'd spotted Pete Veillon talking to several influential supporters of Sojourn—the mayor, a state senator, the president of a large corporation based in New Orleans. Marly Toups. Travis. Tal. Of course he knew she was related to the Robichauxs, sort of. But, all things considered, she believed Veillon had departed with a favorable impression. Still, there was the pending interview on Wednesday.

Even Dwayne Duplantis had been nice. He'd brought his sister, as he'd promised, but there had been no mention of trying to force Tessa to accept his nephew at Sojourn. She wasn't naive enough to think she'd heard the last of that, but at least Duplantis had left it alone for today.

She headed back to the kitchen with the wineglasses, pausing just short of the door and listening to the voices of her family. Keely's bright talk, Steph's soft laugh. Tal crooning something in a deep, low tone to his sleepy boy. Steph was right. She had a lot. So why was she feeling there was something missing?

Daniel. She longed to share the satisfaction of this day with Daniel.

"Ta-dum!" Keely pulled a two-liter bottle of ginger ale from the fridge as Tessa set the beautiful crystal on the table. "It's not champagne, but it's the same color."

Smiling faintly, she waited for Keely to pour, then she lifted her glass and toasted the success of the open house with her family.

IT WAS NEARLY MIDNIGHT when Tessa turned out all the lights and slowly climbed the curving stairs at

Sojourn. At the second landing, she paused, ever sensitive to sounds from the bedrooms of the girls, but all was quiet.

Halfway up the stairs to the third floor, she saw the light go out in Keely's room and heard the rustle of bedclothes as her daughter settled in to sleep. She'd intended to look in, to have a final gossip about the day with Keely, who was almost as committed to the program as Tessa, but now it would have to wait until tomorrow.

With her hand on the railing, she hesitated, looking down to the foyer and beyond through the polished glass doors. The grounds were dark and silent, the crowds gone, the kids settled. Not a creature stirred.

Then Daniel came to mind.

As silently as a night creature, he stole into her thoughts. She looked up at the closed door of her bedroom. When had she started to notice how empty it was? How lonely? She put a hand to her breast, feeling her heart begin to race at the images taking shape. Tempting her. Then, as though pulled by an invisible cord, she turned and made her way down the stairs.

CHAPTER TWELVE

DANIEL HEARD the soft knock at his front door as he came out of the shower. Frowning, he gave himself a few quick swipes with a towel, then pulled his jeans on. His first thought was for Teddy, but no cop on official business would ignore the doorbell in favor of a soft, almost timid, knock.

His heart kicked like a mule when halfway down the hall he recognized Tessa through the glass door. In four long strides, he reached it and pulled it open.

In the shadows of his porch, her eyes were huge and dark. Highlighted by the moonlight, her streaky blond hair seemed to have a pale gold halo. He'd done some repairs in her apartment at Sojourn, and she smelled like the stuff that was on her vanity, the same flowery fragrance he'd recognized that day in the elevator at NOPD. Deep, long dormant emotions moved through him. Longing. Hunger. Desire for a particular woman.

"Tessa."

"I know it's late," she said, standing where she was. "I shouldn't—"

She looked ready to turn and run, and every instinct in him rejected that possibility. He reached for her. "Come in." Having her leave before he found out why she had come was not an option.

She stepped hesitantly over the threshold, but she came. He'd forgotten to turn on the light in the foyer, and they stood with only the dim porch light to give him a hint of what she was thinking.

"I interrupted your shower," she said, her gaze fixed on his chest. "You're still wet. I hate when someone does that, don't you?"

"Not if it's you." He tossed the towel toward the nearest chair, then realized he had nothing to do with his hands. He suspected that what he wanted to do would send her back the way she came. God, he couldn't believe she had trusted him enough to come here. "Have you had dinner?"

She gave a wobbly little movement of her lips, hardly a smile. "It's midnight, Daniel. I didn't come for dinner. I came to tell you some things."

The open house hadn't gone well. She was going to send Teddy away. Pete Veillon had somehow dug up Daniel's past. A dozen thoughts came and went in his mind like debris in a strong wind. Duplantis had done something. He couldn't guess what, but it had to affect Sojourn to put that look on Tessa's face. The place was everything to her, and with Duplantis's threat hanging over her head and that reporter nosing around, it had been just a matter of time before disaster struck anyway. Hell, he was lucky Teddy had been allowed inside Sojourn to begin with.

"Maybe we should sit down," she said.

"In here." He gestured toward the den.

Tessa followed him into the room directly off the foyer. She was surprised when a gray cat jumped from the back of an armchair and darted past her. "I didn't know you had a cat," she murmured.

"I don't. We barely tolerate each other." He rubbed a hand over still-damp hair, sending droplets of water flying. "What was it you wanted to tell me, Tessa?"

She wrapped her arms around herself. "About myself."

"Yourself?"

Tessa realized he must think she had bad news about Teddy. Or Sojourn. Although she was concerned about Teddy, that problem was a lot simpler than the can of worms she was about to open, depending on the way things went in the next few minutes.

She tried not to look at his naked torso. "Teddy's fine. The open house was wildly successful. The mayor promised to look into allocating new funds to expand the program." Why she thought she would be calmer and more logical face-to-face with Daniel, she couldn't imagine. "I didn't come to talk about any of that."

"No?"

"I don't know what's happening between you and me, Daniel, but for the first time in a long time, I...I'm tempted."

He reached out to touch her face, but she stepped backward. "No, let me finish." She forced herself to meet his eyes. "The people close to me—Steph, Keely, Tal, even Travis—they've all got this idea that I'm...we're attracted to each other. And it's crazy."

"It's not crazy."

"It's crazy because of who you are and what I did and the situation..." She looked around helplessly.

"You can't deny that it's bizarre that we're even contemplating..." she waved a hand "...this."

His expression went cool and blank. "I thought you had come to accept that those charges were false."

"I did. I do." She met his eyes, knowing now how he reacted to rejection, imagined or otherwise. "I always had doubts about your guilt, Daniel. But if we...start something...I wonder if we can ever get beyond the part I played in the whole debacle. It cost you your children and your career!"

He stared at her as though not quite certain he understood what she was saying. "Does that mean you *do* believe me?"

"Yes, I believe you."

"I need to get this right. You don't have a tiny doubt, even in the back of your mind, that I might have done it?"

"No, Daniel." She held his gaze steadily. "I don't believe you tried to seduce Judy Lovell. I've watched you with the kids at Sojourn and with your daughter, with my own daughter. There's no way you could do something so heinous. You're too decent. Too straightforward."

He stood stock-still for a minute, as though he couldn't quite believe what he was hearing. Then, with a dazed look, he touched her face, tracing the line of her cheek and jaw with an unsteady hand. "Tessa," he said gruffly.

"I thought I should tell you that." She tried a smile, but it was shaky, rife with all the unresolved issues between them. But Daniel's guilt or innocence wasn't one of them.

With a soft groan, he slipped his hand beneath her hair, pulled her toward him and captured her mouth in a kiss that was everything she'd imagined and feared it would be.

He moved his lips over hers, exploring her softness as if the secret to her belief in him was to be found in touching her. He took his time, until his desire grew into urgency. He seemed to know that in some ways she was as skittish as his cat, and so his touch was gentle and protective, but underneath she sensed fire and need.

For a few heart-stopping minutes, Tessa simply gave herself over to the magic of the moment. He would stop if she wanted, she sensed, but she didn't want him to stop. Not yet. The movement of his mouth on hers was creating sensations that heated her blood, then pooled it into aching pleasure deep inside. God, how long had it been since she'd felt this way? How long since she'd allowed any man close enough to make her feel this way?

Her hand found its way to his bare chest. He was still damp and warm from his shower. She ran her fingers through thick, curly hair, over skin as solid and firm as the thud of his heart beneath her palm. Pausing at one flat nipple, she played her fingers over it and thrilled at the shudder that went through him. With a strangled sound, he stepped between her legs and gathered her close, taking the kiss wide and deep. Now there was possession and male strength in him. She could feel the heavy beat of his heart, matching the frantic pace of her own.

His voice, when it came, was a rumble somewhere

near her ear. "I have such a need, Tessa," he said, holding her tight.

"Me, too." She kissed the hollow of his throat, inhaling the scent of soap and heated male, glorying in the stunning sensations tumbling through her.

He drew back and was dazedly searching her face as if still unsure about her. Then, reassured by something he saw there, he fell to kissing her eyes, her nose, her cheekbones, her chin, until, with an impatient sound, he once again bonded his mouth to hers.

Tessa's arms were around his neck, and she yearned to be closer. To feel him inside her. She might have been frightened by the strength of what she felt, but she was too awash in sheer sensation, her usual caution utterly forgotten in the heat of the moment. She couldn't get enough of him. He was breathing hard now; the dampness on his skin was sweat, not the aftermath of his shower. She closed her eyes as his hand slid downward, gripping her and pressing her to that part of him that throbbed with heat and power.

Power. Rape was about power. Like bullets ricocheting off rock, her thoughts flew into the craziness that always claimed her in the rare times she'd come close to reaching this point with a man. And that was what always spoiled it, stopped her from acting on a woman's natural need to feel connected to another human being. To feel wanted. To feel pleasure. Desire. Completeness. With a tiny leap of her heart, Tessa realized she felt all that now. Oh, God, she could feel all that with Daniel.

He was kissing her neck, her shoulder, undoing buttons to reach the soft swell of her breasts. She tipped her head back, wanting to let him take her away in a tide of desire so intense her mind would be robbed of all reason and she could simply let her body's need for release take over.

And she wouldn't have to think.

She wouldn't have to worry about what happened next. Not tonight or even next week...

With a moan, she pulled away from him, turned and began frantically stuffing her shirt back into her waistband. She tried to gather her wits as she straightened her collar, smoothed her hair.

"What's wrong, Tessa?"

"This isn't what I came for, Daniel." She scooped hair from her cheek, holding it with one hand as she turned and looked at him. He was breathing hard, his chest filmed with perspiration. The front of his jeans was extended with his arousal. She gave a pained groan, knowing she hadn't played fair, and repeated, "This isn't what I came for, but it's exactly what I feared."

"What's to fear from two people being attracted to each other and acting on that attraction? We're both free. We're over twenty-one. We're alone here. So why not, Tessa?"

"Just hear me out, Daniel. You don't know anything about me. Hardly anybody in my new life does."

He managed a smile, just. "You have an old life?"

"You think your past is bad? Well, mine is worse."

"Come on."

"It's true." She secured a button on her shirt with a trembling hand.

"You embezzled a million dollars from your last employer?" he asked, still smiling.

"No."

"You stole a car when you were a kid?"

She shook her head, closing her eyes.

He tipped her chin up. "How many guesses do I get?"

"My past is far more ugly than anything you imagine."

With a skeptical sound, Daniel gripped her shoulders and led her over to the sofa. "Wait, I'll get some wine," he said, urging her down gently. At the door, he stopped. "You can drink wine? Your secret's not that you're a recovering alcoholic?"

"Actually, you're close. I don't drink alcohol."

If he was surprised, it didn't show. "Iced tea, then? I've got it, I think."

"Whatever. Anything." Tessa leaned back against the cushions and felt the stress of the day weighing on her. What had possessed her to come to Daniel tonight? She was in no condition to handle something so delicate. So devastating. So damning.

When, then? If she wanted to explore her feelings for Daniel, when was the right time to deal with the baggage that stood in the way?

From his kitchen came the clink of glasses, the rattle of ice cubes. She imagined him pouring the iced tea. Wondering.

Opening her eyes, she allowed herself to study his house. It was orderly, everything in place. Spartan, almost. No frills. With a frown, she sat up a little, intrigued in spite of her own troubled thoughts. No little added touches at all. She didn't expect his house to be crowded with decorative cushions or pretty vases and the like. But she would have thought there'd be something.

Was his life so empty?

"I spoke too soon," he said, handing her a tall glass. "It's soda. I guess I finished the iced tea this afternoon." For himself, he had chosen whiskey over ice. He sat on the edge of the sofa beside her. "Cheers."

She sipped her drink, then rested the glass on one knee. She was here now. She might as well go for broke. "I'm not an alcoholic, but I'm no stranger to drugs. So I don't tempt fate."

Without looking, she knew she had his full attention.

"I almost destroyed my life and..." she drew a deep breath "...my daughter's. Keely was in and out of foster care from the time she was seven. We weren't really reunited until she was fourteen." She paused, her eyes still on the glass cupped in both hands. When she spoke again, there was a tiny tremor in her voice. Tessa thought if he could have seen the turmoil raging inside her, he would probably be surprised that she could speak at all.

"Fortunately for us both, Stephanie had made all the right choices as opposed to my tendency to make all the wrong ones. She'd wisely finished high school, college and medical school, and was practicing at Women's in New Orleans. Keely had the good sense to search for Stephanie, who took her in, so I can't even take credit for rescuing her."

Daniel carefully set his glass on the coffee table. "What about your parents?"

"We never knew our father. Steph and I went into foster care when we were very young. Our mother... couldn't cope."

"Is she still living?"

"She died when we were eight."

"I'm sorry, Tessa," he said quietly.

"I barely remember her." She traced the rim of her glass with one finger. "They say you don't miss what you've never had, but it's not true. All children have a deep, instinctive need for a mother and a father. For parenting. I see it every day in the kids I deal with."

"How long were you and Stephanie in foster care?"

She gave a derisive laugh. "Too long. Forever."

"Not a good experience, hmm?"

She leaned forward and put her glass down beside his. "That's one of the things I wanted to tell you." She finally sneaked a glance at him when he remained silent. Not more than four inches separated them, and she was suddenly breathless. Caught again in the same heady sexual awareness that seemed to flare without any warning between them now.

Forgetting what she was going to say, she touched his chest. She simply placed her palm on the mat of curly hair between his nipples.

"Tessa," he said thickly, covering her hand and pressing it against him. "Don't do that if you aren't through talking."

She pulled her hand away and picked up her glass. "Alcohol and drugs aren't the only things I've been avoiding," she said. "There has been no sex."

He drew her chin up so that she had to look at him. "Why are you telling me this?"

She felt her heart stumble at the blaze in his narrowed eyes. "I thought you should understand before we…things…went any further. A couple of days ago in the kitchen, that was…such a surprise. Feeling that way again. Looking at a man—a particular man—with desire. You can't imagine if you—"

She looked away, biting her lip. "At first I was obsessed with putting my life together. Losing touch with Keely was a wake-up call. I wound up in Florida at Cypress House to recover and then eventually became a counselor. I found I liked it. I identified with the people there. I took a lot of courses, and after a while, I was appointed the administrator."

"Sounds like you were their poster child."

"Woman. I was almost thirty by then."

She rubbed her forehead. "Anyway, I had a lot to prove, so I worked hard."

"And now that I know all this, are you here to tell me it's a go?" He leaned over a little so she would have to look at him. "Or it's a no-go?"

"You don't know it all yet." She took in a deep breath. "It was no problem for me to avoid sex," she said, deciding to give it to him flat-out. "I was raped."

Daniel swore, a soft, intense oath that sounded even more fervent because she was so still. "Rape does awful things, Daniel," she said quietly. "Some women become promiscuous, others reject their sexuality completely. I was like that. But the pain is always there. I tried desperately to dull that pain…. I would never have become pregnant with Keely except

that I was drinking at a party the night she was conceived. The whole evening's a blur. I never even remember actually...doing it.'' She gave a bitter laugh.
''I was horrified the next day at school when the boy
sought me out to tell me how terrific it had been and
asked where could we meet again for more of the
same.''

''What about the rape?'' Daniel asked quietly.
''When was it? Who was it?''

''It was at our last foster home, a farm owned by
a couple. They persuaded the Social Services people
to let them manage a sort of home-boarding school
environment. There were twenty of us, all girls, ages
ten to sixteen.''

''Ten to sixteen.''

''Steph and I were fourteen.''

Daniel was up, pacing. ''It was the foster parent?
The father?'' he asked, making the word an obscenity.

''Steph stayed clear of him, but I hated him and
didn't make any secret about it. I knew he saw me as
uppity and rebellious, but it wasn't in me to just stand
by and take what he dished out. So I suppose you
could say I brought it on myself,'' she said, again
tracing the rim of her glass.

''I wouldn't say anything of the kind,'' Daniel
snapped.

''I knew he was evil. I knew he was capable of
violence. I'd seen him slap one of the smaller girls
who mouthed off at him. But I didn't know he'd
do...that. If I'd been less cocky, he might never have
noticed me.''

''In your dreams, lady. Not if you had then the

promise of becoming the beautiful woman you are now."

She looked at him. "What?"

He sat beside her again. "You must have been a lovely young girl, and I'll bet your personality was very much like Keely's is today—all fire and flash. It takes a sick son of a bitch to rape, but to rape a young girl in your circumstances makes him a lowlife without equal. I hope you reported it, Tessa."

"No. Stephanie and I just ran. We took off that night."

"Hitchhiking, no doubt."

"Yes. We eventually wound up in New Orleans, where we were taken in by Camille Landry, a retired nurse. Stephanie took to a normal life like a duck to water, but I seemed to screw up worse with every passing day."

"Don't tell me... You got no treatment for the rape."

"I wanted to just forget it, bury it. I never told anybody and I swore Stephanie to secrecy." When he opened his mouth to comment, she stopped him. "I know now that attitude compounded the problem, but at the time I chose not to think about it, hoping it would go away. You know how it is, you have a nightmare, but you shove it deep into your subconscious and pretty soon it's forgotten."

"Wrong."

"Right." She smiled faintly. "But it took a few years and lots of therapy and mistakes to pound that reality into my head. Actually, as I said, it took losing Keely to bring me to my senses. Unfortunately, by the time I'd gotten all that straightened out, she'd run away.''

"What about her father? Hamilton?''

"Rick Hamilton wasn't Keely's father. I was sixteen when I got pregnant, and as I said, we never had a relationship. The father skipped when he found out. The responsibilities of fatherhood did not appeal to him. I got a job at the hospital where Keely was born, in the administrator's office. I met Rick there. He sold pharmaceuticals. I was seventeen when we got married, and Keely was just a baby.''

Tessa stood up, moved to the window and stared out into the night. "Rick was a decent guy, good to me and Keely. He adopted her and gave her his name. I probably wouldn't have married him, but I was desperate. I didn't want to give up my baby. Anyway, Rick was too fond of cocaine. I was afraid I'd wind up like my own mother, so I divorced him. But instead of getting better, things got worse. Rather, *I* got worse.

"Divorce, the responsibility of a baby, low self-esteem, separation from Stephanie—I felt dogged by failure, but I couldn't crawl back to New Orleans. Steph was there doing all the right things. I was too ashamed to let her see the mess I'd made of my life.''

"Stephanie hadn't been raped.''

There was a glaze of tears in her eyes, but Tessa brushed at them impatiently. She'd cried enough over those years.

"Anyway, like they say, I kept on keeping on, but it was hard.''

"And is that when you decided to try Rick's way?''

She watched the trail of a jet in the night sky. "I didn't actually decide it. I just drifted into it." Although there had been no hint of censure in his voice, she found she couldn't turn and meet his eyes. "Keely was seven when I went into rehab the first time. It meant foster care for her, of course. I personally checked out the couple," she said with irony. "I wanted to be sure she was in good hands."

"That must have been terrible for you," Daniel said, and she realized he was just behind her.

"Yes. I'd followed in the footsteps of my mother. My child was now in the care of the system." Her laugh was bitter. "What was worse, the program didn't take, not that time. I got Keely back when I got out, but I was on a merry-go-round—first rehab, then a job, then a relapse. With Keely the victim. On her thirteenth birthday, Keely ran away. And who could blame her? It brought me to my senses like nothing else could have done. I checked myself into a new program with a changed attitude. That was Cypress House. I've been clean and sober ever since."

She could see him reflected in the window. He was close but not touching her. Maybe after hearing the sordid details, he wouldn't ever want to touch her again. She rubbed her hands over her arms to try to warm herself.

"Remember that time you told me you were jealous of the years I'd had with Keely as a child?" She was shaking her head. "I thought then, if he only knew."

"Don't you think Keely's love for you is genuine?"

"Yes, but I cheated her of so much."

He could have made an effort to comfort her with trite words or to dismiss her fear as self-pity or an overreaction, but his face, reflected in the window, was thoughtful. "You weren't there for her then, Tessa, but you've given her something else that may be nearly as valuable as a carefree childhood. You demonstrated how someone can successfully turn his life around against overwhelming odds."

She stood tensely, drinking in every word, hungering for reassurance. Daniel bent and kissed her shoulder, slipping his hands beneath her elbows and wrapping her in the warmth of his embrace. Even more satisfying was the warmth of his admiration.

"But you didn't stop there. You used your experience to make a difference to others, to kids our society too often shuns. That takes compassion and hard work, courage and energy and determination. Keely sees all that. She loves you, yes, and why wouldn't she? You're a wonderful role model. You may have been remiss as a mother all those years ago, but you're a mother and more to the kids whose lives you touch every day at Sojourn."

For a few golden moments, Tessa was struck dumb. When she could manage a word around the tightness in her throat, she turned in his embrace and looked into his eyes. "Could I just say one thing, Daniel Kendrick?" Her voice came out husky with emotion. "Try as I might, I cannot imagine why that woman you married let you get away."

He laughed and she lay her head on his chest, her arms around his waist, and sighed. "I struggle with all that stuff every day of my life, Daniel. I can be doing the simplest thing—writing a report, lecturing a kid, peeling potatoes, watching a movie with Keely—and something will bring it all back. And then the shame comes and takes away so much of the good.''

He held her close, resting his cheek on the top of her head. ''You're too hard on yourself, Tessa.''

''Maybe. But there are more people who'd say the opposite if they knew my past. You're definitely special, Daniel.''

''Special enough that you'll take a chance with me?''

Her smile faded as she looked up at him. ''I want to, but I don't know if it's wise.''

''You say you're tempted, yet it's not wise. Does that mean no? This can't be the first time you've been attracted to a man since your divorce. That was what? Ten years ago?''

''More like fifteen. And, yes, it is.''

He couldn't hide his astonishment. ''You're a beautiful woman, Tessa. There must have been men who wanted to love you.''

''I avoided them.''

''You avoided them.''

''Or I ignored them.''

''What about Travis Robichaux?''

Surprise streaked through her. There was an edge in his voice as he said Travis's name. Could Steph be right? Was he jealous? ''Travis is just a friend, a good friend—one of the first ones I made in New Orleans when I decided to stay here. But there's no spark between us, Daniel. Nothing happens when we're together.''

He fixed his gaze on her mouth. "And something does happen when we're together, doesn't it?"

She drew in a very shaky breath. "That's what I've been trying to tell you. That's why I came tonight— well, that and to share the success of the open house. I didn't expect to feel this way, and I didn't want to come to you under false pretenses."

He dropped a quick kiss on her nose. "You didn't want me to think you were a virgin?"

"I'm serious, Daniel."

His hand was gentle as he tucked her hair behind one ear. "As for all the other stuff, it's in the past. It's over. It doesn't have anything to do with the here and now." He cupped her cheek and gave her a hard kiss. There was nothing careful and tentative about it this time. The effect was dizzying, and Tessa just hung on to the waistband of his jeans, letting him lead her wherever he would. He took his time, getting his fill of her before breaking the kiss.

He spoke into the tangle of her hair. "The only thing I think we should worry about now is whether to go upstairs or to use that couch right over there. Later—much later, we can worry about where all this takes us."

She felt the touch of his lips on her eyelids, erotic and persuasive. Anticipation coursed through her.

And then the phone rang.

Daniel swore, fervently and long.

"Can we ignore it?" she asked, her forehead riding on the rise and fall of his chest.

"Hell, yes." In the kitchen, the third ring ended and his machine kicked in. Holding her tight against him, he heard his voice inviting the caller to leave a message, and in spite of his determination to ignore it, Daniel waited for the response.

"Daniel? Damn it, Daniel, wake up and answer me! This is Beth. I'm in New Mexico and— Oh, hell, Daniel... *Daniel!*"

Daniel snatched the receiver off the hook. "It's me, Beth. What's wrong?"

She made a sound like a feline hiss. "You'll never believe what your son has done, Daniel. I swear, this time I've absolutely had it! I'm washing my hands, do you hear me?"

"Control yourself, for God's sake, Beth," he snapped. "And cut the hysterics. What about Joey?"

"I just got a call from the housekeeper. She's frantic and she's already called the police, naturally, but—"

"Beth!" he roared. "What about Joey?"

"He walked out of the apartment in the middle of the afternoon and nobody's heard a word from him since." She added viciously, "Your son has run away."

CHAPTER THIRTEEN

TESSA LISTENED while Daniel wrapped up a phone call to the housekeeper at the apartment in New York. She gathered from the conversation that the woman—a Mrs. Kowalski—had heard nothing from Joey. The police had been alerted but so far hadn't a clue.

He hung up, then propped both arms against the kitchen counter while he stared blankly at the telephone. Tessa moved closer and touched his hand. "Do you think Joey's on his way here?"

A minute passed before he answered. He rubbed both eyes with a finger and thumb, shaking his head wearily. "I don't know. Probably. I knew he was thinking about this a few days ago. Why the hell didn't I pay closer attention?"

"You're not blaming yourself, Daniel?" She stroked his hand with pained sympathy.

"Who else?"

Beth. Judy Lovell. The judge. The system. Me.

"With his mother in New Mexico," she said, "and Joey barred from seeing his father, plus being abandoned to an elderly housekeeper, seems to me there's enough blame to spread around, Daniel."

"Which doesn't make me feel any better. Joey was giving off signals right and left. When Beth went haring off on one of her trips, I should have anticipated this. I should have been *listening!*"

"Kids threaten to run away all the time, Daniel. That doesn't mean they actually do it."

"Yeah, well, running away worked for Teddy, and that fact wasn't lost on Joey. He warned me he just might try the same thing as his sister if I didn't find a way to get him down here, too."

Tessa walked to the stove top and picked up a kettle. At the sink she ran water in it and put it on a burner. "I hope you have some tea bags," she said, taking two cups suspended from hooks beneath a shelf.

"In there." He glanced at a cabinet but made no move to get them down. Tessa did so, then dropped a tea bag into each cup and stood leaning against the cabinet waiting for the water to boil.

Daniel went to the refrigerator, where a photo of Teddy and Joey was stuck on the door with a magnet. He pulled it off and stared at it, his shoulders slumped. Worry had etched out deep brackets around his mouth, and when he turned to look at her, Tessa's heart turned over at the fear in his eyes. "He's only eleven, Tessa. Do you know what can happen to an eleven-year-old boy on the streets of New York?"

She did, probably better than Daniel. And she knew, too, the gut-wrenching fear and guilt that lived inside a parent whose child was on the streets. Beside her, the kettle began to squeal, but she turned it off and went to Daniel instead. Slipping her arms around him, she nestled her head beneath his chin. "We'll find him, Daniel," she whispered, kissing his throat.

With a shudder, he closed his fist in her hair and

banded his arms around her, letting her feel his fear and need. Share it.

"Joey's smart," she told him, both hands moving up and down his back. "He knows bad things happened to Teddy on the street. He's probably holed up somewhere close to home, somewhere he feels safe."

Daniel was looking out into the dark night, one hand idly stroking her hair. "He was so desperate to leave," he muttered. "I picked up on that, so why didn't I do something sooner?"

"Like what, Daniel?" She leaned back to look at him. "First of all, you're so far away from Joey. You're barred from seeing him without Beth's blessing, and I don't see her making any special effort to ease that situation. Meantime, you've been coping with Teddy's problems here. That alone is enough to send many parents round the bend. And when you talked to Joey, didn't you urge him to wait? Didn't you tell him running away wasn't the way to solve the problem?"

He shifted his gaze to hers. "Yes, but I ought to know how kids are, for God's sake. They get an idea in their heads, no parent can reason it away."

"Did you tell Beth your concern that he might run away? Shouldn't she have been on the lookout? After all, she's right there."

"Yes, and you saw how she took what I told her to heart," he said with bitter sarcasm. He released Tessa to begin pacing the kitchen floor. "I still can't believe he did this. Maybe if we—"

He broke off as the telephone rang and lunged for it. "Hello!"

"Hi, Dad, this is Joey."

"Joey!" The look Daniel sent to Tessa was almost fierce with relief. "Where are you, son? We're all worried out of our minds!"

"I'm not telling you where I am, Dad. But I'm okay. Don't worry."

"Don't worry?" Daniel repeated, struggling to stay calm. "Joey, I get a call from your mother and she's frantic because you've run away, Mrs. Kowalski has almost had a heart attack, and I'm way down here unable to do anything but pace the floor and pray to God you're all right. And you tell us not to worry?"

"It was the only way, Dad."

"The only way to what?"

"To get away. I don't want to make you mad, but I'm not staying with my mother this summer, Dad. Heck, she's never there anyway. And with Teddy gone, I'm getting pretty tired of Mrs. Kowalski's company, you know what I mean? She's a nice lady, but she's old, Dad. And grouchy."

Daniel drew a deep breath. "Where are you, Joey?"

"Like I said, I'm not telling, Dad. If I do, you'll just send the cops to pick me up, and they'll take me back to the apartment and Mrs. Kowalski will get all tight in the face and nag me about leaving and getting her in trouble with Mom. Then nothing's changed and this is all wasted. So I think I'll just hang out here for a while."

"And where is it that you're hanging out, Joey?"

"It's a safe place, don't worry. I'm telling you I'm okay."

Daniel shifted his stance in frustration. He plowed through his hair with his fingers. He kicked at a peach seed on the floor, Cat's toy. It pinged off the bottom of the fridge. "You can't do this, Joey. You can't just decide you don't like things the way they are at home and leave."

"Why not, Dad? Teddy did it, and it worked out just fine."

"It didn't work out just fine. Teddy was miserable and scared until we found her. And she got very sick, in case you've forgotten."

"I'm gonna be careful what I eat, Dad. No kidding, I am."

"And how do you plan to eat at all? Do you have any money?"

"No, but..." Joey was suddenly cautious. "Hey, I'll manage."

"Joey, don't do this, son. New York is a dangerous place. Tell me where you are and let them come and get you and take you home."

"Ha! Shows what you know, Dad. First they'll drag me to the police department and give me a lot of grief about running away and stuff. Uh-uh, no way."

Daniel paced the floor, stretching the cord on the receiver to its limit. "I promise you won't have any hassle from whoever comes to get you, Joey. They'll take you straight home, no questions asked."

"Oh, sure, Dad. You can know that when you're about two thousand miles away."

And so was his mother. And anybody else in the world who loved the kid. Hell, it was no wonder he'd done this. Daniel closed his eyes, desperately seeking words Joey would respond to. "I'll send somebody, but you won't have to stay with them very long, Joey.

I'll get on an airplane right away myself, the first flight available. I'll stay with you until your mother comes home.''

"How can you do that, Dad? You know it's against the rules."

"I'll get around the rules some way, Joey, I swear it." He saw the sympathy in Tessa's eyes. "But first you've got to tell me where you are."

"I'm sorry, Dad. It's like a poker hand, you know? If you let your opponent see your cards, you're outta the game."

Poker? His eleven-year-old son was spouting poker strategy? Daniel looked helplessly at Tessa. "Are you on the streets, Joey? Just tell me that."

"I can't, Dad," he said, sounding close to tears. "So don't ask me anymore, please."

"You don't know what you're doing, Joey." He felt he wasn't getting through, that Joey was on the verge of hanging up, and keeping him on the line was vital. "How will I find you when I get to New York?"

Joey's voice brightened. "You're coming, honest?"

"Yes, I'm coming, Joey, but you have to give me some more information. Even if I could get a flight within an hour—which is impossible because the airport is across the lake from my place—I still wouldn't want you spending a night in some...wherever you are, Joey. Now, please—"

"I'm all right here, really. It's a safe place."

"How can you be sure? Are there adults around?"

"Sort of."

Sort of? "What does that mean?"

"Well, part of the time there are adults around here and part of the time, there's nobody. But it's pretty big and there's lots of places to hide."

Daniel mulled that over. The library? A big supermarket? A museum? God, the city of New York was vast, and although Beth's apartment was in a good area, a walk of a few blocks in either direction and it became inner-city squalor. "Joey, you remember all the bad things that happened to Teddy when she ran away, don't you?"

"Yes, sir, but I'm not going to do the dumb stuff she did. I know I can't hitch all the way to New Orleans. Terrible things happen to kids when they're alone at truck stops and all. No, Dad, the only thing is for you to come and get me. That's a plan. That'll work."

Daniel heard the almost jaunty self-confidence in his son's voice and was torn between wanting to tan his backside and commending him for ingenuity and sheer guts. Provided he didn't get hurt before Daniel arrived to do either.

"I can't talk you into giving me a hint as to where you are, huh, son?"

"No, sir." For a second there was a catch in the boy's voice. "I'm sorry, Dad."

"How are you making this call? Are you at a pay phone?"

"No, sir. I didn't have enough money. I'm on a cell phone."

"Cell phone? Whose? Your mom's?"

"A friend's, but don't bother to trace it so you can ask him where I am, because he doesn't know. Nobody does. Look, Dad, I've gotta go. I'll call the apartment pretty often until we connect there." He was suddenly anxious. "You *are* coming, right?"

"I'm coming, but first—"

"And make plans to take me back to New Orleans with you, okay? Like Teddy."

Daniel banged his fist on the counter. "Joey, I'm giving you a direct order here. Tell me where you are!"

"'Bye, Dad."

Daniel slammed the receiver down, then swung away to pace the floor, almost snarling with frustration. "Can you believe he's done this? He's holed up somewhere in New York, talking as slick as a jailhouse lawyer when I try to pin him down." He watched as Tessa set two cups of hot tea on the table, pulled out a chair and sat down. She sweetened her own, stirring it longer than necessary before lifting it to her mouth and taking a sip.

"He's on a cell phone, for God's sake," Daniel said, snatching a blind aside and staring out the window for a moment. He dropped it with a clack to pace again. "But don't try to trace it, he tells me, because his buddy who owns the cell phone doesn't know anything anyway!" He stopped at a chair in his path and gave it a shove. "He sounded like Johnnie Cochran, one-upping me like that."

"But did he sound safe?"

"Yeah, thank God." He stopped with his hand clamped to the back of his neck and a note of relief in his voice. "But more than that, he sounded cool as a riverboat gambler. Hell, he acted like a riverboat gambler!"

"What's this about gambling?"

Daniel was calming down somewhat. After a second, he gave a dry chuckle. "He couldn't tell me too much, he said, because it would be like showing your cards in a poker game. I tell you one thing, Tessa, when I do get my hands on him, I'm going to find out what he's been doing with his time. He's not nearly as reckless as Teddy was about this. He's thought it all out. He has me and his mother right where he wants us. He'll reveal where he is, but first I've got to go to New York. Otherwise there's no telling how long he'll stay holed up."

Tessa nudged his cup toward him. "Here, have some tea."

"Yeah, thanks." But instead of sitting down, he took the cup and went across the kitchen to get the whiskey he'd used to make his drink earlier. Still standing, he poured a shot into the tea, then came back and sat down across from Tessa.

"So you're flying to New York?"

He gave a shrug as if to say he had no other choice.

Tessa fiddled with the sugar spoon. "I gather from your end of the conversation that he knows you can't stay."

"Yeah, but he's blocked it out. He's counting on me taking him back with me. If I can do it for Teddy, then I should do it for him. Fair's fair. It's the way kids look at things."

"You'll have to be careful, Daniel. Without Beth on the premises, you're committing a crime."

He turned his cup round and round. "What if I called Beth and arranged to keep all this away from the police?"

"What do you mean?"

He tossed back the rest of his drink, then reached for her hands. "Tessa, you could come with me. With your credentials, my son could be released to your custody. We could bring him back to Beth's apartment, have Mrs. Kowalski stay. Everything would be strictly aboveboard. I know Beth would agree. Hell, just a few days ago when Teddy got sick, she was ready to turn her over to me rather than inconvenience herself." His mouth twisted. "She'll jump at the chance to dump this whole problem on me—she'll get to stay in New Mexico. Believe me, she won't like having to come home to a rebellious boy."

"She'll have to do that eventually."

"But not before the end of the summer," he said, giving her a steady look. "If I can persuade her to let me take him back to Louisiana with me."

"But how—"

"I think she'll allow that. Most certainly for the summer. From her perspective, the kids have proved a royal pain lately. With you along to give her a respectable out, I think she'll cave."

"I don't know, Daniel." Tessa rose, pushing her chair back. "I have to think about this. There's still Duplantis's threat hanging over us at Sojourn. Teddy is leaving, remember?"

"Yes, but my kids won't be staying at Sojourn if Beth will agree to release them for the summer. They'll be staying with me."

She wrapped her arms around herself. "Then why do you need me in New York?"

His chair scraped as he stood up and went to her side. "Insurance, for one thing. Just in case Beth gets testy. No, that's not it." He reached to tuck her hair behind one ear. "I want you to come with me because I want to be with you."

"I have responsibilities here, Daniel. I can't just go traipsing off to New York with no notice."

"Why not? The open house is over and it was a big success. From what you say about Pete Veillon's piece on TV tonight, you've got it made."

She rolled her eyes. "Yes, but he's still nagging about that appointment." Recalling it, she looked at him in dismay. "Which is Wednesday, Daniel. I can't just cancel."

"Why not?"

"Well, I..." She couldn't, could she?

His finger trailed down the side of her neck, then snaked beneath the hair at her nape. "Don't you want to go with me, Tessa?"

Silly question. Crazy question. She closed her eyes at his touch and felt the now familiar warmth stealing over her. It had been a long time since she'd done anything even slightly impulsive. The mistakes in her past had taught her well. Was it reckless to go with Daniel? She lifted a hand and covered his, knowing suddenly that whether it was or not, she was going to do it.

SHERIFF WALKER WADE showed up at Sojourn on Monday. Tessa was in her office giving Keely and Jake Raymond detailed instructions on any possible contingency for the next three days when she would be in New York. She still had to pinch herself to believe she was actually going. But ever since she'd decided to go, excitement and a nearly forgotten almost youthful giddiness had kept her stomach in a flutter. This must be what it felt like to anticipate a wedding, she thought, rising to greet the red-faced sheriff. Or a honeymoon.

She shook hands with the sheriff, hoping her thoughts didn't show on her face. She and Daniel hadn't made it to bed yet, but she knew in her heart they would while they were in New York. But it was hardly a wedding. Or a honeymoon.

With a sigh, she signaled Keely and Jake to leave and forced a smile for the top lawman in the parish. "Good morning, Sheriff." She gestured to the chair in front of her desk. "You're out and about early, aren't you?"

He gave her a bluff grin, removed his hat with gentlemanly courtesy and took the chair she'd indicated. "Sorry I missed the party yesterday, Ms. Hamilton. I had some business in Baton Rouge."

It was widely known Sheriff Wade gambled every Sunday on the riverboat docked at the Port of Baton Rouge. "I'm sorry, too, Sheriff. You missed lots of good food and friendly faces. Sojourn has been lucky in the support it receives from the community."

"Well, that's exactly what I'm here about, Ms. Hamilton." He fumbled in his shirt pocket for reading glasses and put them on as he shook the folds out of a document that he'd brought with him. "Comes a time when a setup like this can give a little of that support back locally." He peered at her over the rims of his glasses, still smiling.

She clasped her hands in front of her. "I'm not sure that I understand, Sheriff Wade."

"I've got a man in my department...." He looked up at her again. "Duplantis. Dwayne Duplantis."

"Yes, I know him."

"He's got a nephew...."

"Yes, Kyle. His sister's son, I believe?"

"Yes, yes. That's it. Well, I'm glad you're familiar with the details here. From what Dwayne told me, I wasn't sure you'd understand what's involved. Dwayne's a good man. He's a hometown boy all the way, good solid Southern principles. Which is why he's so distressed over this boy, Kyle."

"Yes, assault with a deadly weapon during a robbery, if I recall from the conversation we had last week. That could be distressing from a concerned uncle's point of view. And from a law-enforcement person's point of view, the fact that Kyle pistol-whipped a defenseless elderly woman is even more distressing, I imagine."

Shifting his bulk in the chair, the sheriff folded the rap sheet and cleared his throat with a loud harrumph. "I told Dwayne it didn't look good, this boy going as far as he did, but he assures me the boy isn't bad. That in the proper environment Kyle can be shown the error of his ways. He'll cooperate with you in every way, Ms. Hamilton, or he'll not only answer to his uncle, but he'll have to answer to me, by God!"

"Sheriff—" Tessa let out a deep sigh. "I've had this conversation with Deputy Duplantis. I can't allow Kyle to come to Sojourn. None of the juveniles here are guilty of serious crimes. None are violent. Kyle is both."

He looked pained. "You've got a lot of riffraff here, Ms. Hamilton. Any kid who runs away from home is potentially violent."

"I'm afraid I don't agree with that, Sheriff. Nevertheless, it changes nothing about my position with regard to Kyle. What if, in spite of Deputy Duplantis's assurances, Kyle does turn violent? Someone could be hurt. No, I'm sorry, but I simply can't take the chance.''

The sheriff sat for a moment in thought, stroking his chin. ''Well, I can see you've made up your mind on this, Ms. Hamilton.'' He got to his feet, shaking his head. ''These kids nowadays…glad mine are grown and gone. Naturally, I can't say I blame Dwayne for wanting to give his nephew another chance—''

Tessa rose. ''It's not that I'm refusing just for the sake of being stubborn or unreasonable, Sheriff. I hope you understand. And please try to explain my position to Deputy Duplantis, if you will. Sojourn is finally getting good press. People are coming to understand why we're here. We simply can't jeopardize the whole program for one boy.''

He eyed her with all the shrewdness that came from forty years in law enforcement. ''Well now, in fairness, Ms. Hamilton, aren't you doing just that—jeopardizing your program for one little girl? Considering who her daddy is, I mean.''

''There were mitigating circumstances, Sheriff, but Teddy's no longer here.''

''Well, I'll be on my way then.'' Moving ponderously, he tucked his glasses back into his shirt pocket and put his hat on his head. ''I'm taking your word on those 'mitigating circumstances,' because I don't have to tell you what would happen if that little tidbit leaked out.''

At the door, he stopped and looked back at her.

"I'll speak to Dwayne, Ms. Hamilton, but I don't think he'll be happy. Sort of a hothead, Dwayne is." Another pained expression crossed his craggy features at having to admit such a thing. "If you want a piece of advice—and I suppose you don't, folks never do—it's this. I'd be real careful handling the situation with Mr. Kendrick and his daughter. If it was me, that is. Just friendly advice, you understand. For what it's worth." And with that, he gave her a courteous nod, touched his hat and left.

Tessa leaned her head on her hands and wished Duplantis and Kyle Whatever-his-name-was to the devil. Sheriff Wade had never been a favorite of hers, but she'd always considered him basically honest. Now she couldn't quite figure out whether he'd been trying to warn her that Duplantis could be dangerous or whether he'd been adding his own not-so-gentle urging to his deputy's to get her to admit Kyle. Whatever his motive, her hands were tied. Why couldn't they see that?

"Hey, pretty lady."

"Daniel." She stood up, smiling at him, her heart lifting. "Hello."

"We've got a plane to catch, sweetheart."

She nodded, the threat to Sojourn receding in exact proportion to her anticipation of what lay ahead. "Give me ten minutes."

He was now on her side of the desk. "But first, this." Tilting her chin, he leaned down to kiss her.

Minutes later, as she waved goodbye to the kids on her way to the car with Daniel, she thought with amusement that he could have suggested going to Afghanistan and she would have agreed. And for the first time, the possibility of a man having that kind of power over her didn't scare her to death.

BETH'S APARTMENT was in Manhattan. Tessa and Daniel didn't waste any time getting there after arriving at La Guardia. Mrs. Kowalski met them at the door. She was a tall woman, thin and exceptionally neat, with a face that didn't smile easily. Her gray hair was permed to look more like a Brillo pad than a coiffure. It certainly wouldn't irritate her by falling into her face, Tessa thought dryly, chilled by the woman's demeanor. Suddenly she understood part of Teddy and Joey's desperation to get away.

"I made it clear to Ms. Carson when she hired me that I was not a nanny," Mrs. Kowalski said with a put-upon air. "These children have given me fits, and Ms. Carson hasn't been much help. I told her after Teddy ran away that I wouldn't be surprised if Joey did the same thing, but she would make that trip to New Mexico." She adjusted her glasses with a quick punch to the bridge piece. "Naturally I called her the instant I discovered he was gone."

"And when was that?" Daniel asked, fighting an immediate dislike of the woman.

"Around 8:00 p.m."

"It was dark by then, wasn't it?" His tone was almost too quiet.

"Yes." She aligned a slightly askew figurine on the coffee table. "But it wasn't unusual for Joey to hare around the streets until the last minute of his curfew."

"Curfew?"

"Yes, of course. His mother made it clear that she expected both of them to be in the house by dark."

"And did you know where he was supposed to be with darkness coming on?"

She was instantly defensive. "Have you ever tried to keep up with two hooligans? If they didn't tell me, I never knew where they were—neither one of them."

"And on the night Joey ran away, you finally got curious around eight o'clock?"

"Well, naturally," she agreed, missing the outrage in his tone. "And that's when I realized he had pulled the same trick."

"The same trick."

It seemed to dawn on her that Daniel's gaze was a little too intense and his stillness a little too rigid. "As I said, Mr. Kendrick, I'm no nanny. My principal duties here have to do with the orderly management of the household."

"And two children are incidental?"

"Hardly. You try coping with two unhappy children and the chaos they cause."

"Nothing could make me happier, Mrs. Kowalski," Daniel said through his teeth. "Unfortunately, I didn't have any choice in that until now."

Her mouth pursed into a prune. "Yes, well, Ms. Carson called me last night to tell me there'd been a change." She flicked a glance at Tessa. "You're to stay here in the apartment with Ms. Hamilton in case Joey calls."

"Have you heard from him?"

"No." Spotting a smudge on the coffee table, she bent and polished it. "Although there have been some nuisance calls. Someone's been ringing the number, then hanging up when I answer." She gave a grimace of distaste. "People dialing numbers willy-nilly just to see who they can harass."

Tessa touched Daniel's arm. "It could be Joey," she murmured.

Daniel nodded. "If we're lucky."

Mrs. Kowalski stared at them, clearly offended. "If it was Joey, why wouldn't he speak to me, for heaven's sake? He knows I'm responsible when his mother is away. At least he could let me know he's safe. This is very hard on my nerves, Mr. Kendrick. First Teddy, now Joey." She whipped her dust cloth over the glass table once more, then marched toward the door. "You can be certain of this. I'm never contracting for another situation with children involved."

"I WANTED TO FIRE HER on the spot," Daniel said grimly as he paced beside the phone in Beth's living room. "And the minute I have Joey safely in my custody, I'm demanding that Beth get rid of her. I don't think the woman's capable of saying a kind word, let alone managing a smile."

"She didn't complain when you gave her the afternoon off," Tessa said from the depths of a huge white sofa.

"Hell, it's going to be tough enough waiting around for Joey to call. I didn't think we should have to cope with Nurse Ratched, too." After a moment, he added with a wicked smile, "Did you notice how suspicious she looked when I suggested it?"

"I'd have to be blind not to."

He waggled his eyebrows. "She thinks we're planning some hanky-panky."

"Silly woman." Tessa's heart fluttered like a trapped bird.

He studied her in silence for a minute, his smile fading. "You know what I'd like to do, don't you?"

She did. It was written all over him. "We need to wait for Joey's call."

"Yeah."

"What did that police lieutenant say when you phoned a few minutes ago?"

"They've got nothing. Joey vanished into thin air, and the only communication anybody's had with him is that one phone call to me in Louisiana."

"And the cell phone number? Couldn't they trace it?"

"They did. It was a pal of Joey's at school. He told his mom exactly what Joey told me. He lent it to Joey but he doesn't have a clue where Joey is." Walking to the window, he pulled the drape aside and gazed out over the Manhattan skyline. He spoke quietly, fearfully. "He could be anywhere out there, Tessa."

Tessa's gaze drifted to the telephone on the end table. "He'll call, Daniel. He will."

The silence of the apartment echoed around them. From the back somewhere came the sound of a clock striking the hour. Daniel released the drape and walked over to the sofa. He sat down beside her, leaned back and took her hand, lacing his fingers with hers. His mouth had a wry slant when he looked at her. "This isn't exactly the way you imagined your first night in the Big Apple, is it?"

"This isn't my first night in the Big Apple."

"No? I took you for a Southern girl all the way."

"I spent a week here once looking for a runaway from Cypress House."

After a moment's silence, he sighed and shifted so that he could slip both arms around her. When they were reclined on the deep sofa, spoon-fashion, he tucked her head beneath his chin. "And here you are again, looking for a runaway. There's got to be a message in that."

"Fate, Keely would call it."

"Did you find your runaway then?"

"Would you believe, I did." She looked up at him. "And we'll find Joey, too."

HIS CALL CAME just after six o'clock. At the first ring, Daniel reared up from the sofa where he and Tessa were watching the evening news and grabbed the receiver. "Hello!"

"It's me, Dad."

"Joey."

A sniff. A strangled sob. "You came, Dad. I—I d-didn't know if you would, for sure."

"I'm here, son. I want to come and get you. Where are you?"

"You won't tell any cops or anything, will you?" Joey asked cautiously.

"No. I'm with the lady who runs Sojourn, Ms. Hamilton. The two of us will come, nobody else."

"That's the same lady who's been keeping Teddy, huh, Dad?"

"That's right."

There was another sniff, but Joey's tone had strengthened. "Is Mom with you?"

"No, she's still in New Mexico. But she's okay

with letting me do this, Joey. Tessa and I will pick you up and bring you back to the apartment. Flights leave daily from New York to New Orleans. We could leave sometime tomorrow.''

''And you're taking me with you?''

''Yes. I promised, didn't I? You're coming.''

''Well…''

Daniel heard the hesitation, and it wrenched at his heart. If he'd doubted the damage done to his relationship with his children, here was the evidence in Joey's reluctance to trust him. Swallowing his bitterness, he strove to reclaim some of that trust. ''I wouldn't lie to you now, son,'' he said quietly. ''You're going to spend the summer with me in Louisiana. You just have to tell me where you are.''

''Saint Patrick's Cathedral,'' the boy said after a long moment.

Daniel closed his eyes. ''Saint Patrick's.''

''Yeah, Saint Patrick's, Dad. Do you know where it is?''

Daniel was shaking his head. ''Yeah, I know where Saint Patrick's is.'' He turned to look at Tessa. ''That's where you've been hiding for almost three days, Joey?''

''Yes, sir. I told you I was in a safe place.'' His natural self-confidence had returned now. ''I slipped inside during mass and nobody even noticed. I snuck my sleeping bag in and some stuff to eat. In a way, it was neat.'' He paused with a hint of uncertainty. ''I knew I was taking a chance. Sort of. You might be mad enough you wouldn't come and get me.''

''I would have come, Joey. Never doubt it.''

''Okay, Dad.''

"Right. Now, how're we going to do this?"

"You can pick me up at the side entrance. There's an old guy—not a priest—who hangs around a lot, and I'd rather not have to explain what I'm doing with my sleeping bag and all, so when you show up, I'll sneak past him, okay?"

"I'm on my way."

"HE'S ADORABLE, DANIEL."

"He's a little scamp. He's a con artist. He's slick as an eel," Daniel said, rummaging in the linen closet for a clean towel. "But I'm crazy about him."

Tessa gave him the pj's and clean underwear she'd found in Joey's room. "And he knows it."

He found a bloodred towel, a color he assumed Beth had chosen to coordinate with the stark black-and-white bathroom. The more he poked around the apartment, the less appealing he found it. The decor was sharp and modern, the art trendy and avant-garde. Every blank space was a spot for something obscurely beautiful—Beth's choices. The place was an artist's lair, not a home for Teddy and Joey. Even the things in his children's rooms were chosen for their artistic appeal by Beth. He could see no evidence that the kids had been allowed to express themselves as individuals. When he'd been married to her, he had managed to curb her self-absorbed personality somewhat. Now, in the freewheeling life-style she'd chosen, it seemed she had almost forgotten that she was a mother as well as an artist.

"I'll take this towel to Joey," he told Tessa, "and then we'll figure out something for dinner."

"Sounds fine to me," she said. "Why don't you

take a minute to talk to Joey? After all, it's been a long time since he's had his dad strictly to himself. And I'll put in a quick call to Keely to see if things are okay at Sojourn.''

He didn't move.

She gave him a little shove. "So, go."

"Right." But he didn't head for the bathroom. Instead, he shifted the towel and pj's to one arm and slipped his hand beneath her hair to pull her close.

"Daniel!" She could hear Joey splashing in the shower.

He spoke in a low tone with his mouth hovering just over hers. "I hope you're not keeping a list, because I'm going to be in your debt for about the next ten years."

"Daniel..."

He meant the kiss to be quick, a lover's expression of appreciation. A promise of a special thank-you to come later. Instead, it was sweet and hot and dizzying. Her lips were smooth and warm; they parted under his, telling him she felt the same hunger and need he felt. He dropped what he was carrying and wrapped his arms around her. How had he thought he could touch Tessa with such casual intent?

He lost all thought then and went deeper into her sweetness, greedy for this woman. With one hand, he skimmed the side of her breast. That wasn't enough. He wanted to remove her blouse and feel her breasts. See them. Taste them.

"Dad...Dad, you out there? I need a towel, Dad."

He groaned, trapping her between his forearms against the wall, breathing like a man who'd run a fifty-yard dash. He muttered something profane and sexual in her ear. Savored the weak, aroused sound it provoked from Tessa.

"Dad?" The shower stopped and the door banged.

"I'm coming!" He kissed her ear, then with a groan he turned her loose. Bending, he scooped up the fallen towel along with Joey's clothes and headed for the bathroom. When he looked back, Tessa was smiling.

CHAPTER FOURTEEN

"WOW, THIS PLACE is something else, Daniel." Tessa stood in the middle of the swank kitchen surveying the stark white tiles and stainless steel appliances. "But I can't see a person doing much cooking in here."

"No problem for Beth. She doesn't cook."

She turned to look at him. "Mrs. Kowalski's job?"

"You heard her. It sure wasn't taking care of the kids."

Tessa drifted to a window. Beth's condominium was in a four-story building, one of a row of tony dwellings on West 54th Street. "I don't know much about New York, but even I know that with Fifth Avenue only one block away, this is a very good address." She turned as Daniel moved to her side. "Relocating to New York proved a good career move for her."

"In more ways than one." Resting a shoulder against the window frame, Daniel crossed his feet at the ankles. "She's worked hard, I won't deny that. She's had several successful showings, but she's not earning the kind of money it takes to live like this."

She decided not to ask for an explanation of that. "I assume your children attend a private school."

He straightened and shoved his hands in his pockets. "Nobody in Manhattan sends their kids to a public school. So, the answer's yes."

Tessa heard the bitter mockery in his voice. Recalling the austerity of the farmhouse he rented, she decided he must send a crushing portion of his income to his ex-wife to keep his children in the style she had chosen.

A hint of her thoughts must have shown on her face. "Even if I sent her every dime I made," he said dryly, "I couldn't put her up in these digs. No, my ex-wife has friends in high places with very high incomes. One of them owns this block of apartments."

"A patron of the arts."

He gave a low chuckle. "Not exactly, but you get the idea."

She'd wondered about Beth's personal life and whether she had any misgivings about the influence her life-style had on her young children. Daniel hadn't commented, but after coming to know him, she suspected he would prefer a more traditional upbringing for Teddy and Joey. But that was just one more detail of his children's lives that was beyond his control.

Moving away, she gestured toward the kitchen. "Shall I try to put something together for us to eat? I'm no Martha Stewart, but all kitchens are pretty much the same and there's stuff in the freezer. I looked while you were talking to Joey."

"Thanks for offering, but I thought we might call for Chinese or something from a good deli. There are tons of places nearby where we can get excellent food delivered." He touched the small of her back and urged her down the hallway. "We'll check with Joey, but I don't think he'll want anything. He was almost nodding off as we talked.''

At Joey's bedroom, he paused and looked inside. His son was curled up with his pillow, comforter askew and out like a light.

"Looks like you were right," Tessa whispered.

"He's exhausted." Daniel closed the door quietly. "Running a scam takes a lot out of a kid."

"You have to admire his ingenuity in a way," Tessa said, turning back down the hall. "He took a chance, but it paid off. He's reunited with his dad and his sister, plus he gets a summer vacation in Louisiana." She smiled at Daniel, shaking her head. "I can only imagine what kind of shenanigans he'll think of when he gets to be sixteen."

He stopped her and with a smile, touched her cheek. "I'm just thankful I'll be a part of his life then. Beth's opened the door now, Tessa. There's no going back."

"I hope so, but—"

"I've got an appointment with her lawyer tomorrow morning," he said. "If she's instructed him as she promised me she would, that should be it."

"You spoke to Beth again?" she asked.

"A few minutes ago. Joey and I both. Between the two of us, we persuaded her that turning over responsibility for Teddy and Joey to me for the summer in Louisiana was best for everybody."

"And she agreed to simply ignore the circumstances that have kept you from sharing custody of your children for five years? Just like that?"

"Just like that." Seeing her amazement, he let out a long sigh. "You'd have to know her. The decision happens to suit her at this time. She's caught up in a new phase of her art and she wants to devote all her time and energy to that. She doesn't want distractions, which is what Teddy and Joey are to Beth right now.''

Tessa was beginning to understand the insanity of what Daniel had been coping with since his divorce, although she would never understand Beth's casual attitude toward her children. Even when battling addiction and divorce and abandonment by Keely's teenage father, Tessa had worried about her child. Studying Daniel's face, she wondered if she would have coped as well as he. "But what she's saying in effect is that she used trumped-up charges to keep your children from you."

"Exactly." He rubbed a thumb over her lips, then captured her hand in his and started down the hallway. "I told you all along she never believed what that girl said."

"This is so incredible," Tessa murmured.

"It's simple. Beth wanted to live in New York without having to cope with the hassle of shared custody and air travel for the kids and visitation, with all the inconveniences that parents who split have to contend with. She also knew that she was going to live a life-style I wouldn't approve of for Teddy and Joey."

"And with you out of the picture, she could safely disregard your opinion."

"More or less."

Tessa stopped at a gorgeous tapestry hanging on the wall, and wondered which of Beth's "friends" had sprung for it. She was quickly finding that noth-

ing of Beth's appealed to her with the exception of
the woman's children and her ex-husband.

"Did you call Keely?" Daniel asked.

"Yes, everything's fine so far. Just keep your fingers crossed."

Daniel was standing very close when he spoke
next. "So, does deli takeout sound okay?"

She turned, knowing her thoughts were reflected in
her eyes, and lifted her gaze to his. "Sure."

"Now? Or after?"

"What?"

She watched his gaze dip to her mouth and linger
there, then climb slowly back up to her eyes. She
didn't realize he still held her hand until he lifted it
to kiss her palm. "After we make love, Tessa."

She conquered the urge to close her eyes as desire
bloomed, then curled warmly through her. And then
he was drawing her close, lifting her arms and linking
them around his neck. As her body met his, he en-
closed her fully in his embrace. "This is the guest
room," he murmured, his lips skimming over to her
ear.

She gave a murmur of confusion. Guest room?
They stood at an open door, but they could have been
standing on the edge of a cliff and she wouldn't have
noticed. He nipped the lobe of her ear and repeated,
"This is the guest room. I don't want to be with you
in Beth's bed."

No. God, no.

"And I want to be with you, Tessa. Now. Tonight."

She turned and met his mouth, warm and deli-
ciously smooth, silky and erotic. Confident. Male to

her female. She sighed with sheer joy, and then, as the kiss heated, could do nothing but surrender to it.

She'd been passive until now, content to feel and enjoy, to savor, but passion suddenly brought her alive. She opened to his exploration, tangled her tongue with his, pushed her body tight against the throbbing heat between his thighs.

She put her arms beneath his pullover and explored his chest with both hands. The skin there was warm and firm, the muscles hard and flexing. She gave a murmur of protest when he began backing away, then realized he was trying to draw them into the room and close the door.

The guest bedroom, she realized dazedly as she heard the sound of the lock click into place, but she had stopped thinking the instant she'd turned into his kiss. He took her face in both hands and forced her to look at him.

"Are you sure?" he asked in a gritty whisper.

She'd been on the brink of absolute surrender, and now he was giving her one last chance to decide. To reconsider. Something inside her turned over, and for the first time in her life, she knew that whatever else might happen, this was right. Maybe this moment had been predestined. Maybe the Fates had intertwined their lives—not so happily at the beginning, but now everything in her was telling her this was no mistake. She had fallen in love with Daniel Kendrick. She wanted to feel his fire, his passion. She needed his loving more than she'd ever needed anything.

"Tessa..."

"I'm sure." Pushing again at the bunched pullover, she began trying to work it over his head. Seeing her intent, Daniel wrenched the shirt up over his shoulders, then sailed it away, catching something on a small table nearby and knocking it over. Neither noticed. Before he could undress her, Tessa had wrapped her arms around his waist and was burying her face in his chest, inhaling the heady scent of Daniel.

And then, with throaty moans and murmurs, she was kissing him. Gliding her lips over him was incredibly delicious. She pressed her mouth to a nipple, flicked it with her tongue. Daniel groaned, standing slack against the wall and letting her have her way, breathing hard, fully aroused. They'd reached this point before, and the memory was an aphrodisiac. She knew what came next and she needed it. Wanted it. All of it, this time.

"Tessa," he said thickly, fumbling with his zipper. "Touch me."

In answer, she slipped her hand into his open jeans and closed it around him. She heard his head bump the wall, sensed him weaken by her touch, and she gloried in her power. Still stroking him, she raised her mouth to his, and he seized on her like a wild man. Then all power was wrested from her as Daniel took charge.

She moaned as his hands moved over her, sweeping past her waist to cup her bottom and hold her there. She trembled from kisses dropped at her cheek and chin and along her throat. And then he was going lower and lower, pushing impatiently at collar and buttons, his breath hot and harsh and out of control.

She closed her eyes as his hands worked under her shirt and closed possessively over her breasts. She had removed her bra earlier after a shower, and now her mind went blissfully blank when he skimmed his thumbs over nipples that were rigid and tingling. Then his mouth once again greedily fastened on hers, swallowing her moans, absorbing her shudders.

By the time they reached the bed, her clothes had been flung in the same general direction as his shirt. But he was prevented from removing his jeans by his shoes. He cursed, groping for them, then when he'd kicked them away, he realized Tessa was laughing.

"You'll pay for that," he rasped, licking one pebble-hard nipple.

"Please," she said, throwing her head back to enjoy it. His teeth nipped, his tongue soothed. She felt pain and pleasure and ached for more.

And then he was sliding his hands beneath her hips, poised to enter her. "Look at me, Tessa."

From a daze of pleasure, she met his eyes.

"This is forever, Tessa."

"Daniel..." Desire threatened to drift away like smoke.

"There's no going back, Tessa."

She shifted restlessly, unwilling to lose this feeling. "Daniel..."

Never taking his eyes from hers, he pushed a hand between them and touched the part of her that throbbed with desire for him. He watched as her gaze blurred, her vision narrowed. Relentlessly, rhythmically, he pushed her beyond thought.

"No...going...back," he ground out, watching heat bloom within her, coating her skin with sweat. Suddenly she cried out. And only then did he thrust inside her.

"Daniel—" The force of the orgasm broadsided her with the force of an oncoming train. But there was no time to savor it. While she still quivered with the aftershocks, she was caught up in another fast, dark tide that erupted with the rhythm of his passion. But this was better. With Daniel inside her, sensing the need in him, holding at bay his unsettling words. And when she'd almost reached that cataclysm of color and sensation, Daniel took her further, until he joined her in the blinding, shattering explosion.

THEY LAY IN A SWEATY, sated tangle as hearts calmed and blood cooled. He turned a fraction until he felt her hair against his face. He inhaled, enjoying the scent.

"Are we still alive?" she asked, lifting a shoulder to capture and hold him there.

Chuckling, he raised on an elbow and treated himself to the look of her sprawled on the plush duvet. "Give me a minute and I'll let you know."

She reached up and brushed the hair from his forehead, a casual, yet openly intimate gesture. "That was an unforgettable experience Daniel."

"The first of many, I hope." A playful look appeared on his face as he skimmed a hand down over her breast to her waist, past her thigh, which he lifted gently. When Tessa realized he was trying to roll her over, she resisted. "Wait, wait," he said, trying to see her backside. "Ahhh, there it is. I thought so." He grinned at her. "You've got a tattoo."

Still pushing at his hands, she scrambled for her shirt, which hung drunkenly from the bedpost.

"A butterfly on your butt," he said with delight.

"I was almost out of my mind with lust when I got to that part, but I saw what I saw." He was caressing the curve of her bottom, his expression gleeful. "I have time now to kiss it."

"No way." She was up on her knees, working to turn her shirt right-side out. It should have been a simple feat, but because her hands were all thumbs, the damn thing was in a tangle.

"Hey, it's cute."

Still smiling, he bent low, trying to get a better look, but Tessa recoiled as if he'd tried something obscene.

"It's tacky. It's cheap. I hate it!" Finally getting the shirt right, she rammed her arms into it.

Daniel looked puzzled. "You hate it?"

"Yes." Now that she was covered, she was suddenly self-conscious.

Unabashed by his own nudity, Daniel stretched out, one knee raised, and looked at her. "Okay, sweetheart, let's talk about this."

"Let's don't," she started to get up from the bed, but he caught her ankle. Startled, she shot him a look, but something in his eyes made her sigh and settle back against the pillows.

"I got it when I was a stupid teenager," she said, not looking at him. "It's...I just want to forget that time, but the butterfly is always there to remind me."

"That'll be a trick. You can't even see it."

She refused to be teased. "This is not a joke, Daniel. I hate that tattoo."

After another good, long look at her, he said, "Correct me if I'm wrong, but I think I'm hearing more of that bad baggage you've been carrying around far too long, Tessa.''

''No one likes to be reminded of a time in their life when all the choices they made were wrong.''

His hand was now moving up her calf, higher, then curling around her thigh. ''All your choices weren't wrong, sweetheart. Most of the major problems in your life were thrust on you before you could choose at all.''

No one had ever defended her so staunchly, but something deep inside Tessa still made her hang on to her guilt. ''Stephanie doesn't have a tattoo,'' she said, but the words were unsteady.

His hand had reached her waist now and was slipping beneath her shirt to stroke her breast. But he stopped. Looked at her.

''Why do you do that?''

She looked bewildered. ''Do what?''

''You always compare yourself to Stephanie.'' He raised himself on one elbow. ''You know, the more I get to know you, the less alike I think you and Stephanie are. And it's no mystery why that is. From the moment you were raped, your lives were irrevocably set on separate paths. I suppose you could say Stephanie was luckier. She certainly didn't have to deal with the aftermath of rape, she didn't wind up pregnant at sixteen, but most important in my opinion, was that Stephanie was safe with a substitute mother while you were coping alone at seventeen.''

''You call it luck,'' Tessa said, ''but I see it as choices. She made the right ones, I made the wrong ones.''

''Maybe, but even so, we are as we are,

personalitywise. Once traumatized, you couldn't hide in a tidy little room, going to school every day and pretending you were just like all those other kids—and I'm including your twin sister. I see your rebellion and those wrong choices stemming from your efforts to deal with the ultimate abuse—rape.'' He leaned in to kiss her, a gentle, but erotic leftover from their recent passion.

''It's in your past now, Tessa,'' he said, breaking the kiss, his mouth still hovered over hers. His gaze roved her face tenderly. ''Let it go, sweetheart.''

Her arms were somehow around him as she lost herself in the seduction of his words and another heart-stopping kiss. She realized with surprise that he wanted to make love again, when only a few minutes earlier she'd been sure neither of them had enough energy left to do more than pull the covers up and go to sleep. Daniel proceeded to show her how wrong she was. With his hands, his mouth, his body, he pushed her dark secrets away and released the passion inside her. And as the hours of the night passed, he made her forget.

IN AN INCREDIBLY short document, Beth's attorney cut the strings that had tied Daniel in legal knots and kept him at arm's length from his children for five years. With Joey sitting between him and Tessa at the lawyer's office, Daniel read the legalese that renounced Beth's belief in the charges lodged against him by Judy Lovell and proclaimed him fit to have Teddy and Joey live with him in Louisiana all summer long. After being assured that the document would go to his lawyer and, just to be on the safe

side, to the sheriff's department in Louisiana, Daniel
had slipped a copy in his briefcase, then ushered his
son and Tessa outside. A quick trip to the apartment
to pick up their luggage and they could head for La
Guardia.

"Don't we have to notify the police or something?" Tessa asked after settling back in the cab.

"No way," Joey told her, almost beside himself
with excitement. "I already asked Dad. As soon as
you two picked me up at Saint Patrick's, Mom called
and told them I'd been found."

Tessa met Daniel's eyes over the boy's head. "And
they didn't question that?"

"They were happy to remove one kid's name from
a long list of missing children."

"And no complications...otherwise?" She didn't
know how much Joey actually understood about the
reason his father hadn't been allowed access to his
children alone. They'd discussed it last night and
Daniel had decided to wait until they got to Louisiana,
when he and Tessa could explain the situation to
Teddy and Joey together.

"None. I don't think NYPD ever had anything on
file about me one way or the other," Daniel explained. "The papers were sealed at the time of the
custody hearing by order of the judge in Florida. But
I thought Beth should be the one to call and tell them
Joey would be flying to Louisiana with me. Any problem would have cropped up then. Luckily, it didn't."

They stopped at the intersection of 56th Street and
Avenue of the Americas, and she watched the hurried
pace of pedestrians crossing in front of their cab, but
her thoughts were back in Florida at the time of the

court hearing. If the judge had ordered the file sealed, it shouldn't have become common knowledge, but somehow it had been leaked. After that, it was a certainty that Daniel couldn't stay in his job.

Over the boy's head, their eyes met. She wanted to touch Daniel. To take his hand in hers and hold it against her cheek. Calling what had been done to Daniel unjust and unfair was like the state apologizing when freeing an innocent man after several years in prison. Nothing could cancel the pain and suffering.

She realized Joey was looking up at her, studying her with a mix of curiosity and friendly interest. "Are you my dad's girlfriend?" he asked.

A quick glance at Daniel and she saw instantly that he wasn't going to help her with this one. "We're very good friends," she said.

"Is that a yes or a no?"

She looked into his eyes, the same silver-gray as his father's. With the same directness. "It's neither. We've known each other for several years and we're friends."

"Are you married to somebody?"

"No. I'm... No, I'm not married."

"Do you have any kids?"

"One. A daughter."

"So, how old is she?"

"Eighteen."

He looked disappointed, then flashed a quick grin. "But I bet you have some kids at Sojourn who are about my age, huh?"

The tension in Tessa eased at the direction he was going. He was looking for a buddy to hang out with. She smiled at him. "I hate to disappoint you, Joey,

but mostly they're fourteen and older. If you're looking for a friend when you get to Louisiana, you won't
have any trouble, though. Your dad lives in the country, but there are neighbors nearby. Somebody's
bound to have a boy about your age.''

As he beamed at her, Tessa realized how much the
boy was like his father. That same grin had been on
Daniel's face as he'd teased her about her tattoo.

Joey turned to his dad. ''Do you know anybody
with puppies, Dad?''

''Puppies?''

''Uh-huh.'' All innocence, Joey studied the land-
scape now whizzing by on the busy route to the airport. ''I was thinking since I'm gonna be in Louisiana
and at a farm and all, that I should get a puppy.''

It was Daniel's turn to appeal to Tessa for help,
but she was carefully studying the clasp on her purse.
''I don't think I know anybody with puppies to give
away, but—''

''We could try the Humane Society,'' Joey suggested helpfully.

''Joey, you're only staying for the summer. A
puppy needs care all year long.''

''Yeah, but it's not like there's nobody around.
You're there all year long, Dad.'' His shoulders
slumped as he gazed at his hands. ''Mom would never
let us have a pet. We always lived in apartments
where they weren't allowed.''

''I have a cat.''

''You do?'' For a second, Joey was disconcerted.
But only for a second. ''A cat or a kitten?''

''A cat. He's full-grown.''

''What's his name?''

"Uh, Cat."

"That's not very original, Dad."

"No, but it gets the job done."

Joey shifted to present his case more earnestly. "But see, Dad, that cat's *your* pet. I'd like to have a pet of my own now that I'll be living on a farm. You know what I mean?" Without waiting for an answer, he rushed on. "So I think we need a puppy, and I bet Teddy'll think it's a good idea, too. We need to get him when he's small and we'll think of a really neat name for him. He'll be our mascot for the farm and we'll always remember that the summer we got our puppy was the summer we started to be a family again."

"Sucker-r-r."

Tessa's eyes were sparkling as Daniel pocketed their newly validated tickets. He thanked the flight attendant and then, disregarding the crush of people milling around them, he caught Tessa around the neck and gave her a kiss beneath her ear. "I told you he was a slick one, didn't I?"

She laughed, moving into the embrace. "I would have helped you out if you'd come to my aid when he started the third degree, but no. You were so smug, with that glint in your eye, and I said to myself, 'Let him get out of this one on his own.'"

"No kidding, do you know anybody with puppies?" He rubbed his cheek against the top of her head.

"Probably," she said after a moment.

"But don't say anything." He glanced over at the

entrance to the rest rooms, on the lookout for Joey. "I want to surprise him."

Gently, because she suddenly felt her heart turn over, she touched his cheek and repeated, "Sucker-r-r."

He kissed her palm. "I'd allow him a dozen puppies if I thought it would make up for the years we missed together."

"You won't need puppies for that. Just be yourself."

Suddenly the announcement of the flight's departure was broadcast from the loudspeaker. "I guess I'll have to go find him," Daniel said, getting ready to move away.

"And I'll check with Keely again."

He squeezed her hand. "Relax, Mom. All your babies at Sojourn are fine."

She smiled. "Maybe, but I'll just call one more time to make sure."

DANIEL HERDED JOEY and another boy about the same age from the men's room, both grinning and talking a mile a minute. Spotting Tessa, Joey waved and dragged his friend over, leaving Daniel to follow.

"Tessa, this is Baxter. He's gonna be on our flight, and guess what? He lives in Louisiana, too. Baxter, this is my dad's very good friend, Tessa. We're all heading for New Orleans. That's where I live now."

Daniel's smile died when he met Tessa's eyes. "What's wrong?"

"Oh, Daniel." She was pale and her lips were unsteady. "It's Sojourn. They've shut it down."

CHAPTER FIFTEEN

KEELY WAS WAITING at the terminal in New Orleans when they got off the plane. Tessa headed straight for her. "What happened?" she demanded.

Keely took her mother's weekend bag. "A special report on TV, Mom. It was all lies and innuendo, but it was enough to spook every official that had ever supported you and Sojourn. Even Marly Toups is freaked out over this."

Tessa gave Daniel a helpless look, then rubbed her forehead. "I'm trying to understand this, Keely. What kind of lies and innuendo? What was said? Who did it?"

"Pete Veillon, who else?" Keely said bitterly. "You were right about him all along, Mom. He did a real number on us."

Tessa was confused. "But the feature he did after the open house was so positive. It was... He seemed to understand Sojourn and what we're trying to do. What happened to change his mind?"

"I don't know. I guess Sojourn proved more interesting than he expected and he started digging."

"Digging?" Glancing at Daniel again, Tessa saw something in his eyes, and her stomach lurched sickeningly. She touched her mouth. "He knows about me, about my past," she said to Keely.

Keely slung the strap of Tessa's case onto her shoulder. "No, Mom, it's not your past, it's—" She seemed to realize suddenly that Joey was listening intently.

"It's my past he dug up," Daniel said quietly. Following his narrowed gaze, Tessa realized he was looking at the headlines framed in a newspaper vending machine. "'Children's Shelter—Haven or Horror,'" she murmured through lips that barely moved. "My God, it's already in the papers."

Grim-faced, Daniel fed the machine a coin and took out a copy of the newspaper. Tessa had time to read only the first few sentences over his shoulder before he crumpled the paper with a savage curse and rammed it into a side pocket of his garment bag.

She'd seen enough. They'd somehow uncovered Judy Lovell's testimony and worse. They knew Tessa herself had testified against him. There was outrage that she'd welcomed him into Sojourn knowing his background.

She bent her head, willing away the sick flutter in her stomach. Then she faced Daniel, wanting to find something to reassure him, but the look on his face stopped her.

"What is it, Dad?" Joey asked, instantly picking up on his father's distress. "What's in that paper?" He saw the same look on Tessa's face and turned to Keely in bewilderment. "What's the matter?"

Keely managed a smile. "Grown-up stuff, Joey."

Joey swung back to his father. "I'm used to grown-up stuff, Dad. What's going on?"

Daniel put a hand on his son's shoulder. "We'll talk about it when we get home, Joey."

The uncertainty on the boy's face shot an arrow straight into Tessa's heart. They'd removed him from one intolerable situation only to land him in another. How could Daniel's children survive something like this? How could *Daniel* survive it? "Where's Teddy?" she asked Keely in an unsteady voice.

"Aunt Steph still has her. As soon as she saw the TV report, she realized the people from Juvy might want to stick her in a foster home. Aunt Steph told me to tell anybody who asked to call Uncle Tal, then she said she'd make sure he wasn't available." She shifted the bulky case. "But that'll only hold the media off temporarily, Mom. You know how they can be when they're out for somebody's blood—and this time it's yours. They're using this garbage about Daniel to try to destroy you."

"And Sojourn," Tessa murmured. She knew there were people who dismissed what she tried to do as simply pandering to kids. The type who thought troubled teens would straighten up after they were spanked soundly and sent to learn a lesson in a place where they got a good dose of reality. "When did this happen, Keely?"

"Only last night. None of us realized it would be in the paper today or I would have told you when you called. Aunt Stephanie said there was nothing you could do from New York, and besides, you were coming home today." She looked anxiously at her mother and then at Daniel. "Did I do wrong? Should I have called last night?"

Keely suddenly seemed very young. Tessa squeezed her hand reassuringly. "No, it's okay, Keely."

Daniel waited while a huge jet lifted off in a thunderous roar and rose majestically into the night sky. "When did they shut down Sojourn?"

"This morning. They took the kids to the Juvenile Detention Center, every single one of them."

Tessa made a helpless sound. The thought of Leon and Greg and Jacky confined in that cold, impersonal place with seasoned criminals was enough to make her cry.

"We'll get this all straightened out, Tessa," Daniel said in a clipped tone. "Don't worry."

How not to worry? Sojourn—or a place like it— might be the only alternative for kids like Leon and Greg and Jacky. She couldn't let a scandal destroy everything she'd worked for—her reputation, her career, her beliefs. Not to mention the loss of goodwill in the community that was finally coming to fruition.

And Daniel. She couldn't let anything ruin this chance for Joey and Teddy to spend the summer with their father. She'd wrecked his life once. Now it seemed she was the catalyst in another scandal in which Daniel was the victim.

With a hand out to urge Tessa in front of him, Daniel ushered his group out of the terminal into the infamous heat and humidity of New Orleans. They paused at the curb to wait while a shuttle bus and several taxis ignored the pedestrian crosswalk in a rush for fares. Off to one side, a tuxedo-clad man passed out handbills for a strip show on Bourbon Street. A limo slid soundlessly to a stop and four well-heeled businessmen got out. One look at them was enough to tell they'd had a rough night.

"Gosh, Dad," Joey said, wide-eyed. "Those guys are drunk and everybody sees it."

"Those guys have partied a little too well in the Big Easy, son. Sometimes it's tempting to do things in New Orleans that you wouldn't do in your hometown."

In the wide median halfway across the street, a clown was making animals and other whimsical shapes out of long, skinny balloons. Beside him, three young boys in threadbare clothes tap-danced tirelessly to music blaring from a boom box. Slightly to one side, a large metal paint can was conveniently provided with the words *Donations, Please* written in childish block print. Daniel fished a dollar out of his pants pocket and gave it to Joey to "donate."

"I think I'm gonna like it here," Joey said, grinning up at his dad. Daniel turned to look at Tessa, but today neither of them could share the boy's enthusiasm for the sounds and ambiance of New Orleans.

"You're driving, right, Keely?" he asked tightly.

"Yes, the car's in short-term parking. There's a little booth just outside the elevator. Why don't y'all wait there while I go and get it? Joey, you want to come with me?" With a knowing glance at the newspaper sticking out of Daniel's bag, she gave the boy a friendly smile. "Your dad and my mom can wait for us."

After being cooped up in airports and an airplane for most of the day, any chance to escape was enticing to Joey. "Is that okay, Dad?" he asked, poised to dash away.

Daniel nodded, managing a smile. "Sure. Just stay close to Keely in the garage."

Only when their children had disappeared in the maze of parked cars did Daniel trust himself to move. Quivering with fury, he slung his own hanging bag on the bench and then dumped Joey's duffel on top of it. Without looking at Tessa, he pulled the newspaper from the bag and shook it out savagely. With a derisive laugh, he struck it with the back of his hand. "In New York we worried about telling my children why they'd spent five years without a father. Well, Veillon sure as hell solved that problem for us, didn't he?"

Tessa didn't flinch, but her face was chalk white. "Give me the paper," she said. "I want to see for myself what he said."

He handed it over and felt a welling of angry impotence when her saw the way her hands trembled as she smoothed the paper on her lap. Her tawny hair fell forward, hiding her face, but not before he'd seen the brightness in her eyes. She looked ready to cry. Damn it, he hated causing Tessa pain. After all she'd done for him, this was what she got for her trouble.

A ruined reputation.

Her career in shambles.

The end of Sojourn.

She folded the paper and handed it back to him. "Don't worry," Tessa said, her eyes now cool and blank. "This is ugly and embarrassing for you, I understand that, but it won't jeopardize your plans for the summer with your children. I'll do whatever it takes to clear your name, Daniel. Now that Beth has renounced the custody terms, you have all the rights that other parents have who share custody. I'm just sorry that—"

"Wait a minute."

"What?"

"You're talking as if I'm the only injured party here, Tessa. You're telling me you'll do whatever it takes to clear *my* name when Veillon's sleazy feature harms you as much as me." He hunkered down in front of her, taking her hands in his. "I'm the one who should be apologizing—and I do, with all my heart. First I wormed my way in at Sojourn for the sole purpose of using the kids to help me find my daughter. Then I pushed and schemed and badgered until you agreed to take Teddy in, even though I knew all along that if my background ever came to light, it could do untold damage to your mission here."

"I knew the risks, Daniel."

"We both knew the risks and we did it anyway." He reached up and tucked her hair behind one ear. "I wonder why?"

For a long moment, they looked at each other. Car brakes screeched as vehicles made turns from one level in the parking garage to the next. Horns blew inside, aircraft roared outside. "I don't care what they say about me," Daniel said, looking into her damp, shadowy eyes. "I've already been there. Now I've got my kids back. I can face anything they throw at me."

When she started to object, he gave both her hands a little shake. "It's you I'm worried about. You probably should rue the day you ever saw me, but instead you're trying to reassure me that you'll try to smooth over another scandal in my life as if you were responsible for it."

"In a way, I am."

"We both are. So we're in this together. But I don't

give a damn, Tessa. If scandal is the price I pay to have you in my life, then it's a small one.''

"It's not just you and me," she said, her voice high with distress. "What about the kids? They're stuck in that place. You've never seen it, Daniel. You don't know how traumatizing it can be for a girl like Jacky. She was coming along so well. We talked Saturday about calling her parents, but after this who knows what she'll do?''

He got up to sit beside her on the bench, still holding her hands. "I promise you this, Tessa. Sojourn will reopen, we'll get those kids back and you'll still be the heart and soul of it. The document we got from Beth's lawyer takes the teeth out of Veillon's charges.''

She looked away. "I don't know, Daniel. These things aren't so easily reversed." Bringing her gaze back to his, she said simply, "Duplantis did this.''

His gaze fell to the headlines on the battered newspaper. "You think so?''

"Who else? Veillon left the open house Sunday in a good frame of mind about Sojourn. Monday morning the sheriff came by with one last appeal on behalf of Duplantis's nephew. I refused again. They both know they can't force me to take in a juvenile I consider violent.''

"So the sheriff is willing to see a worthwhile program go down the tubes if you won't play ball with the locals? Is that how you see it?''

She waited until a noisy pickup sped past. "I'm not certain the sheriff approved what Duplantis did. After all, Sojourn's been getting a lot of good press, and that fact's not lost on him. He's an astute politician. My guess is that Duplantis did this on his own. His first visit to my office proved that he has no capacity for compassion. He's shortsighted and not too bright. Without giving a thought to the long-term loss, out of sheer maliciousness he's destroyed Sojourn.''

''He may have destroyed his own career while he was busy trashing yours,'' Daniel said. ''If we can prove he accessed those sealed documents illegally, he'll pay with his job. And any access would *have* to be illegal except by express permission from Beth or me through our lawyers.''

She sighed. ''Even so, it will probably be a very long time before I regain the trust of the public, if ever.''

He turned her hands loose and sat back, leaning his head against the wall of the cubicle. ''I've screwed things up royally for you, haven't I?''

She watched another huge jet lift off in a deafening roar. ''Well, things do look pretty dismal right now, but...'' she turned her head with a faint smile ''...I can't seem to make myself regret seeing you again.''

He sat up straight and looked at her. The cubicle where they waited was dingy, like a much used bus stop. Some effort had been made to remove graffiti, but some survived. He laughed shortly as he looked around.

''This isn't exactly the place I would have chosen to say this, Tessa, but we may not have another minute to ourselves again soon. I wanted my kids here in Louisiana with me, but at the moment I'm wishing I could stash them somewhere for a day or so until we get this all sorted out. But since that's impossible, hell, I don't know when I'll get another chance to tell you. I love you, Tessa.''

"Oh, Daniel..."

"I can't believe my good luck in bumping into you just at the right time in my life."

She groaned helplessly. "If this is good luck, Daniel, then please deliver me from bad. First Florida, now this. My God, it's almost as if I'm personally fated to be the instrument of your destruction.''

"Why can't it be exactly the opposite?"

One tawny brow lifted skeptically.

He leaned forward to make his point. "Just think about it. Tessa, you and only you had the power to bring Teddy and me together at Sojourn. You've already admitted you were reluctant to testify against me in Florida. That you had grave doubts even then about the charges. What are the odds that we'd meet again, that you'd have a chance to explore that? And yet we wind up in the same city, we meet by chance at NOPD when I'm looking for my runaway daughter, and you've actually seen her." Daniel almost held his breath. He needed her to believe as he did that they were meant to be together.

"Finding Teddy alone is enough to make me believe in a benevolent fate, Tessa. And the frosting on the cake was Beth signing that document. Having you along—a person she knew to be of high integrity and dedicated to the welfare of children—made it happen.''

She got up and moved to the back of the cubicle. Looking down, she watched cars and shuttles and taxis jockeying for space. She wanted to believe him. She wanted to seize any shred of hope that would link her heart and his, this man she'd never dared to dream could love her.

She felt him come up behind her, and her eyes closed as he slipped his arms around her waist.

"I love you, Tessa," he said, drawing her closer. "And I think you love me, too."

With a soft sigh, she turned into the haven of his arms. "But we're in such a mess, Daniel. How can we ever survive it?"

"Together, sweetheart. We'll survive it together. I was alone the last time I was in a big mess, but if I know I have you to come home to, in my life and in my heart, then I can take on anything they throw at me."

"Oh, Daniel…"

He pressed her against his heart and rested his chin on the top of her head. "Oh, Daniel…what?" he asked, and she felt him smiling as he stroked her back.

"I love you, Daniel."

"Ahh, that's what I wanted to hear, darling." He gathered her to him forcefully, almost lifting her off her feet, and covered her mouth in a soul-stirring kiss. And then a sharp honk from a car horn broke them apart.

"It's Keely." Flustered, Tessa scrambled to smooth her hair and find her purse, refusing to look at her daughter. Daniel was unabashed. He scooped up his bag and Joey's as if they weighed nothing.

"Pop the trunk, Keely," he ordered in a jubilant voice. While Tessa waited, he strode to the rear and slung their baggage inside, then banged the lid down. Since Joey had claimed the passenger seat beside

Keely, he and Tessa climbed into the back. She was even more unsettled when Joey turned around, obviously intrigued.

"Is this another thing people do here they wouldn't do in their hometown, Dad? Kissing right in front of everybody?"

Keely made a choked sound.

Daniel squeezed Tessa's hand. "Yeah. I guess you could say that, Joey."

Joey's gaze centered on their clasped hands, then looked up at Tessa, who was beet red. "I guess it's a good thing you aren't married, huh, Tessa?"

"Turn around and buckle your seat belt, son," Daniel said.

Keely stayed studiously quiet, but when Tessa finally met her eyes in the rearview mirror, she was laughing.

"YOU'VE GOT a ton of messages, Mom."

Tessa tossed her bag onto the bed and wearily kicked off her shoes. "Don't tell me, let me guess. Pete Veillon wants to reschedule our interview."

"Here, see for yourself." Keely separated half a dozen pink message slips and handed them over. "And those are just the ones from him that I picked up on. Your voice mail is loaded, too."

Tessa tossed the messages from Veillon aside unread. She'd like nothing better than to ignore him until hell froze over, but if she wanted to save Sojourn, she would have to talk to him. First and foremost, however, she needed to get her thoughts in order. She put a hand to her temple and rubbed a spot that throbbed painfully. Veillon was no fool. Now that he'd drawn first blood, he would be thirsty for more. He wasn't the type to drop something so juicy before milking it of every drop of scandal.

Off the top of her head she hadn't a clue what strategy to use. About the only thing she knew for certain was that she wanted Daniel with her when she talked to the reporter. Daniel was just as much a victim in this fiasco as the kids at Sojourn.

She drew in a deep breath and reached for the remaining phone slips. "Is there anything pleasant in here? Doesn't anyone believe we are what we say we are at Sojourn?"

"A few, Mom, but you'll have to admit that it looks bad about Daniel. If I didn't know him personally, I might be tempted to believe that stuff about him, too. But I do know him and I know he could never have come on to teenage girls at his school. It's ludicrous."

Tessa smiled. "You'll have to tell him that when you see him next, Keely. He could probably use some moral support right now."

"You love him, don't you, Mom?"

She shifted her gaze from the phone slips to Keely. "Yes. Are you okay with that?"

"Only if you're going to marry him."

"He hasn't asked me. Yet."

Keely grinned. "But he will. He's got that look."

Tessa's smile faded as she frowned at a phone message. "Who's this, Keely? Judith Winston."

Keely leaned over to read the message, then took it from Tessa. "I'm trying to recall... Winston...Judith Winston." She tapped the pink slip against her lips, thinking. "Oh, yeah, I remember her now. She was obsessing over this big time, Mom. Most of the calls were people just wanting to diss us. You know how people get over sex and scandal nowadays. I didn't even take down names for those. But this lady had watched Veillon's piece on TV and she wasn't calling to trash Mr. Kendrick—that's what she called Daniel. She asked if I knew where he was, because she'd called his place and he hadn't replied to any of her messages. She insisted on leaving her name and number for you, but all she said was that she had to speak to you or Daniel.'' Keely handed the slip back. "I remember that, specifically. She said she *had* to talk to you."

"Judith Winston," Tessa murmured again, trying to put a face to the name, but drawing a blank. Then after a moment, she put the slip in the meager stack to be answered. Most of the others she'd crumpled up and tossed into a trash can. People could be so cruel.

When she finished, there were very few calls she chose to return. Marly Toups was the most difficult. Tessa suffered through a severe tongue-lashing over the backdoor tactics she had used to get Teddy into Sojourn. When Marly had vented enough, Tessa filled her in on Beth's about-face.

Marly was somewhat sympathetic when she heard that Daniel's wife had petitioned the court to allow him to have his children, but she was cautious about commenting on whether or not she would recommend reopening Sojourn. Tessa made an appointment for her and Daniel to meet with Marly in two days. She *had* to persuade Marly to give her a second chance.

She called Travis, who'd left an encouraging message, and thanked him for his support. Also a nurse at the free clinic who was a good friend. And Camille Landry, the woman who'd taken her and Stephanie in when they arrived in New Orleans. All in all, Tessa made about a dozen calls before dialing the number left by Judith Winston.

She glanced at the time as the number rang and debated whether to have a snack. She hadn't eaten anything since leaving New York, but maybe she would forgo a meal in favor of a long soak in the tub, then crawl into bed. Alone.

Her thoughts drifted to Daniel, as they so often did. After swinging by Stephanie's house to pick up Teddy, Keely had driven him and his children to the farmhouse.

Tessa smiled now thinking of the look on the kids' faces as they'd pulled up in front of the rambling old homestead. Cat had been sitting on the steps as if he knew just when to expect his new family. To everyone's astonishment, when Joey had darted over and scooped him up, Cat had suffered the indignity calmly.

Then, while Daniel got their luggage out of the trunk, Teddy had discovered the porch swing. She'd shoved off, leaning back in it with her eyes closed as it squeaked on its metal chains, back and forth, back and forth. For a second, Daniel had simply stood watching her, then he'd unlocked the front door to let them inside before turning back to Tessa and pulling her into his arms. "I wish you could stay," he'd whispered.

"Not tonight," she'd told him, reluctantly backing away. "Tonight's for you and Teddy and Joey."

In spite of the scandal that had met them when they

landed in New Orleans and the shadow cast on Daniel's name here where he had hoped to put his past behind him, there was quiet joy in his face as he walked her back to the car.

"I'll call first thing tomorrow," he promised, squeezing her hand. He'd waited until she was seated beside Keely, then he'd bent down and given her a quick goodbye kiss before turning to go inside to be alone with his children for the first time in five years.

Tessa was still recalling that moment when someone finally answered the phone. "Hello."

Tessa straightened, looking at the pink slip in her hand. "Hello. Is this Judith Winston?"

"Yes." The tone was coolly polite.

"Ms. Winston, this is Tessa Hamilton."

A gasp. "Oh, thank God. I've been waiting and worrying. I'm so glad you called, Ms. Hamilton. When it looked like Mr. Kendrick wasn't going to let me talk to him, I hoped I would be able to get through to you. I know this is a bad time. I can only imagine what it must be like for you, but I felt like I just had to try one more time. Mr. Kendrick has ignored all my messages, so—"

"Ms. Winston," Tessa said, forced to interrupt the woman, "Why are you calling me when it's Daniel you want to talk to?"

There was an instant of silence. "Of course, it's... Naturally, you don't know who I am." She gave a nervous laugh. "Well, actually, you do, but you wouldn't recognize my married name. I didn't think—" She took a breath, then ended in a rush. "I'm Judith Lovell, Ms. Hamilton."

Tessa sat up straight. "Judith Lovell?" she repeated. "Judy. *Judy Lovell.* From Florida?"

"Yes, that's me. Or rather, it was me." She paused. "Dear God, this is so...difficult. After all I've done..." She took a deep breath. "Ms. Hamilton, could you please tell me how I can get in touch with Mr. Kendrick?"

CHAPTER SIXTEEN

TESSA FOUND DANIEL in the barn. "What on earth are you doing out here?" she asked, stepping inside the wide door. "It's after midnight, Daniel."

Daniel threw down the plane he'd been using to shave the edge from a piece of heart pine. "What's wrong? What's happened? Has Duplantis—"

"No, no. It's Judy Lovell."

"What?"

"Judy Lovell. Daniel, didn't you pick up the messages on your answering machine?"

"I heard as much as I could take, then I just quit listening and erased the tape." He stripped work gloves from his hands and tossed them aside. "What about Judy Lovell? Did you hear from Cypress House? Do they have an address?"

She gave him a jubilant hug. "You're not going to believe this," she said, stepping away to pace around his work space. "She tried to call you and tell you herself, but all she got was your machine, because you were in New York. Which she wouldn't have any way of knowing." She stopped, pulled her hair away from her face with one hand and smiled. "That's when she decided to call me, although I was gone, too. So she left a message with Keely."

"And the message was..." He leaned against his

workbench with his arms crossed over his chest, waiting.

"She's retracting everything she said about you, Daniel. Everything. It was all lies."

His face went slack. He dropped his arms slowly to his sides. "What?"

"It was her father, Daniel, not you. She apologized over and over."

"She admitted, straight-out, that she lied?"

"Yes."

He turned away, thrusting a hand through his hair. "Why, for God's sake?"

She came up behind him, touched his back gently. "Maybe you should hear it from her, Daniel."

"I don't want to hear it from her. I couldn't trust myself to speak to her without—" He kicked at some wood shavings at his feet. "Maybe I should just leave it at that."

"I know how you feel. She wrecked your life, she knows that. She's trying to make amends."

He picked up a hammer with a bitter twist of his mouth. "Can she give me back five years without my kids? Can she erase a thousand insults and rejections? Can she give me back my job?" The hammer landed in a tool tray with a clatter. "Can she give me back my freaking *life!*"

Tessa leaned against his arm, shaking her head silently. Without looking at her, Daniel touched her hair, pressed her face against him.

"It's too late, Tessa."

Tessa lifted her head to look at him. "No, it isn't, Daniel. It's never too late to right a wrong. Besides, this is your chance to clear your name publicly. Even though Beth has agreed to let you share custody of Teddy and Joey, everyone's aware of the details now, thanks to Veillon's exposé on TV. The only person who can make a difference is willing to go public and retract everything she said. Only Judy Lovell can wipe the slate clean, Daniel.''

''I've just got my kids for the first time in five years. I don't want them to see my name splashed all over the papers and TV. I don't want them to hear that garbage.''

''They will. They probably already have, Daniel. Do you think Teddy hasn't heard the scandal?''

''If she has, she didn't mention it tonight.''

''Possibly because she thought that if she didn't mention the elephant in the kitchen, it wouldn't exist.'' She clutched his arm, keeping her eyes on his face. ''But she's smart, Daniel. She's putting two and two together, you can bet on that.''

Tessa's hand was moving, caressing his arm as if to comfort and persuade. ''You're going to have to deal with this, Daniel. Judy Lovell is doing the right thing.''

He drew in a deep breath. ''I didn't want to have to explain everything to Teddy and Joey until we could do it together the way we discussed in New York. They were tired tonight. They could barely keep their eyes open long enough to eat a sandwich and fall into bed. I was going to call you tomorrow morning and ask you to come over.''

She nuzzled the point of his shoulder with her cheek. ''And I would have, Daniel. I will. But this must be done, too.''

After another moment of silence, he asked, "When does she want to talk?"

"Soon, I think. And she's willing to tell it to Veillon, too, in front of a camera."

He turned and pulled her close, resting his chin on her head. "God, it'll be a circus."

She nodded, feeling the beat of his heart, warm and strong.

"Well, one good thing," he said, holding her fast, "is that this will vindicate you, and Sojourn can be opened again."

It probably would accomplish that, but she wished he and his children could be spared the publicity. From the haven of his arms, she gazed around the old barn. He had an expensive array of equipment, everything well maintained. Cabinetry was stacked here and there in various stages of completion. Toward the rear were several ornate antiques in various stages of restoration. Daniel had built a prosperous business here. It dawned on her suddenly that he'd been working.

"Have you fallen so far behind that you've got to work at midnight?" she murmured, sifting her fingers through the hair on the back of his head.

"Nah, I couldn't sleep." He paused, looking at his workplace without actually seeing anything. "I was trying to figure some way to head off the scandal and restore Sojourn to you."

"Enter Judy Lovell."

"I guess."

Tessa peered through the darkened rear of the barn to the old horse stalls. "I bet you're going to get horses for the kids now, huh?"

She felt his smile at her temple. "How'd you guess?"

"Smells like new hay."

"I ordered it before we left for New York."

They were both silent for another minute or two. Daniel's hands moved sensuously over her shoulders and down to her hips. She made a little sound and pulled back to look at him. Even in the dim light of the barn, she could see that look in his eye.

"What?" she said.

"Are you thinking what I'm thinking?"

She smiled, enjoying herself suddenly. "I bet hay isn't half as romantic as it's supposed to be."

"We could always check it out, sugar." In two beats, he had her hand and was leading her toward the last stall. Before she had a chance to say anything else, he pulled her down on the fresh hay. "Well, what d'you think?" he asked, his mouth a scant inch from hers.

She drew him into a kiss. "It's scratchy, but who's complaining?"

In another second he had pulled her on top of him and was tugging at the tails of her shirt. The shirt went one way, her bra another, and she sighed as he kissed one turgid nipple.

"Are the kids going to be okay while we do this?" she managed to ask. "What if they call and you don't hear?"

"No problem. I've got a baby monitor." He fumbled at the snap of her jeans.

"A *baby* monitor?" She gasped as he kissed her belly button.

"It gets the job done," he said thickly, working his

way down. "Now, just close your eyes and enjoy, sugar."

No problem.

JUDY LOVELL ASKED to meet with Daniel and Tessa at Sojourn, and then afterward, Pete Veillon, armed with crew and minicam, was coming to interview her. He planned to air the feature on the late-night newscast.

Judy arrived on time, a tall, slim brunette in pale yellow silk blouse and white linen pants. "I was afraid if we were in a restaurant or some place more public that I'd get emotional and people would stare." She made a face. "The embarrassment's going to come soon enough. There's no virtue in being a glutton for punishment." She gave them a brief smile. "A quote from my therapist."

Tessa met Daniel's eyes. His expression was unreadable.

Judy gazed around, taking in the spacious foyer and the sweeping curve of the staircase. "This is such a nice place. But so empty. My fault, huh?" She gave Tessa a nervous smile, clutching her purse with both hands. "I admire you for the work you do, Ms. Hamilton. I'm so sorry to be the cause of Sojourn's trouble. But for once maybe I can be the cause of something good." Except for that first brief greeting, she studiously avoided looking at Daniel.

Tessa gestured toward her office. "We can talk in here."

Daniel waited while both women sat on the sofa, then took the chair nearest Tessa. She suspected he'd like to be up and pacing, he looked that ill at ease, but he sat anyway, crossing his ankle over one knee. The only evidence of his nervousness was the way he jiggled his foot. As soon as he realized it, he stopped.

Judy Lovell was tense, too, but determined. She was a beautiful young woman, and her outfit hadn't been bought at Wal-Mart, Tessa thought. She tried to recall if at sixteen, she had guessed how lovely Judy would grow up to be, but she could bring to mind only a shattered, scared young girl. As a professional, Tessa spotted some signs of that girl, but like many victims of sexual molestation, Judy had learned to disguise her damaged soul.

She dropped her bag—a signature Chanel—on the floor beside her, clasped her hands tightly, took a deep breath, and looked directly at Daniel. "I'm sorry, Mr. Kendrick."

Daniel sat unmoving, his expression stern. Unforgiving.

"I know those words mean nothing compared to the pain and suffering I caused when I told those lies, but I wanted to say them anyway. Janna—she's my therapist—Janna says taking responsibility for what I did instead of shifting it to my father is the first step to healing. The problem is, I keep wanting to explain so you'll understand that I lied because my father had been having sex with me since I was eleven and I didn't think I could take it another day. Or because he threatened to hurt my mother if I didn't keep my mouth shut. Or because my ten-year-old sister was going to be his next victim and I had to say something—to bring attention to what was going on—or it would continue."

Tears welled in her eyes and she put her clasped

hands to her unsteady mouth. "But none of that can excuse the horrible injustice to you and your kids," she said huskily. "Can it?"

Daniel stood abruptly and walked to the window. With his back to them, he stared out at the grounds of Sojourn. He wanted to throw her words back in her face, beautiful and young and wounded as she was, goddamn it. He wanted to yell at her that the sordid, ugly picture she painted of her childhood didn't cut any ice with him. He wanted to say nothing justified what she'd stolen from his kids—*his kids, damn it*—when she'd shifted her old man's sins onto him.

Behind him, he heard the rustle of movement, then the clasp of her handbag opening. She blew her nose discreetly. "I'm so sorry, Mr. Kendrick."

"Daniel," he said shortly.

He sensed her surprise and turned around. "I'm not the principal any longer, Judy. I'm a carpenter."

More tears poured down her face. "I hated that...when you lost your job. You were such a good teacher. Everyone...was so...sh-shocked."

"Yeah, me most of all."

"I don't think I realized the harm I'd done until I heard all the nasty things they said about you."

Even now, the memory of it made Daniel sweat.

She wiped her eyes with a wad of tissue. "I wanted to take it all back the minute I saw the trouble you were in."

"The custody hearing would have been a good time."

"But my father—" She stopped and shuddered. "The day of that hearing I told him I was going to tell Ms. Hamilton the truth and try to straighten everything out. He said if I did, there would be a divorce, I could count on that, because my mother would surely want to divorce him. And he'd go to prison, too. And if he did, there would be no money coming in for my mother to keep the family together. We'd be homeless, her, my sister and me. And I had the power to prevent all that, he told me. I was sixteen, Mr. Kendrick. I believed him.''

Daniel walked back to the chair and sat down heavily. "So what happened?"

"With you conveniently tagged with his crimes, he walked. I mean, he left us. Looking back, I think he knew he was incredibly lucky that he wasn't serving a jail sentence.''

"So even though you went ahead and ruined me, he still abandoned your mother and everything he threatened came to pass.''

"No, he dropped out of our lives, but he sent checks regularly. He was an engineer and made good money, but an accusation coming from me would ruin him. I haven't seen him since, and neither has my mother.''

"You never told her?''

"I did, but only after I went into therapy. That was eighteen months ago. I enrolled at Florida State University, but I had trouble concentrating.'' She was silent for a minute, wiping her eyes again, burrowing for another tissue, closing the handbag. She turned her hands palms up and held them out for him to see. "I only went into therapy when this happened.''

Daniel stared at the fine red lines crisscrossing her wrists and felt a sick twist in his gut. He wanted to break something—the old man's neck was a good place to start. God, the atrocities some men were capable of.

Beside Judy, Tessa made a soft, sympathetic sound and put her hand on the young woman's knee. "This must be so hard," she whispered.

Daniel scrubbed his face with both hands. "God, I'm sorry, Judy."

She smiled sadly. "Everyone's sorry. Except Daddy."

"Where is he now?"

"Denver. Or somewhere in Colorado, I suppose. The checks were from a bank in Denver."

"Won't they stop when you go public with this?" Daniel asked.

"Who cares? Once I got the courage to tell my mother, she stopped cashing them anyway." She shrugged with a humorless laugh. "Besides, maybe somebody who knows him will find out about it and they'll throw his ass in jail."

"Better late than never," Tessa murmured.

"Exactly," Judy said.

"How did you find me?" Daniel asked.

"It was just a twist of fate, I guess. I've been trying to locate you on the Internet for a while now to make amends, but I haven't had any luck. I didn't know where you'd gone, you see. So Janna was here in New Orleans for a psychiatric conference this past weekend and she saw the feature that reporter did. And even though they didn't mention my name, they talked about Cypress House in Florida, and naturally, from hearing my sessions, Janna knew that was where I had been. She also recognized Tessa's name. She called me right away, and I called the TV station and identified myself as the victim.''

Daniel snorted with disgust. ''That must have made their day.''

''Knowing I was now legally an adult, they jumped at the chance to air all the details.'' She smiled. ''However, I didn't leave a name or number. I knew I had to talk to you before I blew Mr. Veillon out of the water. But first I had to reach a real live person…'' she shot Tessa a grateful look ''…so, once Ms. Hamilton—Tessa—returned my call, I drove straight to New Orleans. It's not too far. I live in Pensacola now.''

Tessa glanced at her watch. ''Are you still serious about going public with this? Because Veillon's due in about fifteen minutes.''

''Yes. Absolutely.'' She looked at Daniel. ''Provided you're okay with this whole thing, Mr. Kendrick?''

''Daniel,'' he repeated. ''*Okay*'s a mild word for how I feel. If you tell them what you've just told Tessa and me, it will reverse about five years of bad history. Plus, it will give a big boost to Tessa's case for reopening Sojourn.''

''If certain people like Marly Toups won't hold a grudge and Sheriff Wade won't get on a high horse,'' Tessa put in cynically.

''I don't know about Sheriff Wade,'' Daniel said, ''but I bet Marly will be in your corner again by the time the credits roll on the newscast tonight.''

''My husband has some pretty strong connections in the mayor's office,'' Judy said. ''He'll pull out all the stops to help you.''

"Your husband?" Daniel glanced at Tessa, who looked blank.

"His brother's your state senator. For this parish, you know?"

Daniel stared for a second. "Roscoe Winston."

"That's him." Judy sat up a little straighter. "So, I guess we're all clear for the main event, huh?"

"It'll be brutal once the media gets hold of this, Judy," he warned, still distracted by how casually she'd dropped the name of one of the state's most powerful politicians. "Although a lot of people will admire you, there'll be some who won't dismiss what you've done lightly. Veillon's already told the world that I've been kept from my kids for five years for fear I'll molest them, and he insinuated I was at Sojourn to prey upon adolescent girls. With your sudden appearance on the scene, the scandal gets even juicier. He'll be so smooth switching sides that he'd make a seasoned debater look like an amateur."

"I can handle it," she said firmly. "The hard part was telling you."

He added dryly, "I wouldn't mention Roscoe Winston if I were you."

"Okay," she said.

"Uh-oh, guys." Tessa watched from the window as a TV minivan pulled up in front of the house. "It's show time."

TESSA SAT in front of the TV in the living room at Sojourn as the newscast wound down. As soon as the spot with Judy Lovell had run, Keely had taken Teddy and Joey to get ice cream, making it clear they would be gone a long time. Daniel was in the kitchen getting a beer when the phone rang.

Tessa stared at it, debating whether or not to let the machine take it. Whoever it was, she thought, if it was favorable and friendly, she'd take it as an omen that Judy's confession was enough to correct the five-year-long injustice to Daniel and to restore Sojourn. If it was mean and ugly...

She picked it up. "Hello?"

"Evening, Ms. Hamilton. This is Sheriff Wade."

She took in a deep breath, but it was too late to hang up. "Sheriff. How are you?"

"Fine, fine. You catch that newscast just now, Ms. Hamilton?"

"I did, Sheriff."

"Incredible the way that little gal absolved your friend of any hint of wrongdoing 'way back in Florida, wasn't it?"

"I like to think it was heartwarming, Sheriff."

"Oh, yes. 'Course, as I mentioned a few days ago, I was disturbed by the rumors circulating about Sojourn and the company you were keeping out there, Ms. Hamilton. Not being privy to the truth, you understand."

"I do understand."

Daniel appeared with his beer. She patted the space beside her, and when he sat down, she tipped the receiver so he could hear the sheriff.

"You know, when there are children involved, we can't be too careful."

"I agree with you there, Sheriff. Absolutely."

"And I got a good feeling about your place when we talked last week. I was impressed by you personally, Ms. Hamilton, I don't mind saying that. I understood perfectly why you couldn't accept a young hoodlum like Kyle Faciane into your care."

"I appreciate that, Sheriff." She rolled her eyes at Daniel.

"Which brings me to the point I'm wanting to make." She heard the sound of his chair creaking. Was the man in his office at this hour? "I don't condone vindictiveness in my staff. Law enforcement is a sacred trust. When that power is used to bring harm to any constituent in my jurisdiction, I take umbrage, ma'am."

"I don't quite follow you, Sheriff," she said cautiously.

"The inner workings at Sojourn should never have been made public the way they were—suspicions based on half-truths, personal vendettas, plain old meanness. No, ma'am, I don't condone that kind of behavior in my people. A lawman takes a wrong turn like that, it can bring about a lot of grief. Then I got to clean it up."

"Uh-huh."

"It was pure spite that made Dwayne leak the details of Mr. Kendrick's sealed court records."

"We suspected your man, Sheriff."

"Not my man anymore, ma'am. I stripped Duplantis of his badge and gun as of an hour ago."

She gazed dumbfounded at Daniel.

"You still there, Ms. Hamilton?"

"Yes. Oh, yes, Sheriff. I'm right here."

"He went off half-cocked, I'm sorry to say. Can't have him blackening a man's name, forcing troubled kids into more trouble...makes the voters nervous, that kind of stuff.'' There was a harrumphing sound. ''I take full responsibility, of course.''

''Of course,'' she said faintly.

''I'll drive on out to Mr. Kendrick's place tomorrow morning and express a formal apology on behalf of my department.''

''He'll probably be very glad to get it,'' she said with a wicked look at Daniel.

''And I'll be going into Noo Awlins right afterward and have a talk with Ms. Marly Toups. In Juvenile, you understand?''

''Oh, yes, sir.''

''We'll see if we can't get you up and running again before the week's out, you hear?''

''Thank you, Sheriff Wade.''

''You have a good evenin' now.''

''You, too.''

''And drop by my department any time you find there's something we can do to help you turn those kids around. Worthwhile project, ma'am. We need more people with good hearts, yes, indeed we do.''

''Goodbye, Sheriff.''

She hung up the phone and threw herself into Daniel's arms. ''He's fired! Duplantis is history, the jerk!'' She reared back to look at him. ''Could you believe that blarney Sheriff Wade was laying on me? I'll bet he was shocked to get a lot of calls in support of Sojourn. He's having to do some major damage control.'' She grinned. ''What d'you think? It just doesn't get any better than this, right?''

''Blarney?'' Daniel repeated, lifting his eyebrows.

''I'm Irish. I never told you.''

''First a tattoo, now this.'' He grabbed her and fell

on top of her among the soft, oversize cushions on the sofa. "What other secrets are you keeping from me, woman?"

FOR THE PAST ten minutes, the late-night staff at McDonald's had been directing looks at Keely and the kids hinting that it was almost closing time. Glancing at her watch, Keely saw they'd been gone almost an hour. She stood up after collecting used napkins, plastic spoons and sundae cups from the table and carried the lot to the disposal bins at the front door.

"You can bring your drinks if you want to," she told Teddy and Joey, who trailed behind. "Just don't spill anything in Mom's car."

"Okay." Joey moved ahead and went outside. Keely caught and held the glass door for Teddy. First they'd driven by the lakefront, killing time, then they'd decided to take a walk along the shore before stopping for the promised ice cream. It should be safe to go back now, she decided.

Teddy grabbed her arm before she could unlock the Camry. "Keely, look! It's Jake, and he's driving Sojourn's van."

Keely blinked in surprise as the long Chevy van with the shelter's logo on the front door panel pulled up in the space beside the Camry and stopped. The side door slid open and Leon jumped out, following by Curtis.

"Yo. How you doin', Keely?"

With a dazed look, she lifted a hand to high-five Leon. Behind the two boys, she could see Greg and Jacky sharing a seat. Farther back were half a dozen more Sojourn alumni. As she gaped, Jake Raymond got out from the driver's side and came toward her. He was grinning.

"Is this a jailbreak?" she asked Jake.

"With this group, it might look like that, but we're legit."

She was shaking her head. "What's going on? Who... How... You're all supposed to be at the parish correctional center!"

"Uh-uh." Leon rearranged his cap so that the bill was in back. "We been sprung. After the TV spot tonight, Mr. Jake here called the sheriff and talked him into lettin' us go back home."

"Home," she repeated faintly.

"Sojourn, girl, what you think?"

Keely looked at Jake. "Is that right?"

"More or less. After Veillon's piece exonerated Daniel, I suspected that it would behoove the sheriff to get Sojourn's kids out of correctional and back where they belong as soon as possible." He shoved his hands in his pockets, fighting a grin. "He agreed."

"You called Mom?"

"I thought we'd surprise her."

"She's going to be so happy," Keely said, still flabbergasted.

"Yeah, the sheriff said he'd spoken to her, which probably relieved her mind, but she'll like having the kids back at Sojourn." Jake gestured at the Golden Arches. "They conned me into stopping for burgers and fries before we went back."

"She's missed everyone so much. She's there with Daniel right now. We were just heading back." She put a hand on Joey's shoulder. "This is Daniel's son, Joey."

Leon blinked in mock amazement and stepped back, making his eyes go round and white. "Who'd you say this little dude is?"

"You heard right. Daniel's son. He's visiting from New York. Joey, meet the gang from Sojourn—Leon, Curtis, Greg, Jacky, Rachel..." she bent to see deeper into the van and introduced half a dozen others who called out in friendly voices.

"Hi," Joey said cheerfully.

"Hey, kid, are you really Mr. Dan's boy?" Leon pretended to study him thoughtfully.

"Yeah," Joey said a little warily now.

"Well, show me somethin', my man!" He held up his palm to high-five Joey. "'Cause if you're anything like your daddy, me and you gonna be tight. Real tight."

"You like my Dad?"

"Like him? Mr. Dan's the Man, son. They don't come better'n Mr. Dan."

Joey turned a bright face up to Keely, then gave them all a big smile. "I think I'm gonna like it here."

BACK AT SOJOURN, Tessa scrambled to gather up her clothes and find her shoes, to pick up cushions and toss them back onto the sofa. She scooped up Daniel's jeans, but just before throwing them at him, she had to stop and admire the way he looked sprawled on the carpet in front of the sofa, propped on one elbow as naked as the day he was born. He looked sweaty and sated and...

"Gorgeous. You're gorgeous," she said, holding

her clothes in a wad against herself. "Did I ever tell you that?"

He grinned. "The feeling's mutual."

For a time, too much time, they simply gazed at each other. She was so comfortable with Daniel. She felt so right with him, as if he were the one man she was meant to be with for the rest of her life. But she couldn't stand here all night mooning over him.

"We've got to get dressed, Daniel. Keely's going to drive up any minute with Teddy and Joey." She started to shake out her blouse.

"Wait." He got up and reached for her, pulling her into his arms. "I forgot something."

"Mmm, what?" It was a beautifully erotic feeling, their arms around each other, both of them naked. He was warm, smoothly muscled, strong. She closed her eyes and rocked with him.

"I forgot to propose."

Her eyes popped open and he stopped rocking. Waiting. She pushed back a tiny bit and looked up at him. "Are you sure?"

He dropped a kiss on her forehead. "I've never been more sure about anything, Tessa. I love you. I want to be married to you."

She waited a minute. "What would we do?"

"You mean about Sojourn?" She nodded. "What we're doing now, of course. We make a good team, don't we?"

"Yes, but what about your business?"

"I can still run the business. I'll hire people, but I'll want to live here with you. I've missed teaching. If I can talk the right people into it, I can take on a few of the kids who want to learn woodworking and carpentry. I can't see you being away from Sojourn, not when these kids need so much one-on-one attention."

"You'd do that?"

He smiled, kissing her softly. "I would do whatever it takes to have you as my wife. So, how about it? Will you marry me, Tessa Hamilton?"

"Yes. Of course."

"Yes, of course?" He was still smiling. "You mean I could have gotten a yes even without all those concessions?"

She laughed. "I didn't say that."

They stood quietly again for a few moments, then Tessa pulled away to start dressing.

"She never did ask you to forgive her, did you notice that?"

"Who, Judy?" Head bent, Daniel snapped his jeans. "I'm glad. I don't know if I could have answered yes honestly, and I sure as hell didn't want to say no point-blank, especially after seeing those scars on her wrist."

Tessa shook out her denim skirt and stepped into it. "Do you think you *can* ever forgive her?"

He didn't reply right away. "She was a sixteen-year-old in a helluva bind," he said finally. "I knew there was trouble in her family, but I didn't know what. She was in my office a lot. I thought she was one of those kids with an absentee dad looking for a replacement. It surprised me to find out that her parents were living together." Dressed now, he moved to the window. "Maybe I was partly to blame for not being more astute, for not sensing the danger in being too kind to young girls like Judy."

"Which is a sad comment on our society today,"
Tessa said.

Daniel shifted, then leaned with his back against
the window frame and pulled her between his thighs.
"So, yeah, I guess I can forgive her. I'd be pretty
churlish not to, since she's taken the high road and
faced down the media, wouldn't I?"

"You could never be churlish," she said, tracing
the shape of his mouth. She loved his mouth.

He kissed her finger. "It's her old man I'd like to
see crucified over this, but he'll probably never get
his."

"Oh, I don't know. What goes around comes
around," Tessa said. "Look at Duplantis."

"No, thanks. Never again if I can help it."

She sighed, snuggling a little closer. "Everything
has worked out so well, hasn't it, Daniel? It's almost
spooky. A few days ago, it seemed everything was
unraveling. My whole world, and yours, too. Then
Beth was suddenly willing to give you your children.
Next, Judy showed up ready to clear your name. And
from that, everything else just fell into place."

"Didn't I say we were meant to be together?"

"I just wish the kids weren't marooned in the parish correctional. Even with an all clear, you'd be
amazed how much red tape there'll be trying to get
them back."

"I wouldn't be too sure about that."

"What?" Following his gaze, she looked out the
window. "Is it Keely?"

"Yes, and isn't that the Sojourn van pulling up
beside her?"

"It's Jake Raymond." She looked a little closer.

"And Leon. And Curtis." She fumbled for Daniel's shirtsleeve. "It's the kids, Daniel! They're back!"

She took his hand, and together they hurried to the front of the house. She pulled the door open to find a dozen kids, all kinds of kids—Sojourn's and hers and Daniel's—hurrying up the tall steps. Smiling through happy tears, she threw open her arms to welcome them home.

HARLEQUIN SUPERROMANCE®

HOME ON THE RANCH

Welcome back to the Silver Dollar Ranch, near Tombstone, Arizona. Home of the Bodine men—and their wives.

She's the Sheriff (#787)
by Anne Marie Duquette

Virgil Bodine. He's the oldest brother. One-time sheriff of Tombstone and former bodyguard to the stars. He's come home from California with his reluctant ten-year-old son in tow.

Desiree Hartlan. She's a member of the extended Bodine family—his brother Wyatt's sister-in-law. She's also a DA who's talked herself out of a job...and is looking for a new one.

The position of sheriff is open. When Desiree decides to run, Virgil runs against her.

Next thing he knows, he's calling her sheriff. And boss. And...wife?

Available May 1998 at your favorite retail outlet.

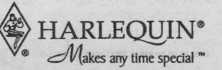

HARLEQUIN SUPERROMANCE ®

COMING NEXT MONTH